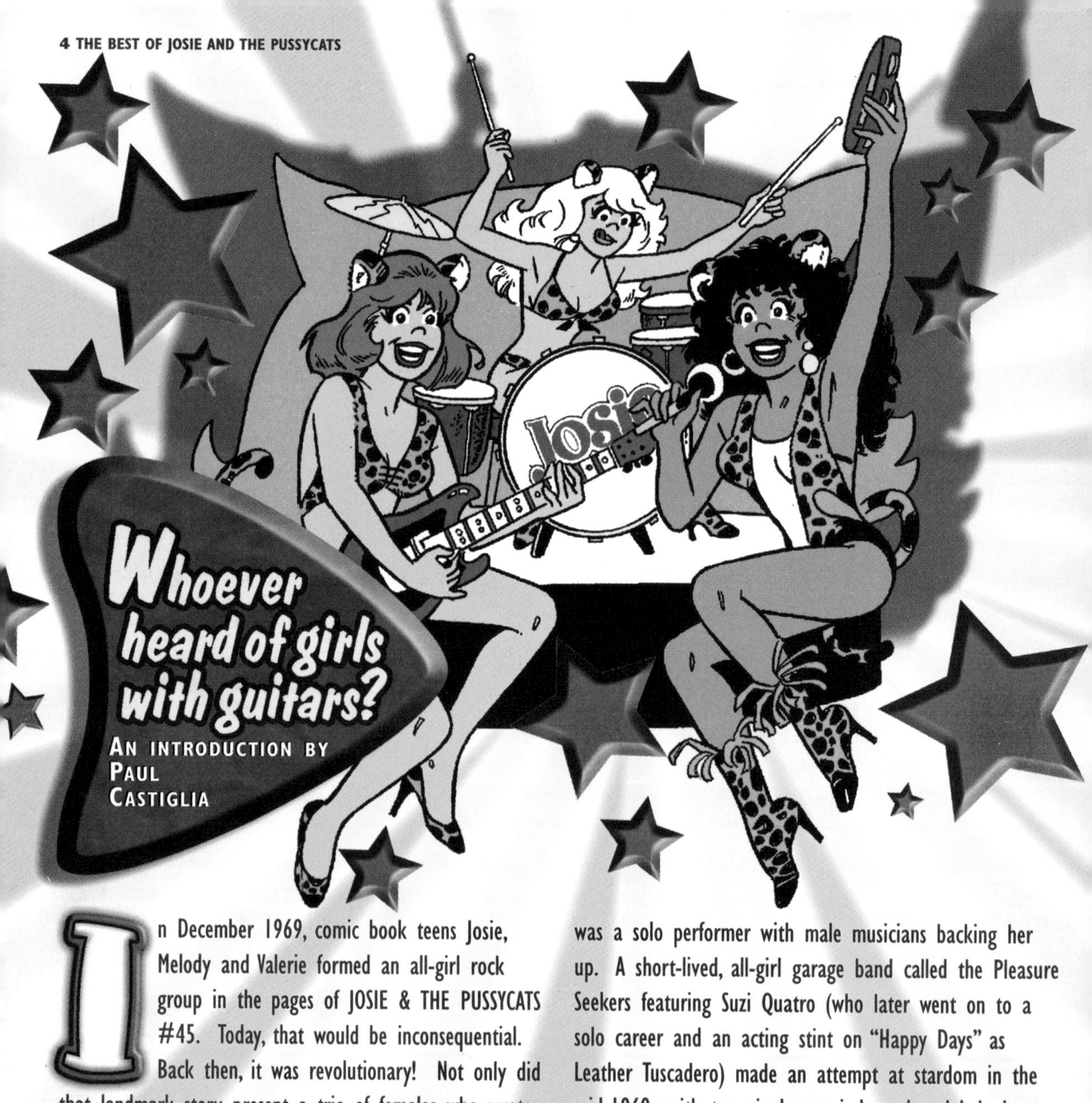
josie

Whoever heard of girls with guitars?

An introduction by Paul Castiglia

In December 1969, comic book teens Josie, Melody and Valerie formed an all-girl rock group in the pages of JOSIE & THE PUSSYCATS #45. Today, that would be inconsequential. Back then, it was revolutionary! Not only did that landmark story present a trio of females who wrote and performed their own music, the band was also a multi-cultural unit, with sensible Valerie emerging as a strong African-American role model. In the process, what could have been written off as just another comic book became a cultural milestone whose impact is still felt today.

To understand the effect of JOSIE & THE PUSSYCATS on the current music scene, one needs to take a look at its past. Simply put, girls with guitars were all but unheard of. Of course, there were exceptions. Wanda Jackson was responsible for some rockabilly scorchers that rank with the best of her 1950s contemporaries like Elvis Presley, Jerry Lee Lewis and Eddie Cochran. However, she was a solo performer with male musicians backing her up. A short-lived, all-girl garage band called the Pleasure Seekers featuring Suzi Quatro (who later went on to a solo career and an acting stint on "Happy Days" as Leather Tuscadero) made an attempt at stardom in the mid-1960s with two singles on independent labels, but never broke beyond local success. While it can be argued that the Pleasure Seekers are an important footnote in music history, they remained an obscure blip on the radar screen in their time. Last and probably least are the Shaggs, another female garage band who owe their existence primarily to the fact that their dad thought they had talent! Their infamous debut album appeared the same year that Josie and the girls donned their catsuits, and they became a cult oddity over the years, leading to a short-lived comeback in the early 1990s. Clearly, however, they were a novelty act appealing to eccentric tastes only. Barely known, neither the Pleasure Seekers nor the Shaggs could have inspired many girls to pick up guitars.

ARCHIE COMIC PUBLICATIONS, INC.

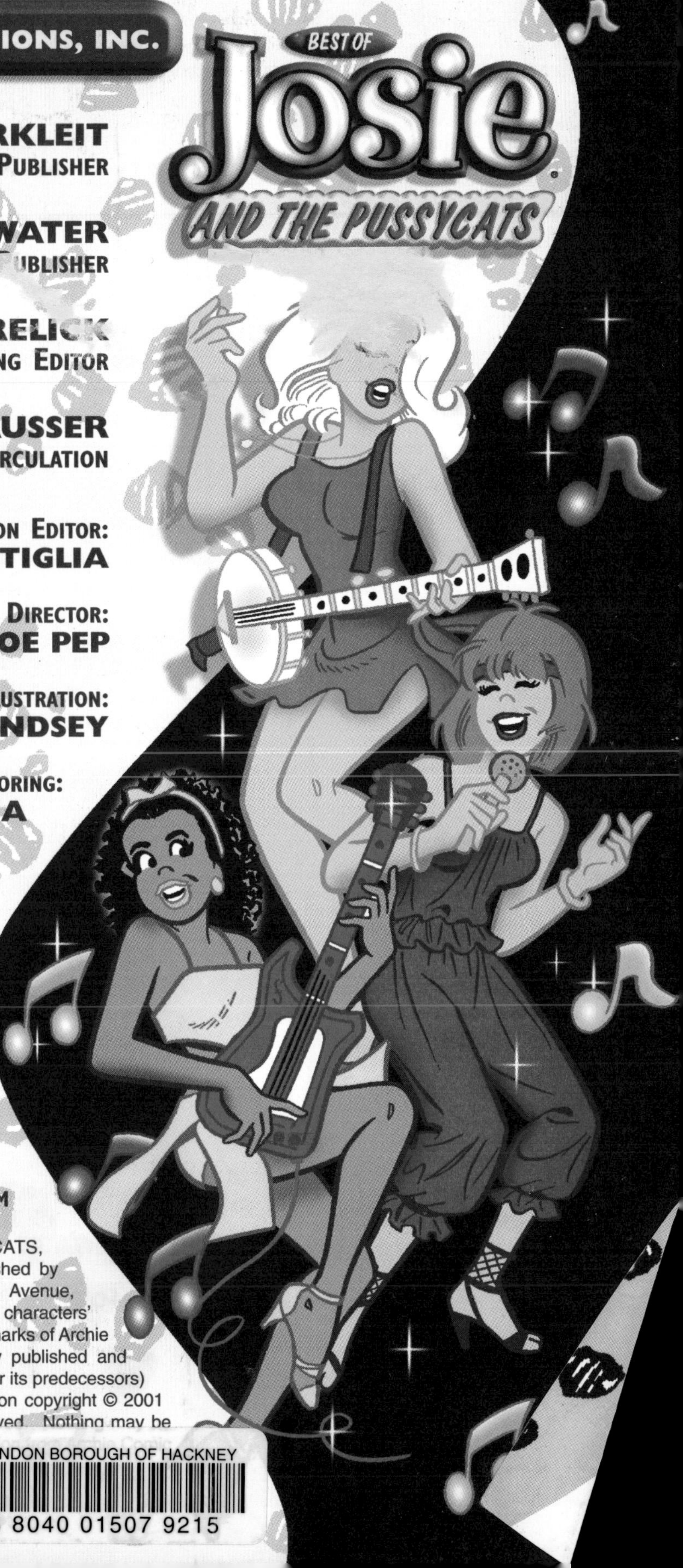
BEST OF
Josie
AND THE PUSSYCATS

MICHAEL I. SILBERKLEIT
Chairman and Co-Publisher

RICHARD H. GOLDWATER
President and Co-Publisher

VICTOR GORELICK
Vice President / Managing Editor

FRED MAUSSER
Vice President / Director of Circulation

Compilation Editor:
PAUL CASTIGLIA

Art Director:
JOE PEP

Front Cover Illustration:
REX W. LINDSEY

Cover Coloring:
ROSARIO “TITO” PEÑA

Production Manager:
ROBBIE O’QUINN

Production:
NELSON RIBEIRO,
CARLOS ANTUNES,
PAUL D’ONOFRIO,
MIKE PELLERITO

Visit Josie & The Pussycats
at www.archiecomics.com

THE BEST OF JOSIE AND THE PUSSYCATS, Volume 1, 2001. Printed in CANADA. Published by Archie Comic Publications, Inc., 325 Fayette Avenue, Mamaroneck, New York 10543.

ISBN 1-879794-07-1

TABLE OF CONTENTS

The notion of an all-girl rock group has its roots in two other musical forms: all-girl vocal bands and female folk singers. From the 1950s through the mid-1960s, "girl groups" were racking up pop hits by the score. Groups such as The Chiffons, The Ronettes, The Supremes, The Shirelles, The Shangri-Las and The Angels sang songs of love lost and found. While many of these songs veered toward the pop ballad style evolved from 1930s crooners—and others were purely novelties—new sounds and themes started to emerge. Tougher songs, both in melody and lyrics, were sung with an authority that let listeners know something was brewing: the early strains of "girl power," perhaps? A listen to hits such as "My Boyfriend's Back," "Leader of the Pack," "Dancing in the Street" and "R.E.S.P.E.C.T" heralded females as a strong force in popular music with something to say. Strengthening this notion were the female folk artists of the 60s—artists like Joni Mitchell, Janis Ian and Buffy-Saint Marie—whose confessional lyrics gave voice to a generation of females where previous generations had remained disenfranchised and unheard.

Which brings us to Josie. Originally presented as a typical, teenage humor comic in the mold of Archie, the success of the filmation cartoon series, "The Archie Show," and the bubble gum recording group it spawned, The Archies, led animation producers William Hanna and Joseph Barbera to option the Josie character for a TV cartoon of her own. Marrying the successful concepts of The Archies' teenage rock band with Hanna-Barbera's own popular *Scooby Doo* (teenagers solving mysteries) and adding a healthy dose of the equal rights movement to the mix, the JOSIE & THE PUSSYCATS TV show premiered in 1970 to much fanfare. Each episode featured a peppy tune "performed" by the Pussycats (a studio band featuring future "Charlie's Angel" Cheryl Ladd as Melody's singing voice!) while depicting the girls as take-charge characters in both their adventures and music. Conceptually and musically, it was as if all the aforementioned female artists were thrown into a stew with the Beatles and all the guitar-wielding British invasion bands that followed them, including the "prefabricated four," the Monkees. The result was a "bubble gum music" concoction not unlike The Archies,

a TV show featuring adventures similar to those depicted in the Beatles' movies and animated TV series, and of course, the Monkees' TV show. Years after its initial run, the Josie series was kept alive in reruns and—what do you know?—wound up inspiring a generation of female rockers!

Strangely enough, it was five years after the Pussycats band debuted in the comics before the first important, real-life all-girl rock group appeared. The Runaways made quite an impression with their energetic, guitar-driven music and take-no-prisoners attitude. Members Lita Ford and Joan Jett would go on to even greater solo fame and inspire other hard-rock girl groups, from the rough and tumble Girlschool to the more pop-driven, fashion conscious Vixen.

The 1980s saw the emergence of many groups surely inspired by Josie and the Pussycats. Chief among these were The Go-Go's and the Bangles. What they had in common with each other—and the Pussycats—was combining fresh pop melodies with a girl power attitude. Throw in a dash of punk, power-pop and new wave influences, and it was easy to imagine a real Josie band sounding that way in the 1980s!

Furthering the girls with guitars motif, the progenitors of the "riot grrrl" movement of the 1990s often cited Josie as a major inspiration. Groups and artists such as Liz Phair, Juliana Hatfield, L7, Bratmobile and Babes In Toyland are in turn inspiring a new generation of female guitar slingers. The power-pop and punk-pop genres are also producing all-girl and girl-led groups at a high rate, to the point where everything's come full circle: Kay Hanley, lead singer of the band, Letters To Cleo, provides Josie's singing voice in the new Josie and the Pussycats, live-action movie!

For three decades, life has imitated art as the ground-breaking Josie and the Pussycats comic book feeds the dreams of hopeful musicians everywhere. In an age where entertainment is seen as the cause of much that is wrong with the world today, is that such a bad thing?

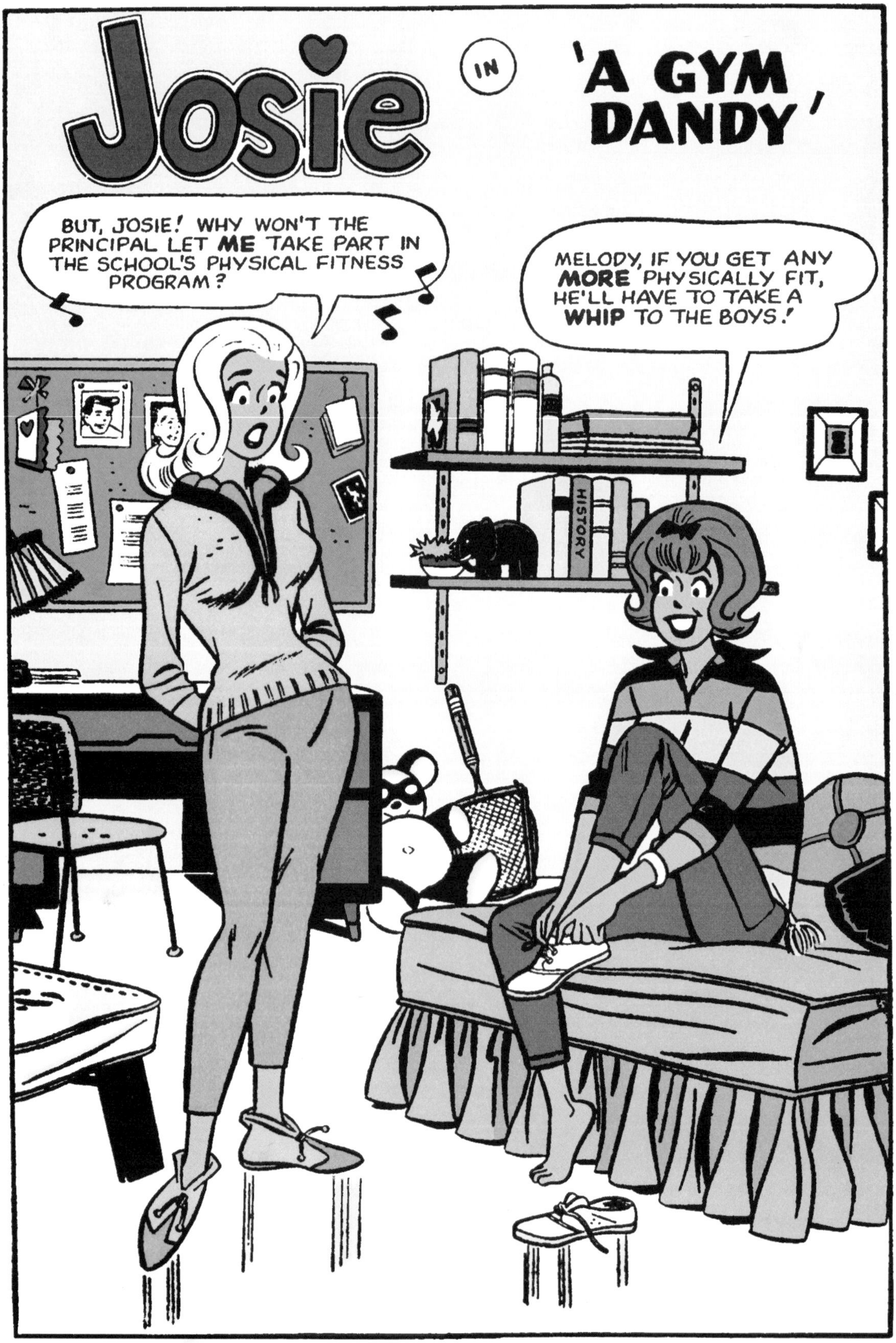
Josie
IN
'A GYM DANDY'
BUT, JOSIE! WHY WON'T THE PRINCIPAL LET ME TAKE PART IN THE SCHOOL'S PHYSICAL FITNESS PROGRAM?
MELODY, IF YOU GET ANY MORE PHYSICALLY FIT, HE'LL HAVE TO TAKE A WHIP TO THE BOYS!
HISTORY

ORIGINALLY PRESENTED IN
SHE'S JOSIE #1, FEBRUARY, 1963

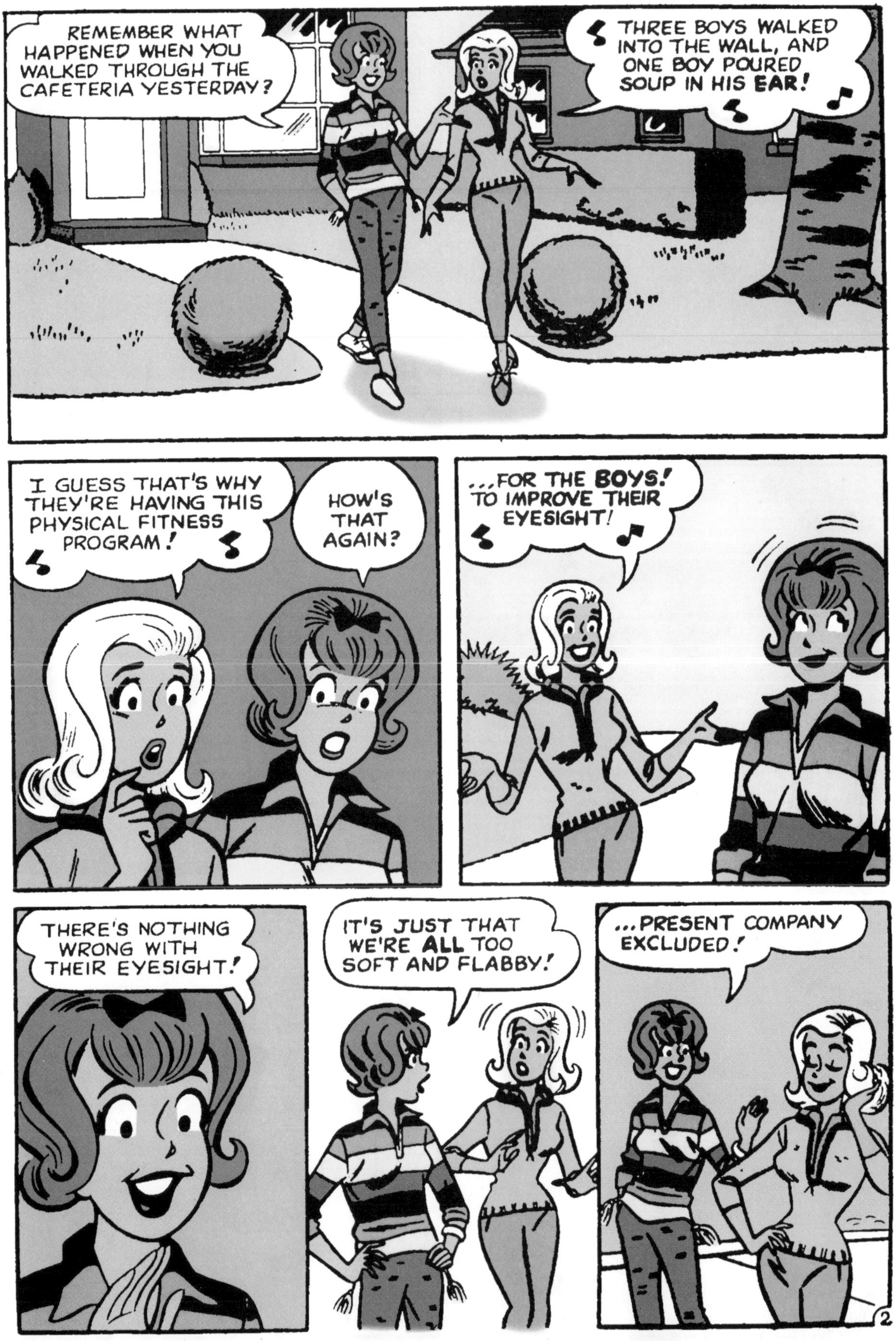
REMEMBER WHAT HAPPENED WHEN YOU WALKED THROUGH THE CAFETERIA YESTERDAY?
THREE BOYS WALKED INTO THE WALL, AND ONE BOY POURED SOUP IN HIS EAR!
I GUESS THAT'S WHY THEY'RE HAVING THIS PHYSICAL FITNESS PROGRAM!
HOW'S THAT AGAIN?
...FOR THE BOYS! TO IMPROVE THEIR EYESIGHT!
THERE'S NOTHING WRONG WITH THEIR EYESIGHT!
IT'S JUST THAT WE'RE ALL TOO SOFT AND FLABBY!
...PRESENT COMPANY EXCLUDED!
2

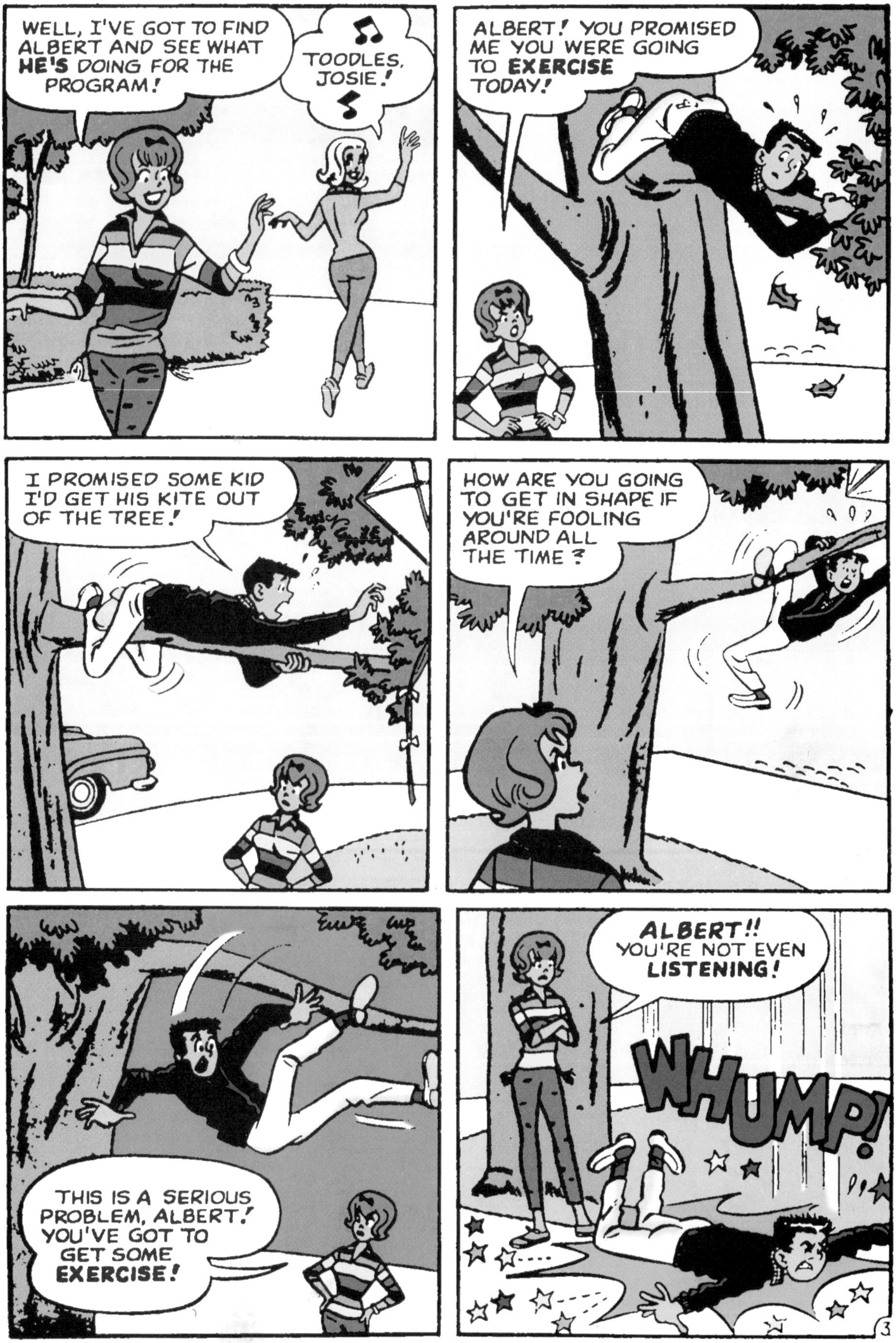

WELL, I'VE GOT TO FIND ALBERT AND SEE WHAT **HE'S** DOING FOR THE PROGRAM!
TOODLES, JOSIE!
ALBERT! YOU PROMISED ME YOU WERE GOING TO **EXERCISE** TODAY!
I PROMISED SOME KID I'D GET HIS KITE OUT OF THE TREE!
HOW ARE YOU GOING TO GET IN SHAPE IF YOU'RE FOOLING AROUND ALL THE TIME?
THIS IS A SERIOUS PROBLEM, ALBERT! YOU'VE GOT TO GET SOME **EXERCISE**!
ALBERT!! YOU'RE NOT EVEN **LISTENING**!
WHUMP!
3

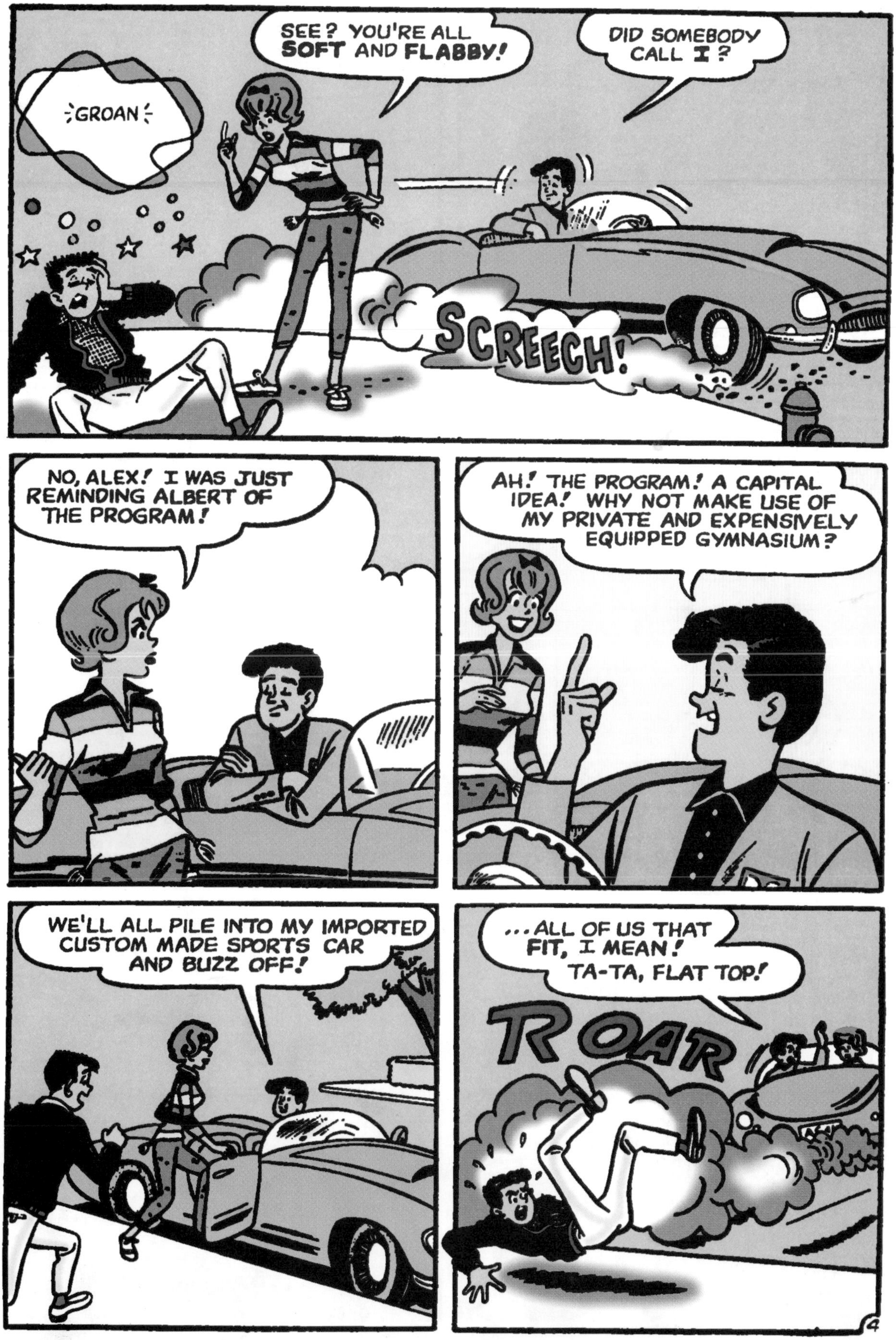
GROAN
SEE? YOU'RE ALL SOFT AND FLABBY!
DID SOMEBODY CALL I?
SCREECH!
NO, ALEX! I WAS JUST REMINDING ALBERT OF THE PROGRAM!
AH! THE PROGRAM! A CAPITAL IDEA! WHY NOT MAKE USE OF MY PRIVATE AND EXPENSIVELY EQUIPPED GYMNASIUM?
WE'LL ALL PILE INTO MY IMPORTED CUSTOM MADE SPORTS CAR AND BUZZ OFF!
...ALL OF US THAT FIT, I MEAN! TA-TA, FLAT TOP!
ROAR
4

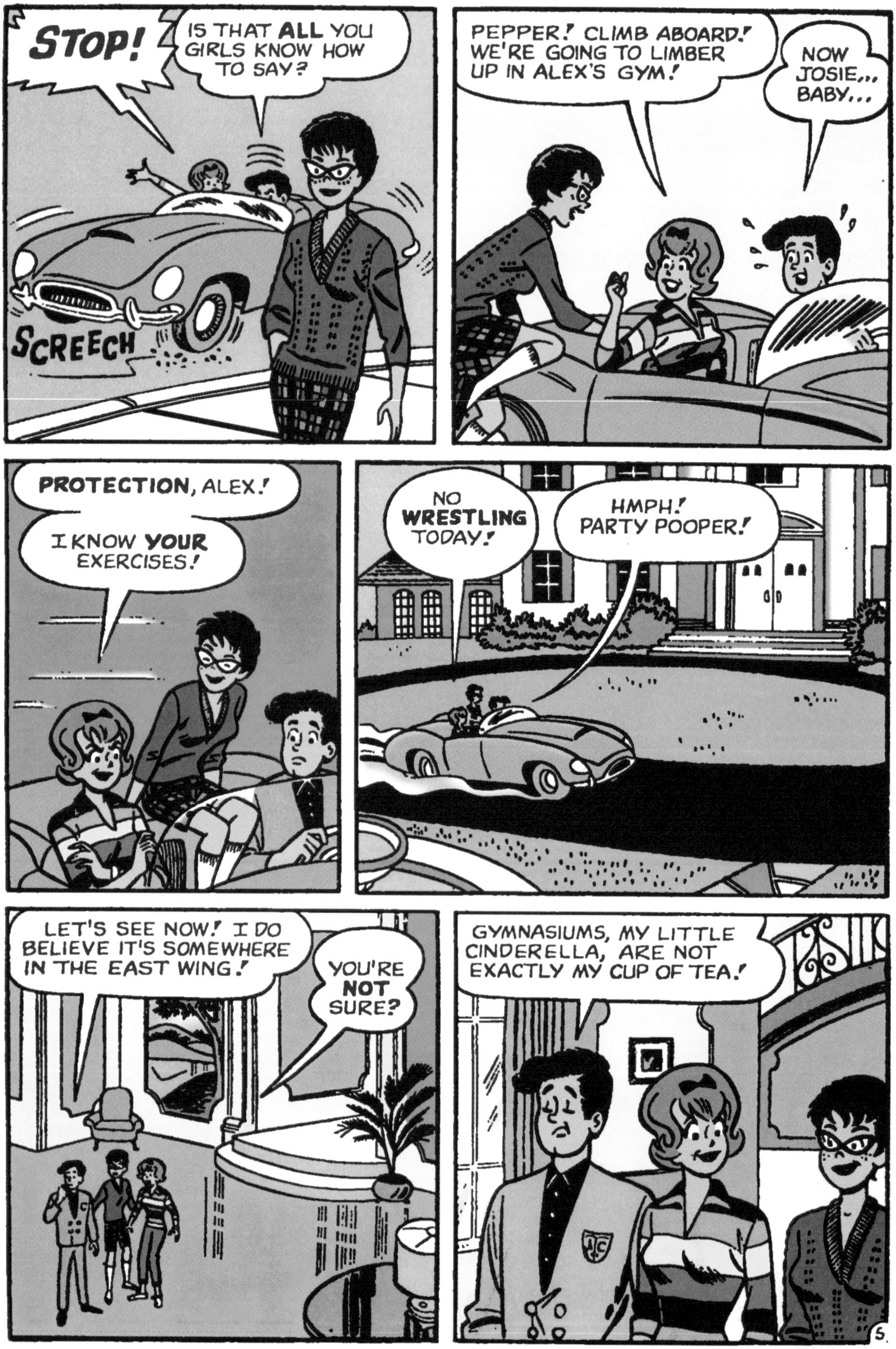
STOP!
IS THAT ALL YOU GIRLS KNOW HOW TO SAY?
SCREECH
PEPPER! CLIMB ABOARD! WE'RE GOING TO LIMBER UP IN ALEX'S GYM!
NOW JOSIE,.. BABY...
PROTECTION, ALEX!
I KNOW YOUR EXERCISES!
NO WRESTLING TODAY!
HMPH! PARTY POOPER!
LET'S SEE NOW! I DO BELIEVE IT'S SOMEWHERE IN THE EAST WING!
YOU'RE NOT SURE?
GYMNASIUMS, MY LITTLE CINDERELLA, ARE NOT EXACTLY MY CUP OF TEA!
5.

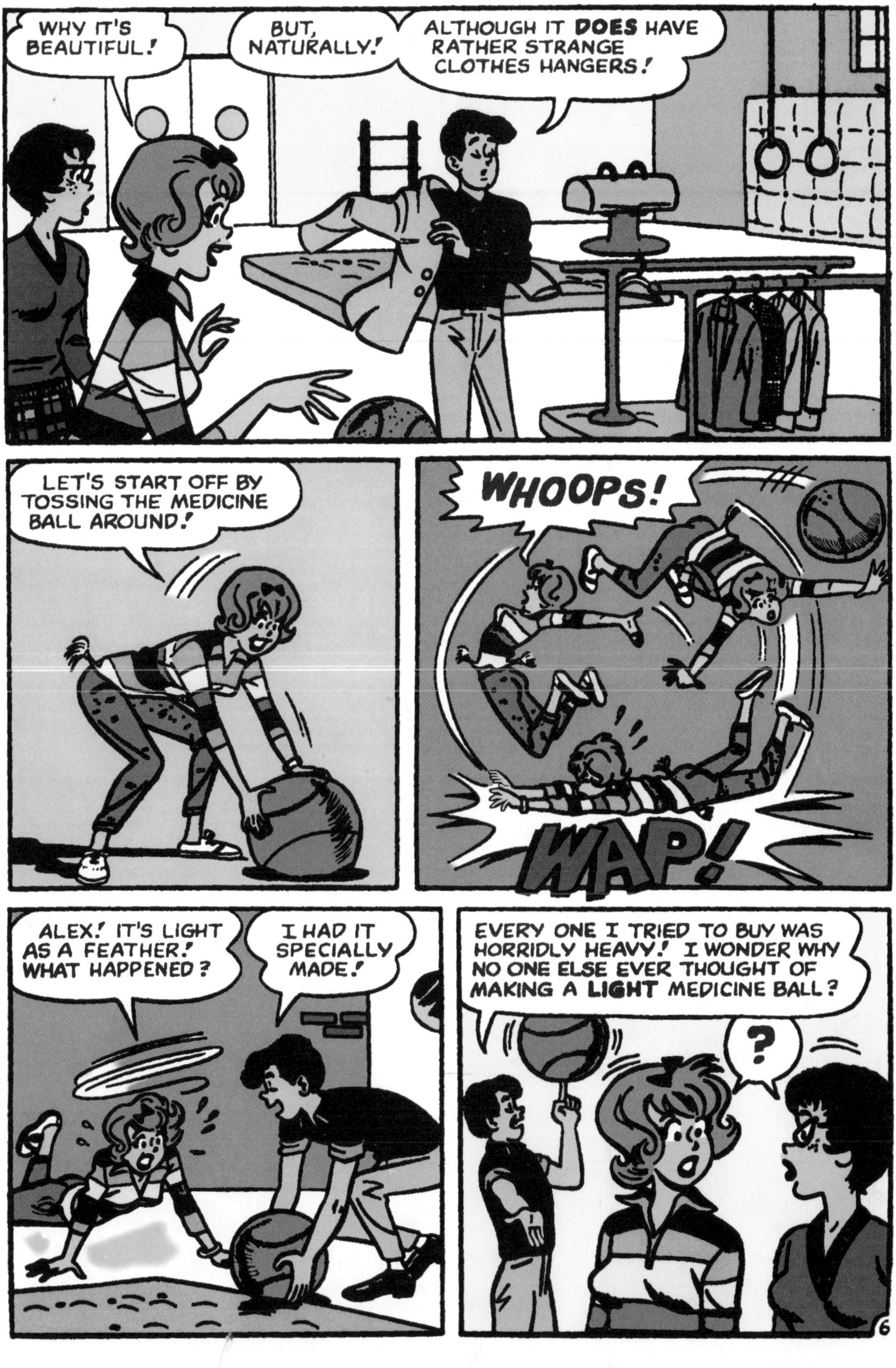
WHY IT'S BEAUTIFUL!
BUT, NATURALLY!
ALTHOUGH IT DOES HAVE RATHER STRANGE CLOTHES HANGERS!
LET'S START OFF BY TOSSING THE MEDICINE BALL AROUND!
WHOOPS!
WAP!
ALEX! IT'S LIGHT AS A FEATHER! WHAT HAPPENED?
I HAD IT SPECIALLY MADE!
EVERY ONE I TRIED TO BUY WAS HORRIDLY HEAVY! I WONDER WHY NO ONE ELSE EVER THOUGHT OF MAKING A LIGHT MEDICINE BALL?
?
6

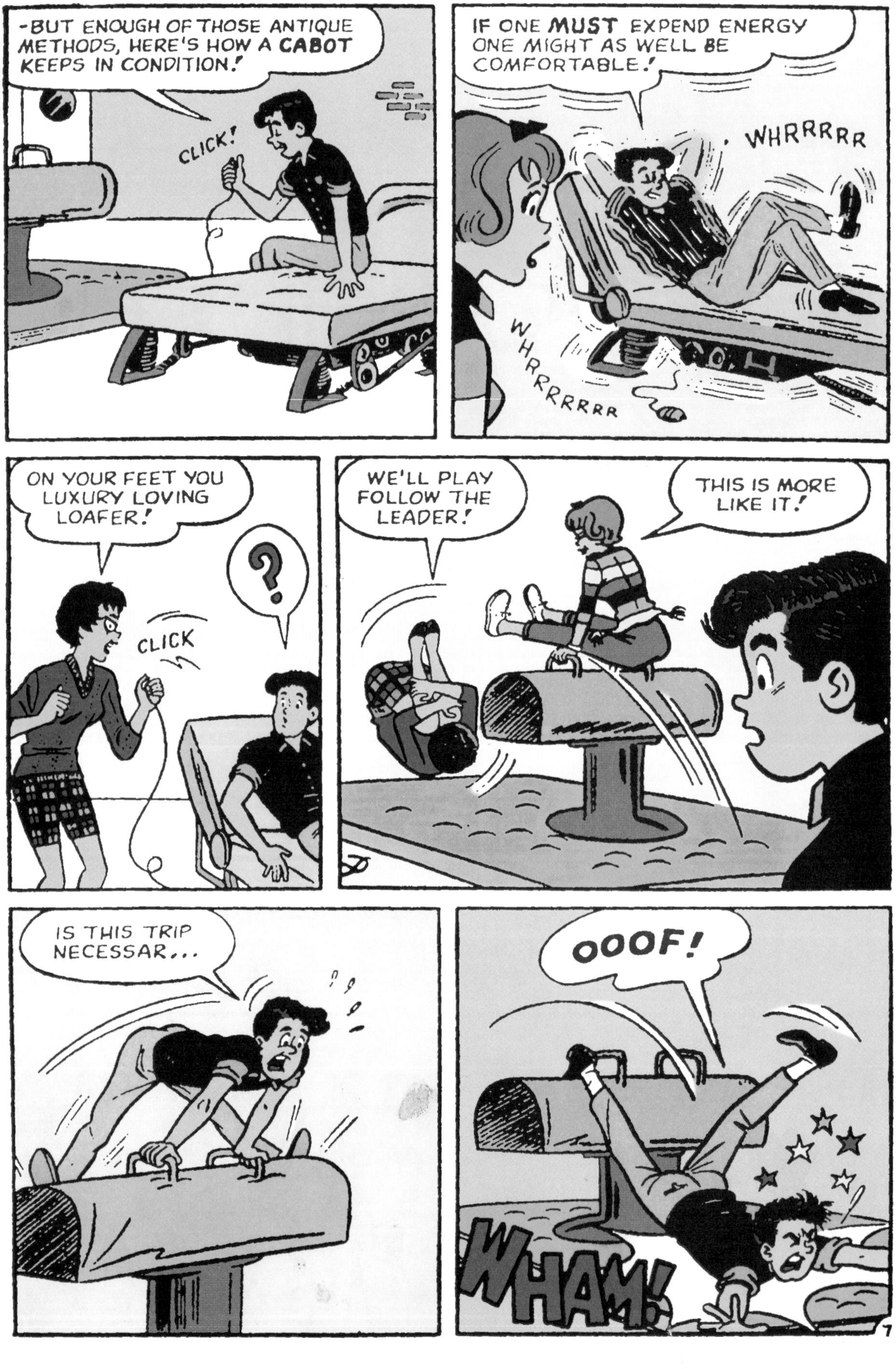
-BUT ENOUGH OF THOSE ANTIQUE METHODS, HERE'S HOW A CABOT KEEPS IN CONDITION!
CLICK!
IF ONE MUST EXPEND ENERGY ONE MIGHT AS WELL BE COMFORTABLE!
WHRRRRR
WHRRRRRRR
ON YOUR FEET YOU LUXURY LOVING LOAFER!
CLICK
?
WE'LL PLAY FOLLOW THE LEADER!
THIS IS MORE LIKE IT!
IS THIS TRIP NECESSAR...
OOOF!
WHAM!
7

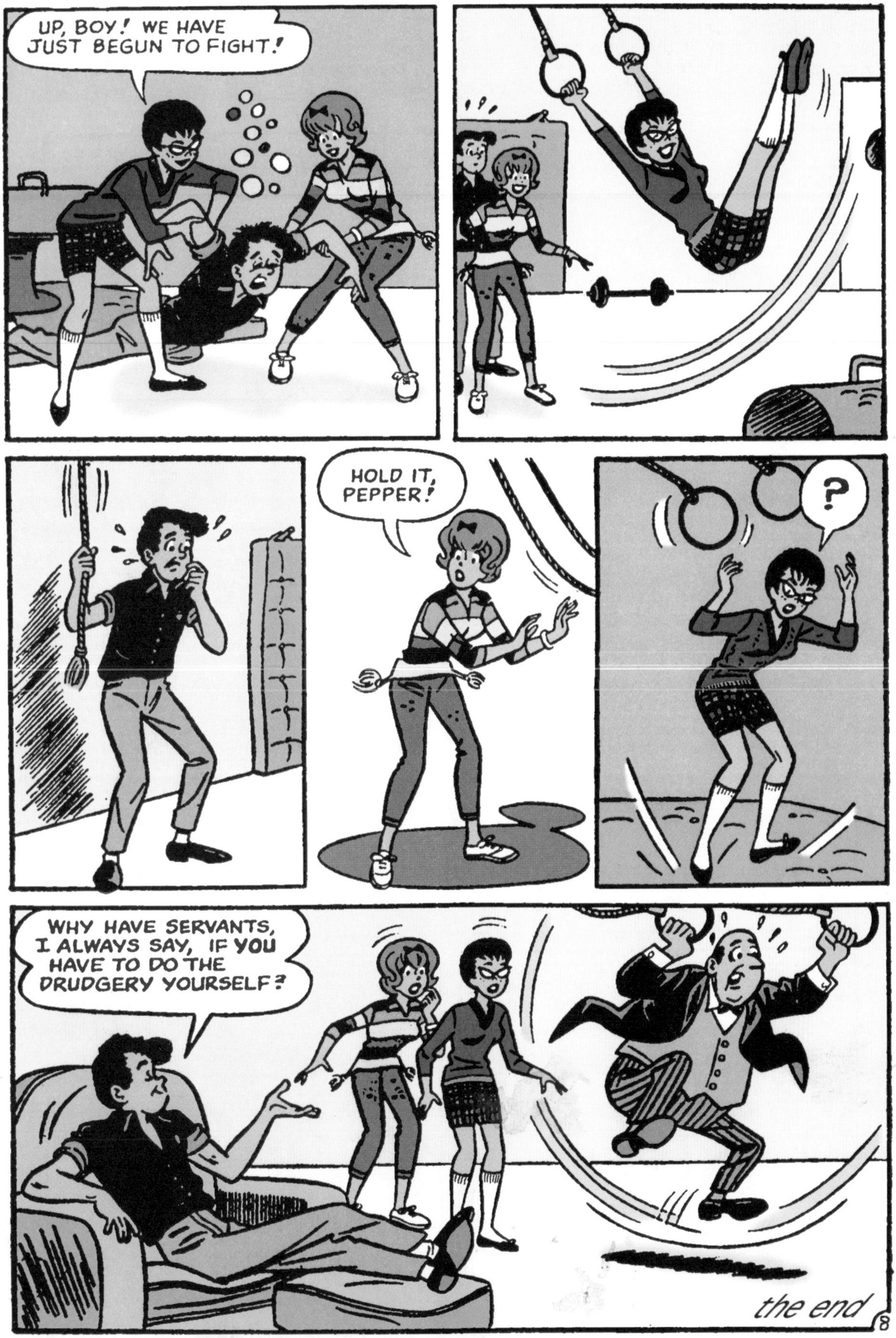
UP, BOY! WE HAVE JUST BEGUN TO FIGHT!
HOLD IT, PEPPER!
?
WHY HAVE SERVANTS, I ALWAYS SAY, IF YOU HAVE TO DO THE DRUDGERY YOURSELF?
the end
8

THE FIRST APPEARANCE OF ALEXANDRA CABOT

SPACE DOES NOT PERMIT US TO REPRINT THIS ENTIRE TALE, BUT WE'LL HUM A FEW BARS WITH SELECT PANELS FROM **SHE'S JOSIE #8, SEPTEMBER, 1964**

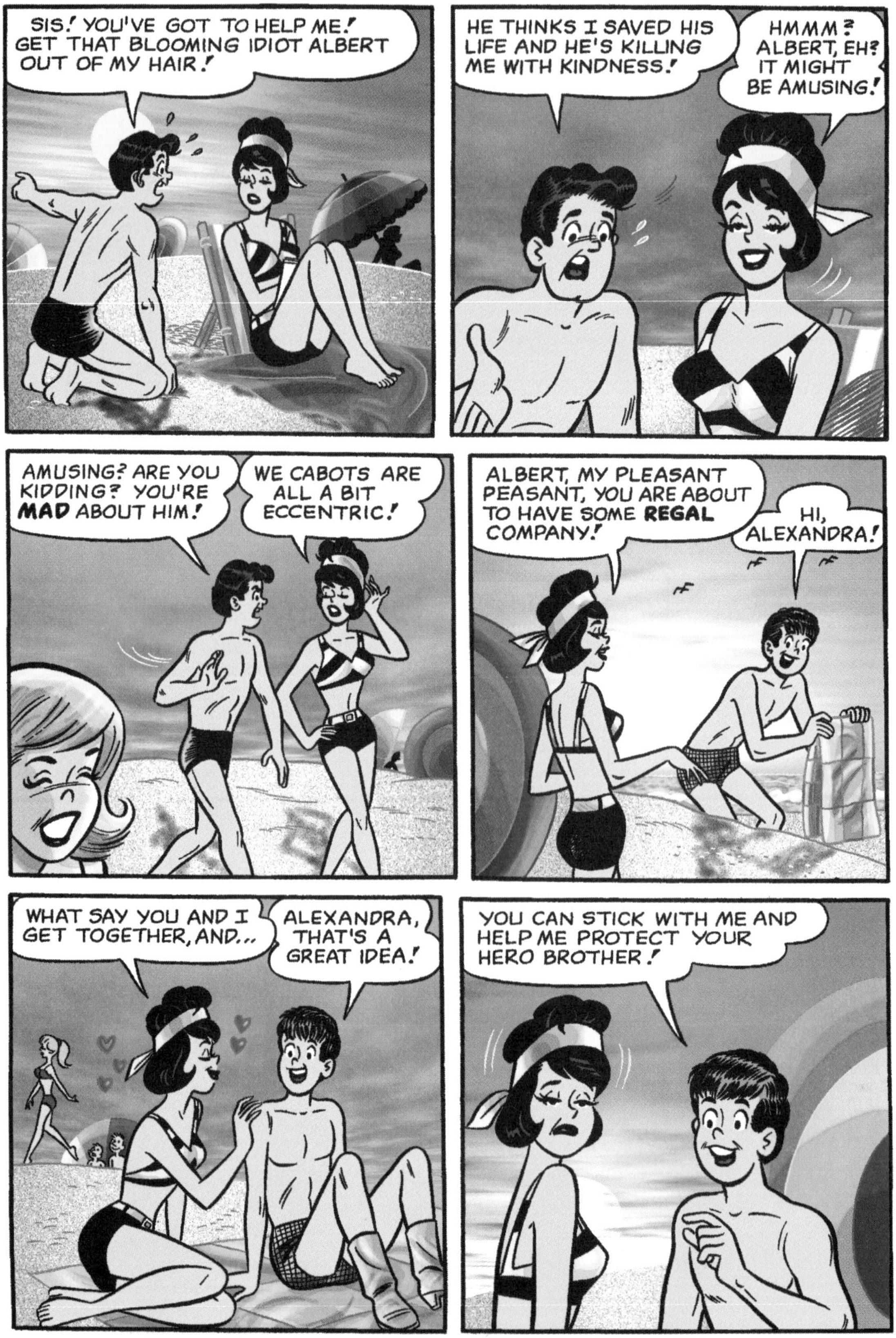
SIS! YOU'VE GOT TO HELP ME! GET THAT BLOOMING IDIOT ALBERT OUT OF MY HAIR!
HE THINKS I SAVED HIS LIFE AND HE'S KILLING ME WITH KINDNESS!
HMMM? ALBERT, EH? IT MIGHT BE AMUSING!
AMUSING? ARE YOU KIDDING? YOU'RE **MAD** ABOUT HIM!
WE CABOTS ARE ALL A BIT ECCENTRIC!
ALBERT, MY PLEASANT PEASANT, YOU ARE ABOUT TO HAVE SOME **REGAL** COMPANY!
HI, ALEXANDRA!
WHAT SAY YOU AND I GET TOGETHER, AND...
ALEXANDRA, THAT'S A GREAT IDEA!
YOU CAN STICK WITH ME AND HELP ME PROTECT YOUR HERO BROTHER!

THE FIRST APPEARANCE OF ALAN M.

SPACE DOES NOT PERMIT US TO REPRINT THIS ENTIRE TALE, BUT WE'LL HUM A FEW BARS WITH SELECT PANELS FROM **JOSIE #42, AUGUST, 1969**

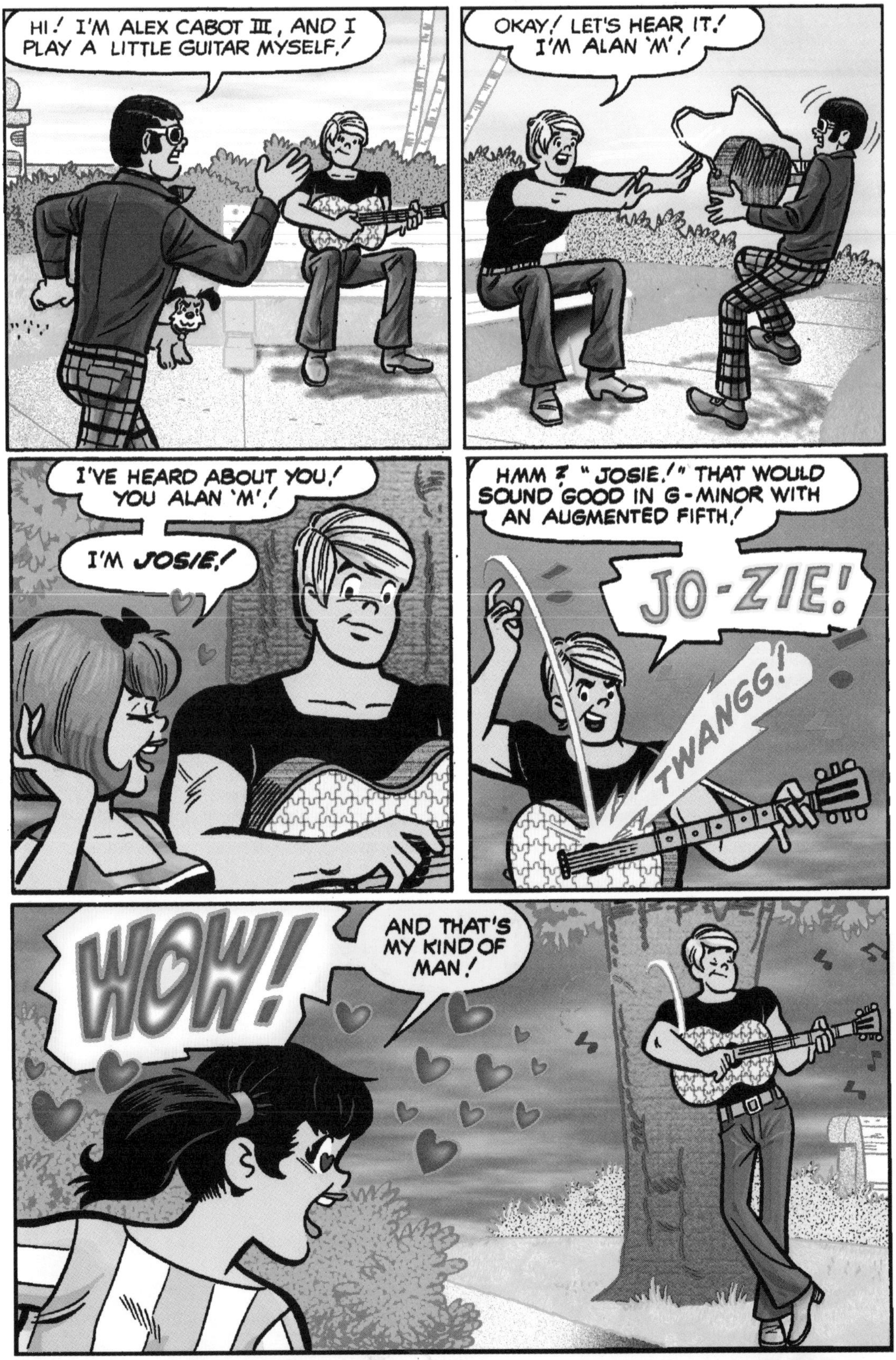
HI! I'M ALEX CABOT III, AND I PLAY A LITTLE GUITAR MYSELF!
OKAY! LET'S HEAR IT! I'M ALAN 'M'!
I'VE HEARD ABOUT YOU! YOU ALAN 'M'!
I'M JOSIE!
HMM? "JOSIE!" THAT WOULD SOUND GOOD IN G-MINOR WITH AN AUGMENTED FIFTH!
JO-ZIE!
TWANGG!
WOW!
AND THAT'S MY KIND OF MAN!

THE EVOLUTION OF SEBASTIAN THE CAT & ALEXANDRA'S STRIPE

SPACE DOES NOT PERMIT US TO REPRINT THIS ENTIRE TALE, BUT WE'LL HUM A FEW BARS WITH SELECT PANELS FROM **JOSIE #43, SEPTEMBER, 1969**

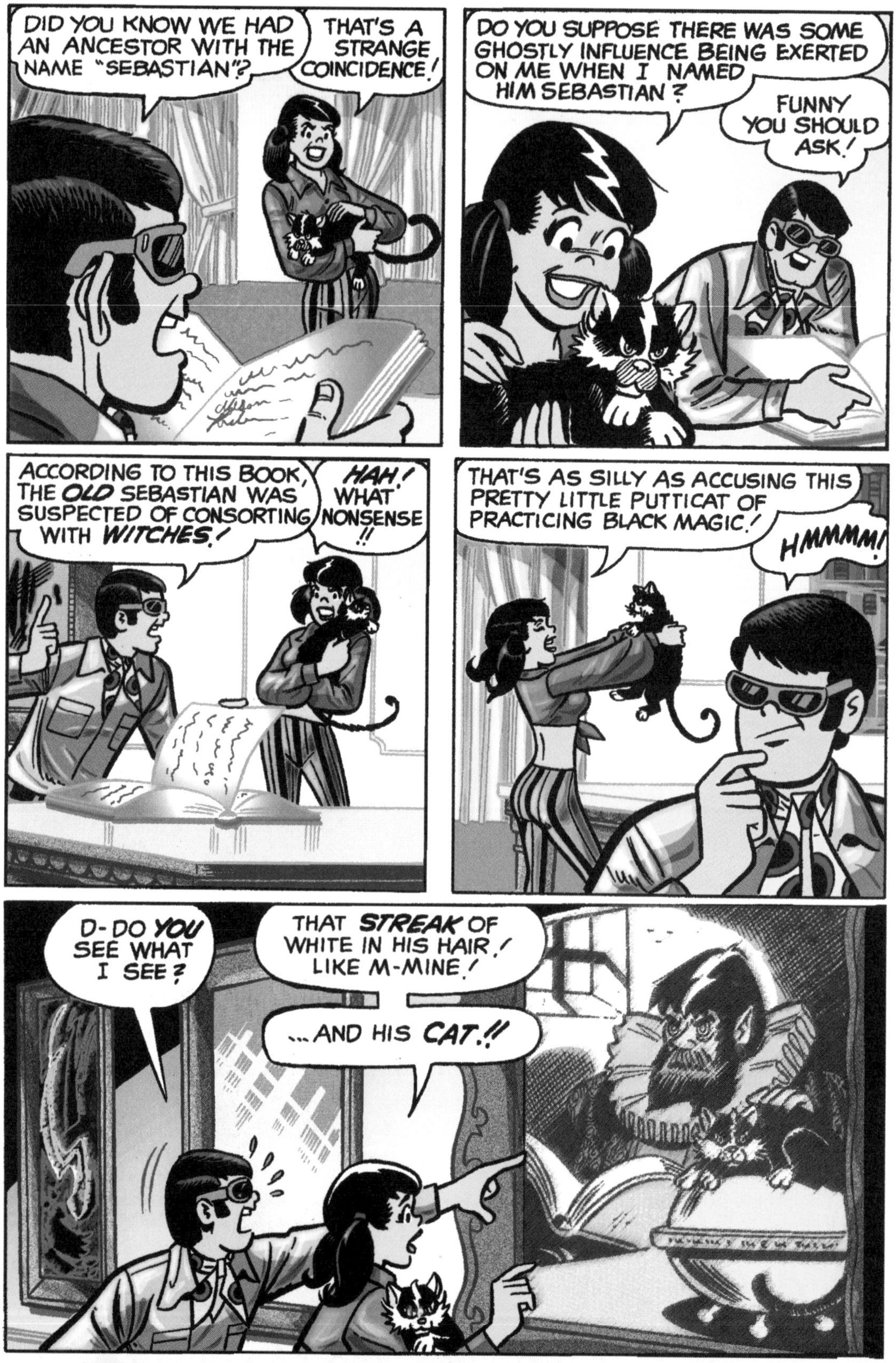

DID YOU KNOW WE HAD AN ANCESTOR WITH THE NAME "SEBASTIAN"?
THAT'S A STRANGE COINCIDENCE!
DO YOU SUPPOSE THERE WAS SOME GHOSTLY INFLUENCE BEING EXERTED ON ME WHEN I NAMED HIM SEBASTIAN?
FUNNY YOU SHOULD ASK!
ACCORDING TO THIS BOOK, THE OLD SEBASTIAN WAS SUSPECTED OF CONSORTING WITH WITCHES!
HAH! WHAT NONSENSE!!
THAT'S AS SILLY AS ACCUSING THIS PRETTY LITTLE PUTTICAT OF PRACTICING BLACK MAGIC!
HMMMM!
D-DO YOU SEE WHAT I SEE?
THAT STREAK OF WHITE IN HIS HAIR! LIKE M-MINE!
...AND HIS CAT!!

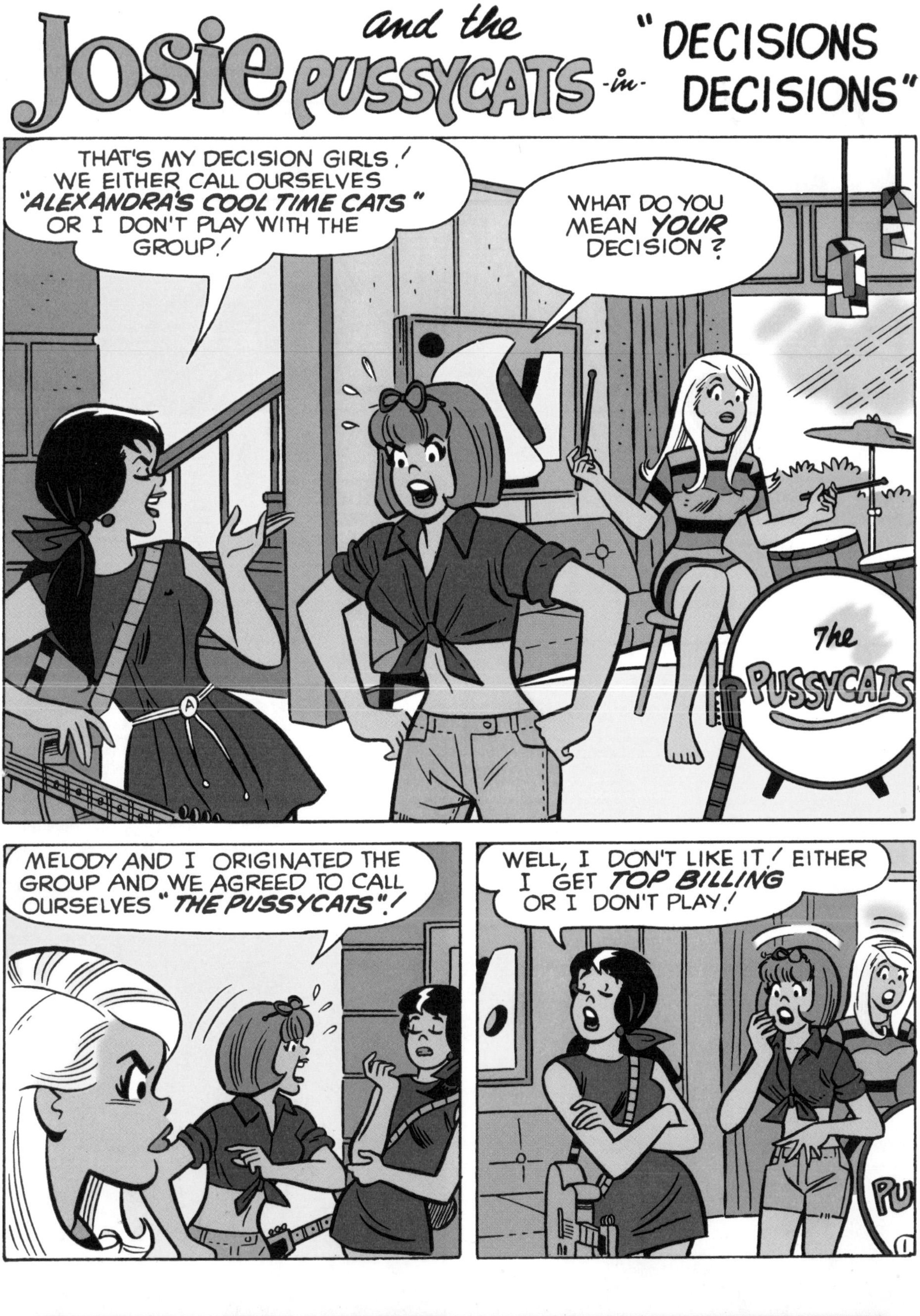
Josie and the PUSSYCATS -in- "DECISIONS DECISIONS"
THAT'S MY DECISION GIRLS! WE EITHER CALL OURSELVES "ALEXANDRA'S COOL TIME CATS" OR I DON'T PLAY WITH THE GROUP!
WHAT DO YOU MEAN YOUR DECISION?
The PUSSYCATS
MELODY AND I ORIGINATED THE GROUP AND WE AGREED TO CALL OURSELVES "THE PUSSYCATS"!
WELL, I DON'T LIKE IT! EITHER I GET TOP BILLING OR I DON'T PLAY!

ORIGINALLY PRESENTED IN
JOSIE & THE PUSSYCATS #45, DECEMBER, 1969

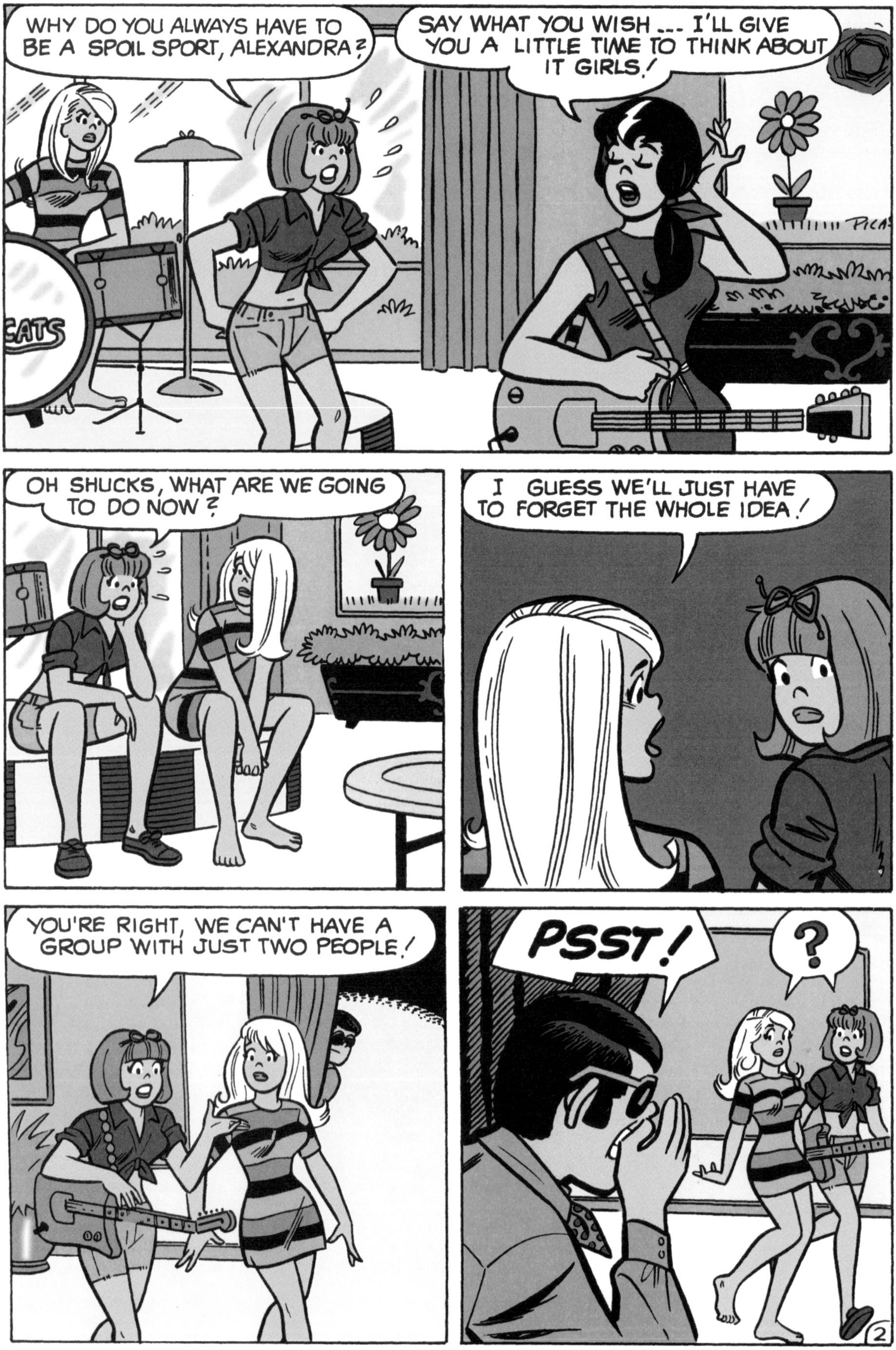
WHY DO YOU ALWAYS HAVE TO BE A SPOIL SPORT, ALEXANDRA?
SAY WHAT YOU WISH ... I'LL GIVE YOU A LITTLE TIME TO THINK ABOUT IT GIRLS!
CATS
OH SHUCKS, WHAT ARE WE GOING TO DO NOW?
I GUESS WE'LL JUST HAVE TO FORGET THE WHOLE IDEA!
YOU'RE RIGHT, WE CAN'T HAVE A GROUP WITH JUST TWO PEOPLE!
PSST!
?
2

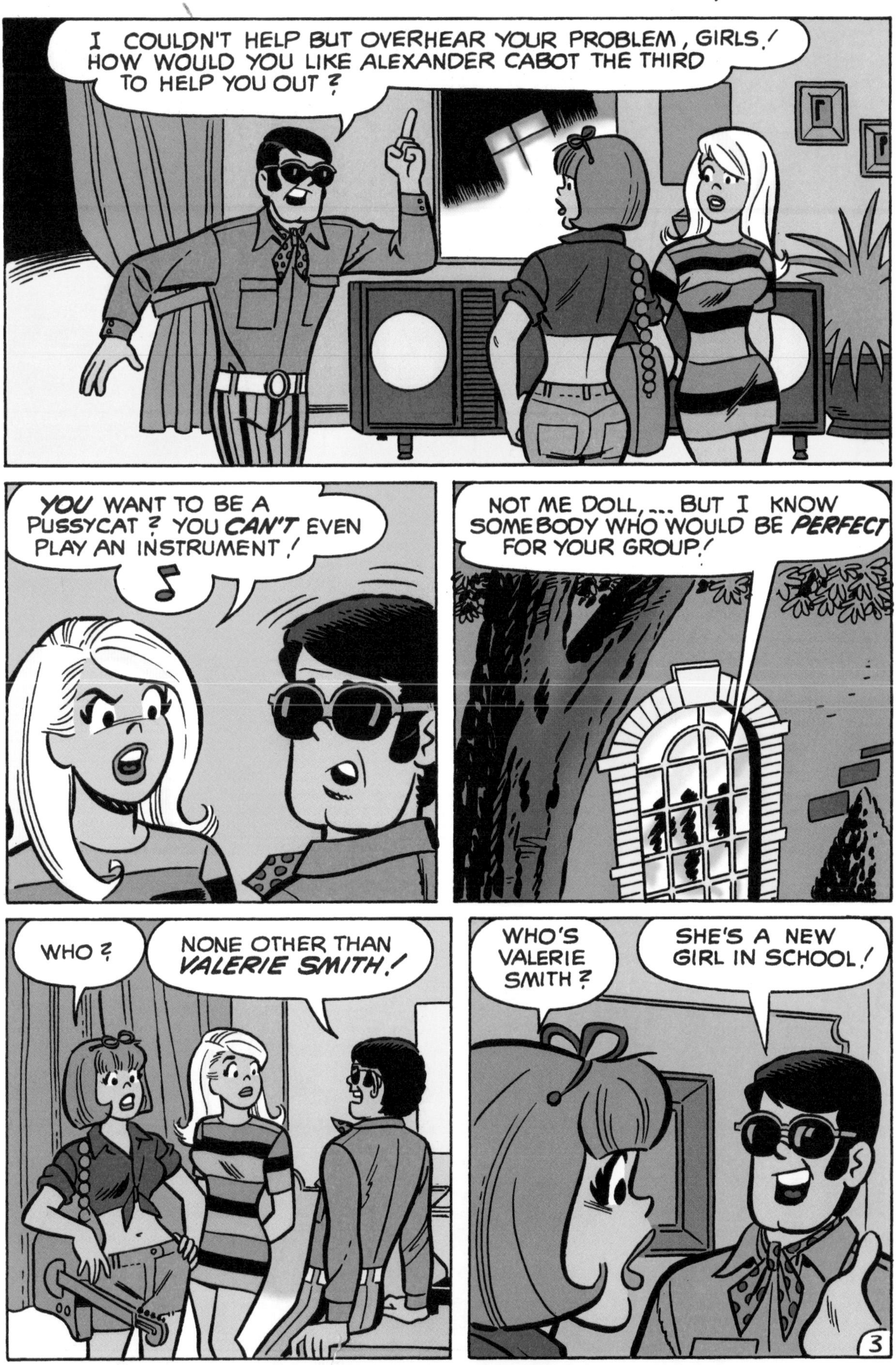
I COULDN'T HELP BUT OVERHEAR YOUR PROBLEM, GIRLS! HOW WOULD YOU LIKE ALEXANDER CABOT THE THIRD TO HELP YOU OUT?
YOU WANT TO BE A PUSSYCAT? YOU CAN'T EVEN PLAY AN INSTRUMENT!
NOT ME DOLL, ... BUT I KNOW SOMEBODY WHO WOULD BE PERFECT FOR YOUR GROUP!
WHO?
NONE OTHER THAN VALERIE SMITH!
WHO'S VALERIE SMITH?
SHE'S A NEW GIRL IN SCHOOL!
3

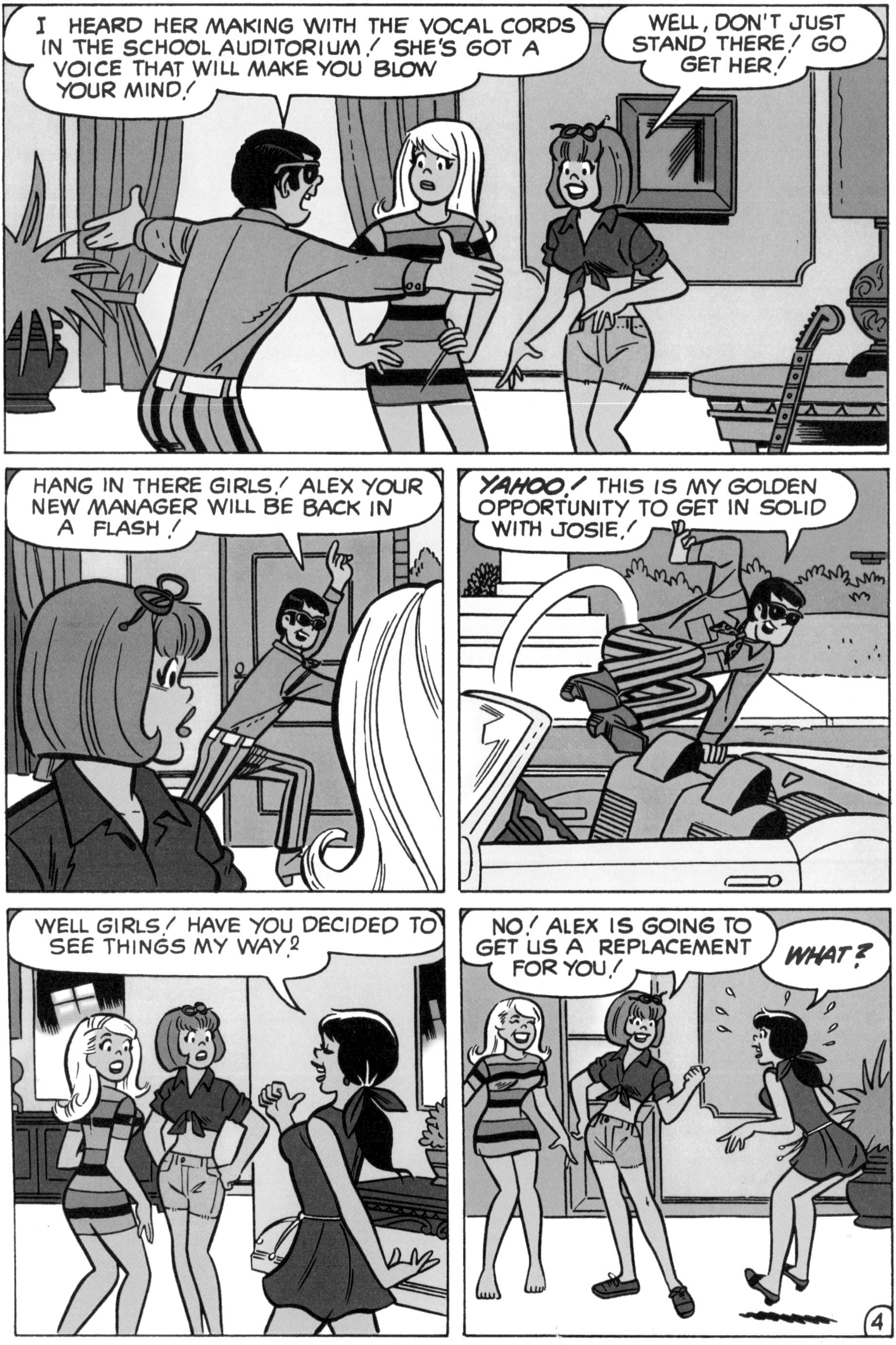
I HEARD HER MAKING WITH THE VOCAL CORDS IN THE SCHOOL AUDITORIUM! SHE'S GOT A VOICE THAT WILL MAKE YOU BLOW YOUR MIND!
WELL, DON'T JUST STAND THERE! GO GET HER!
HANG IN THERE GIRLS! ALEX YOUR NEW MANAGER WILL BE BACK IN A FLASH!
YAHOO! THIS IS MY GOLDEN OPPORTUNITY TO GET IN SOLID WITH JOSIE!
WELL GIRLS! HAVE YOU DECIDED TO SEE THINGS MY WAY?
NO! ALEX IS GOING TO GET US A REPLACEMENT FOR YOU!
WHAT?
4

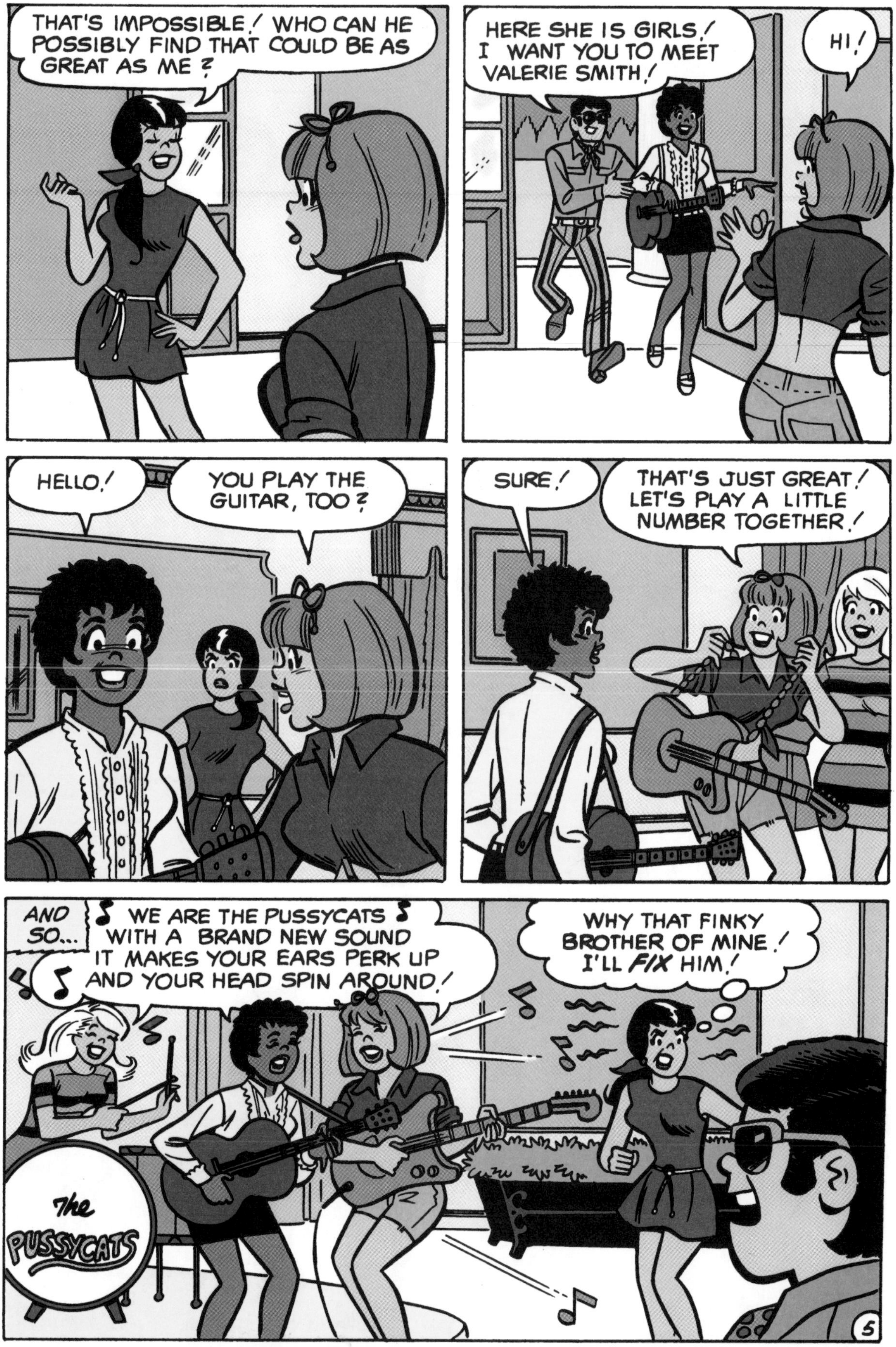
THAT'S IMPOSSIBLE! WHO CAN HE POSSIBLY FIND THAT COULD BE AS GREAT AS ME?
HERE SHE IS GIRLS! I WANT YOU TO MEET VALERIE SMITH!
HI!
HELLO!
YOU PLAY THE GUITAR, TOO?
SURE!
THAT'S JUST GREAT! LET'S PLAY A LITTLE NUMBER TOGETHER!
AND SO...
WE ARE THE PUSSYCATS WITH A BRAND NEW SOUND IT MAKES YOUR EARS PERK UP AND YOUR HEAD SPIN AROUND!
WHY THAT FINKY BROTHER OF MINE! I'LL FIX HIM!
The PUSSYCATS
5

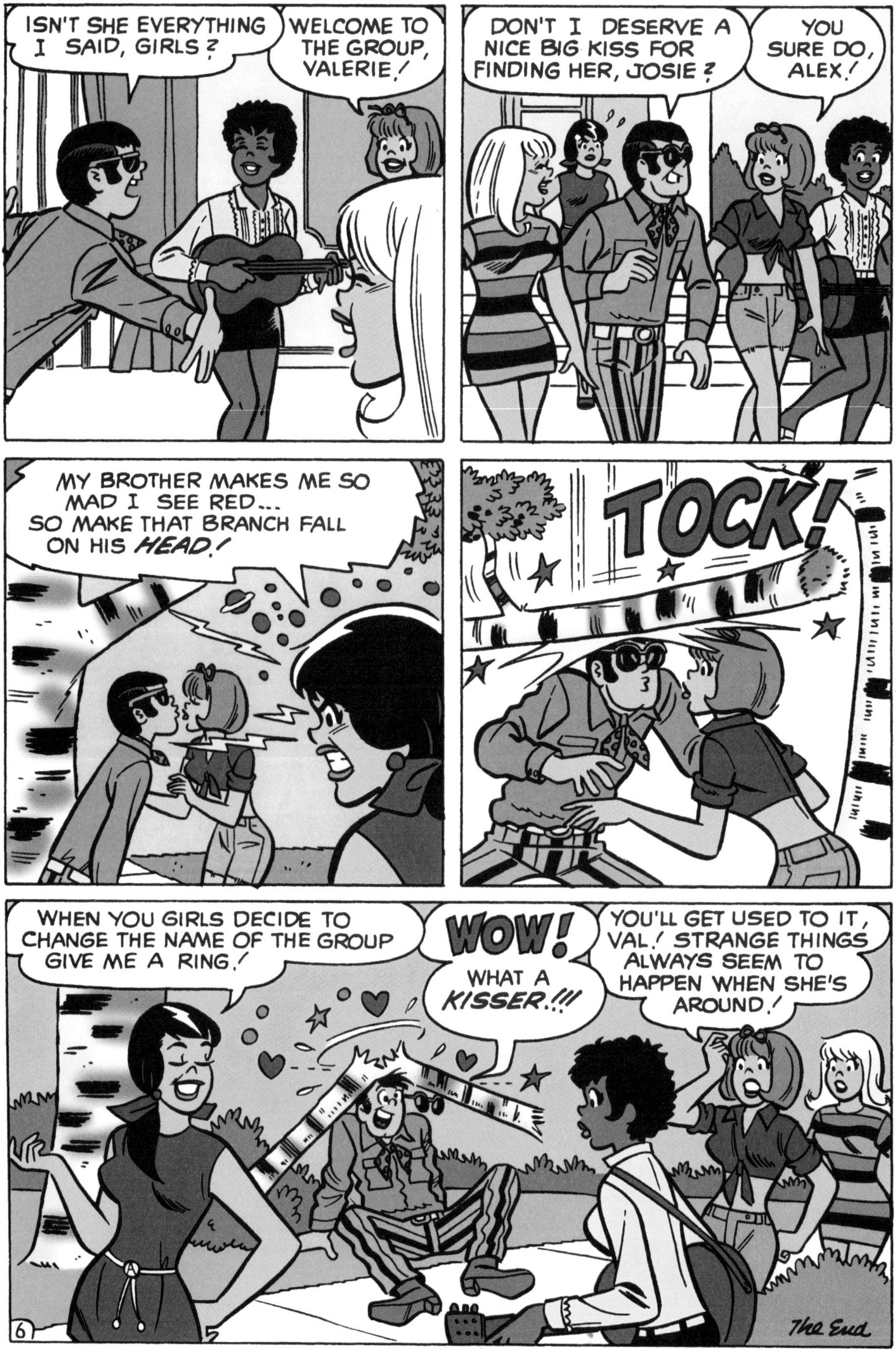
ISN'T SHE EVERYTHING I SAID, GIRLS?
WELCOME TO THE GROUP, VALERIE!
DON'T I DESERVE A NICE BIG KISS FOR FINDING HER, JOSIE?
YOU SURE DO, ALEX!
MY BROTHER MAKES ME SO MAD I SEE RED... SO MAKE THAT BRANCH FALL ON HIS HEAD!
TOCK!
WHEN YOU GIRLS DECIDE TO CHANGE THE NAME OF THE GROUP GIVE ME A RING!
WOW!
WHAT A KISSER!!!
YOU'LL GET USED TO IT, VAL! STRANGE THINGS ALWAYS SEEM TO HAPPEN WHEN SHE'S AROUND!
6
The End

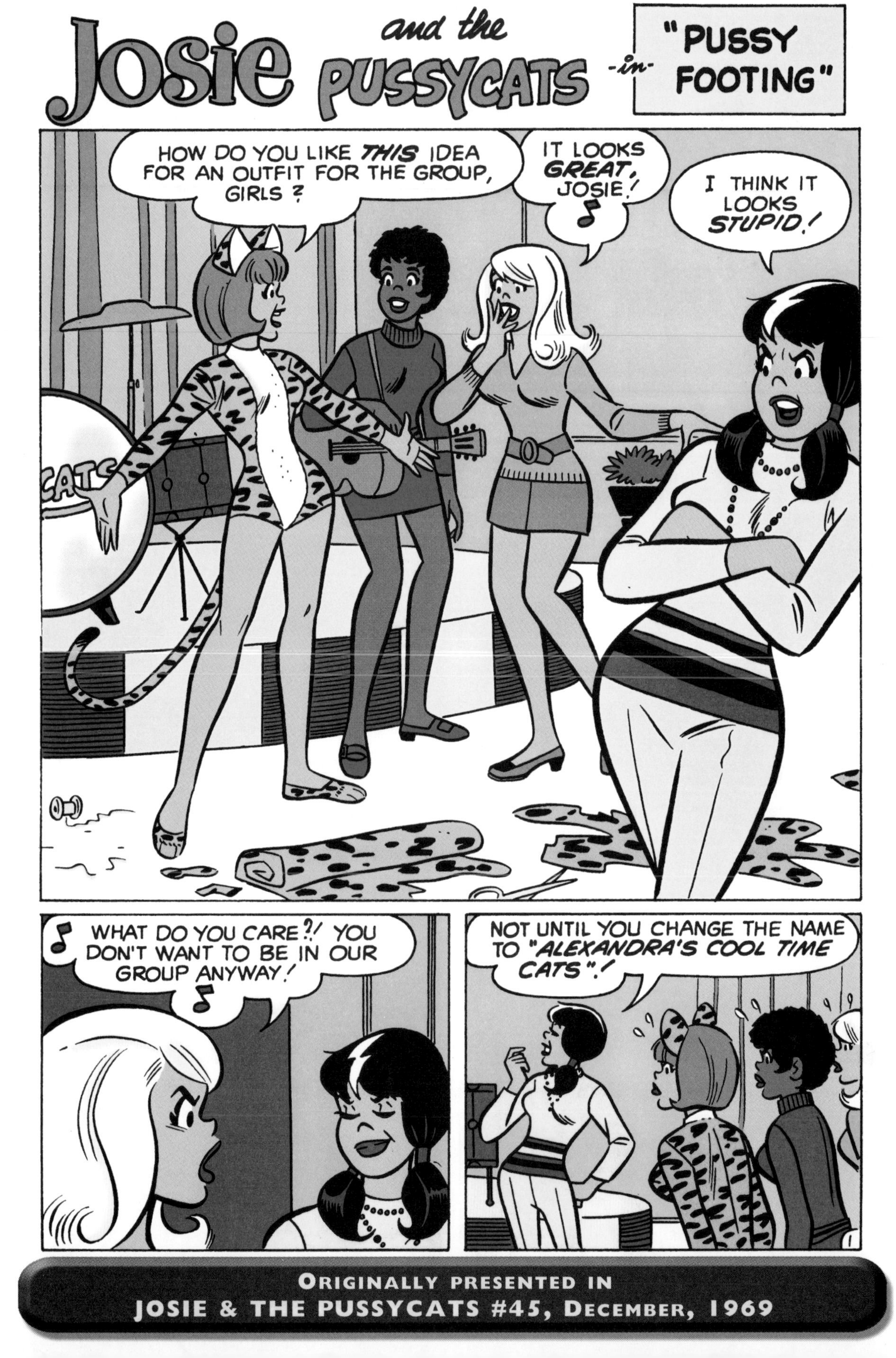
Josie and the PUSSYCATS -in- "PUSSY FOOTING"
HOW DO YOU LIKE THIS IDEA FOR AN OUTFIT FOR THE GROUP, GIRLS?
IT LOOKS GREAT, JOSIE!
I THINK IT LOOKS STUPID!
CATS
WHAT DO YOU CARE?! YOU DON'T WANT TO BE IN OUR GROUP ANYWAY!
NOT UNTIL YOU CHANGE THE NAME TO "ALEXANDRA'S COOL TIME CATS"!

ORIGINALLY PRESENTED IN
JOSIE & THE PUSSYCATS #45, DECEMBER, 1969

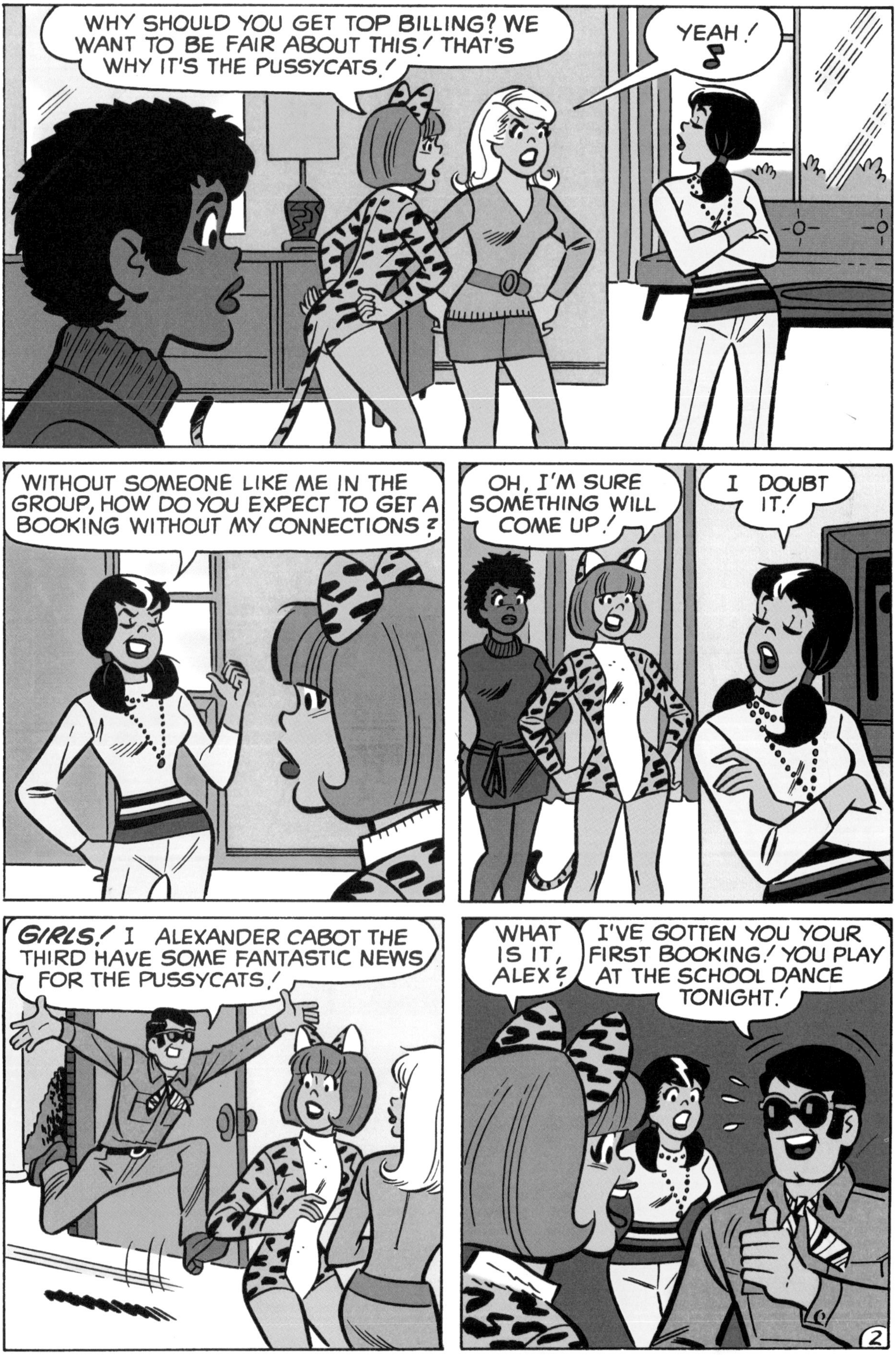
WHY SHOULD YOU GET TOP BILLING? WE WANT TO BE FAIR ABOUT THIS! THAT'S WHY IT'S THE PUSSYCATS!
YEAH!
WITHOUT SOMEONE LIKE ME IN THE GROUP, HOW DO YOU EXPECT TO GET A BOOKING WITHOUT MY CONNECTIONS?
OH, I'M SURE SOMETHING WILL COME UP!
I DOUBT IT!
GIRLS! I ALEXANDER CABOT THE THIRD HAVE SOME FANTASTIC NEWS FOR THE PUSSYCATS!
WHAT IS IT, ALEX?
I'VE GOTTEN YOU YOUR FIRST BOOKING! YOU PLAY AT THE SCHOOL DANCE TONIGHT!
2

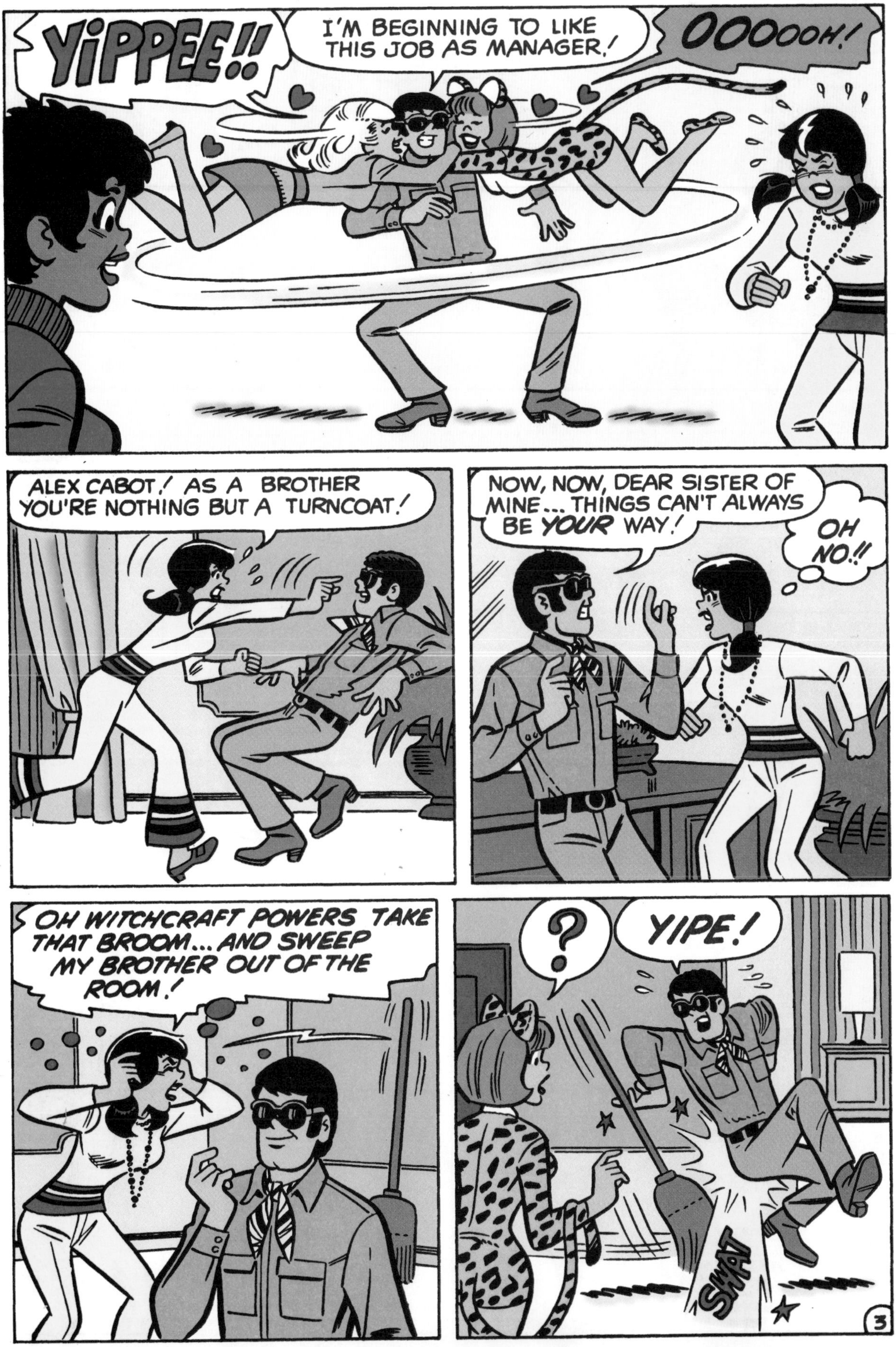
YIPPEE!!
I'M BEGINNING TO LIKE THIS JOB AS MANAGER!
OOOOOOH!
ALEX CABOT! AS A BROTHER YOU'RE NOTHING BUT A TURNCOAT!
NOW, NOW, DEAR SISTER OF MINE... THINGS CAN'T ALWAYS BE YOUR WAY!
OH NO!!
OH WITCHCRAFT POWERS TAKE THAT BROOM... AND SWEEP MY BROTHER OUT OF THE ROOM!
?
YIPE!
SWAT
3

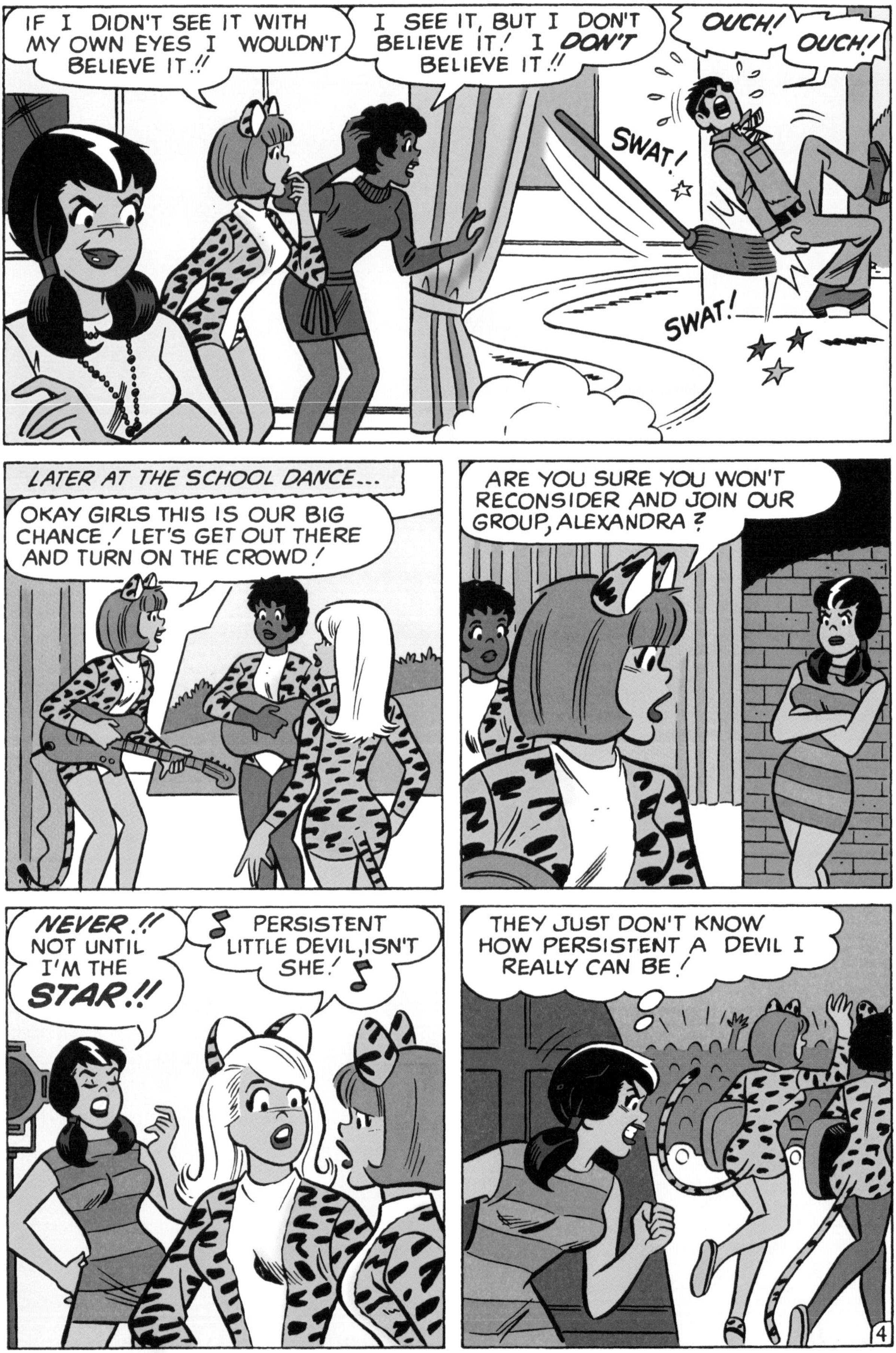
IF I DIDN'T SEE IT WITH MY OWN EYES I WOULDN'T BELIEVE IT!!
I SEE IT, BUT I DON'T BELIEVE IT! I DON'T BELIEVE IT!!
OUCH!
OUCH!
SWAT!
SWAT!
LATER AT THE SCHOOL DANCE...
OKAY GIRLS THIS IS OUR BIG CHANCE! LET'S GET OUT THERE AND TURN ON THE CROWD!
ARE YOU SURE YOU WON'T RECONSIDER AND JOIN OUR GROUP, ALEXANDRA?
NEVER!! NOT UNTIL I'M THE STAR!!
PERSISTENT LITTLE DEVIL, ISN'T SHE!
THEY JUST DON'T KNOW HOW PERSISTENT A DEVIL I REALLY CAN BE!
4

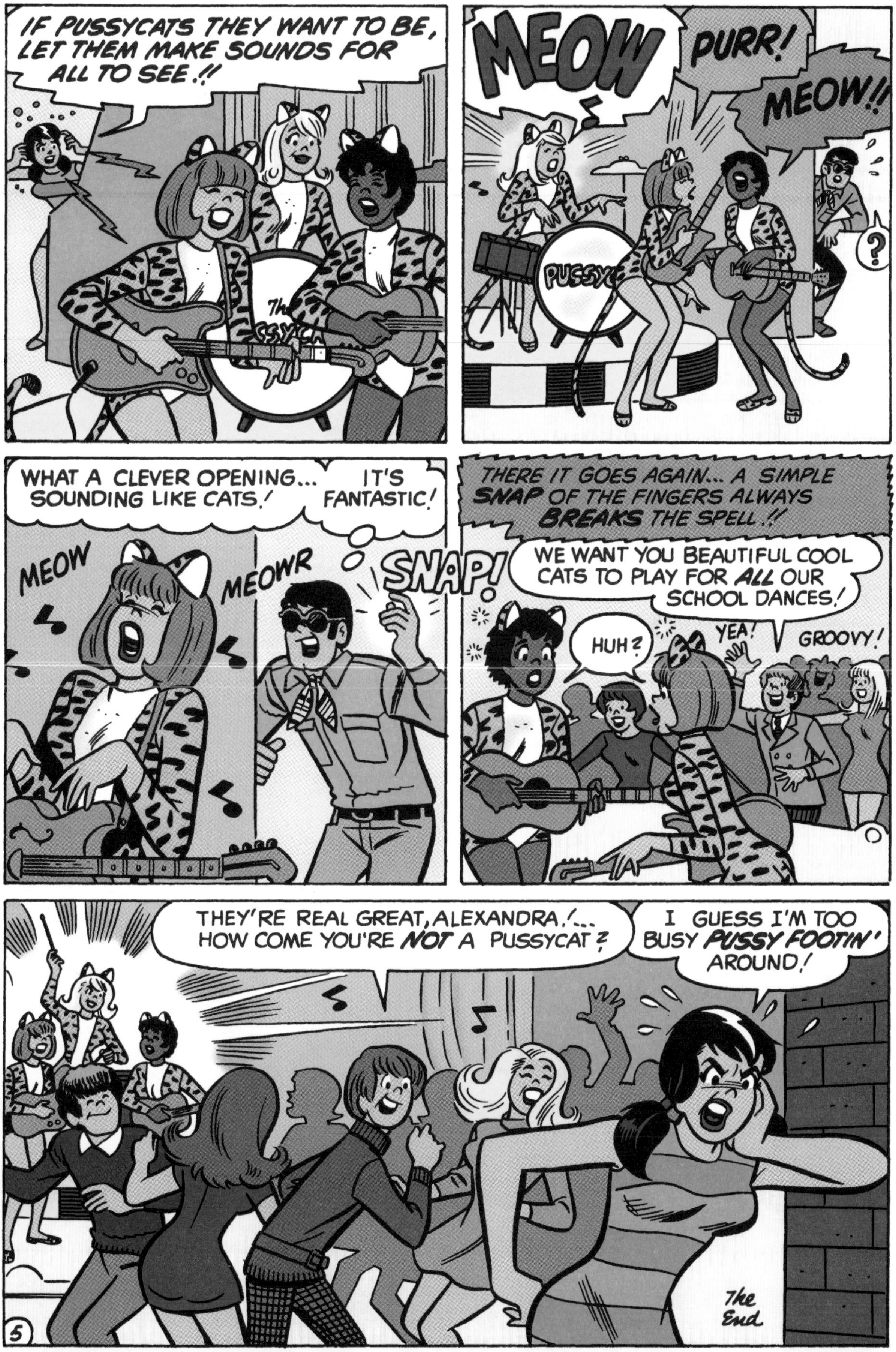
IF PUSSYCATS THEY WANT TO BE, LET THEM MAKE SOUNDS FOR ALL TO SEE.!!
MEOW
PURR!
MEOW!!
?
WHAT A CLEVER OPENING... SOUNDING LIKE CATS!
IT'S FANTASTIC!
MEOW
MEOWR
SNAP!
THERE IT GOES AGAIN... A SIMPLE SNAP OF THE FINGERS ALWAYS BREAKS THE SPELL.!!
WE WANT YOU BEAUTIFUL COOL CATS TO PLAY FOR ALL OUR SCHOOL DANCES!
HUH?
YEA!
GROOVY!
THEY'RE REAL GREAT, ALEXANDRA!... HOW COME YOU'RE NOT A PUSSYCAT?
I GUESS I'M TOO BUSY PUSSY FOOTIN' AROUND!
The End
5

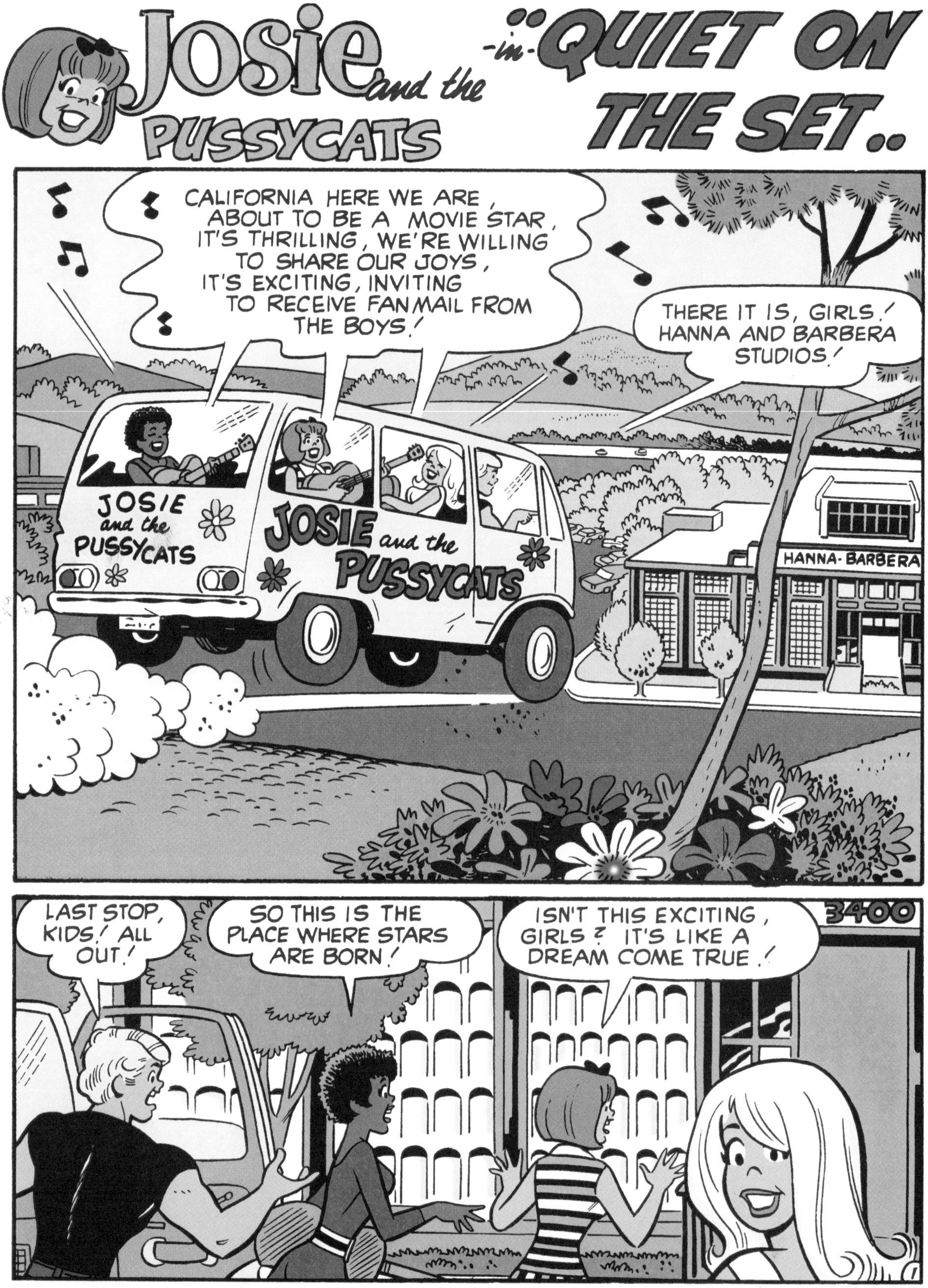
Josie and the PUSSYCATS -in- "QUIET ON THE SET.."
CALIFORNIA HERE WE ARE, ABOUT TO BE A MOVIE STAR, IT'S THRILLING, WE'RE WILLING TO SHARE OUR JOYS, IT'S EXCITING, INVITING TO RECEIVE FANMAIL FROM THE BOYS!
THERE IT IS, GIRLS! HANNA AND BARBERA STUDIOS!
JOSIE and the PUSSYCATS
JOSIE and the PUSSYCATS
HANNA-BARBERA
LAST STOP, KIDS! ALL OUT!
SO THIS IS THE PLACE WHERE STARS ARE BORN!
ISN'T THIS EXCITING, GIRLS? IT'S LIKE A DREAM COME TRUE!
3400

ORIGINALLY PRESENTED IN
JOSIE & THE PUSSYCATS #50, SEPTEMBER, 1970

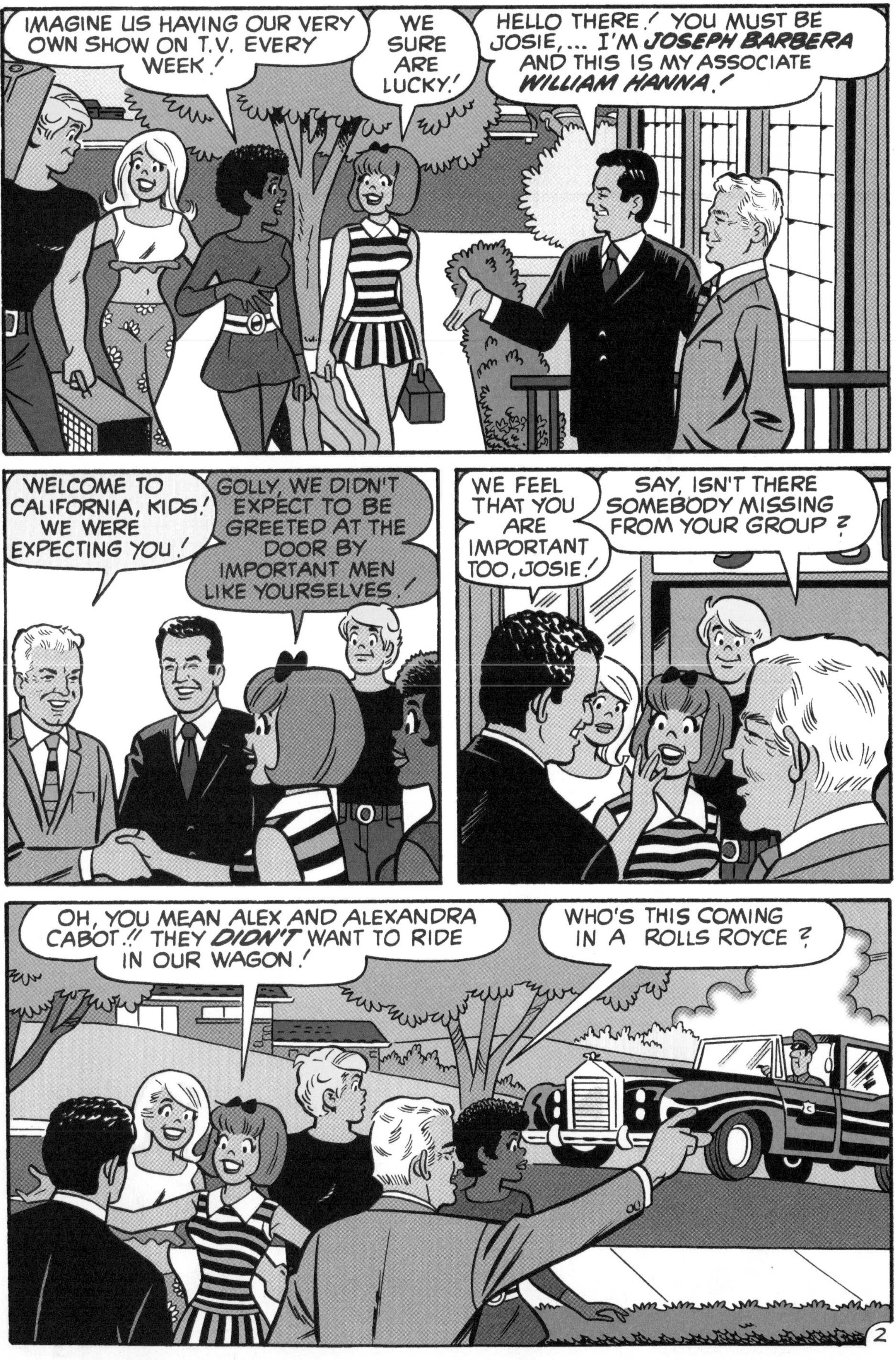
IMAGINE US HAVING OUR VERY OWN SHOW ON T.V. EVERY WEEK!
WE SURE ARE LUCKY!
HELLO THERE! YOU MUST BE JOSIE,... I'M JOSEPH BARBERA AND THIS IS MY ASSOCIATE WILLIAM HANNA!
WELCOME TO CALIFORNIA, KIDS! WE WERE EXPECTING YOU!
GOLLY, WE DIDN'T EXPECT TO BE GREETED AT THE DOOR BY IMPORTANT MEN LIKE YOURSELVES!
WE FEEL THAT YOU ARE IMPORTANT TOO, JOSIE!
SAY, ISN'T THERE SOMEBODY MISSING FROM YOUR GROUP?
OH, YOU MEAN ALEX AND ALEXANDRA CABOT!! THEY DIDN'T WANT TO RIDE IN OUR WAGON!
WHO'S THIS COMING IN A ROLLS ROYCE?
2

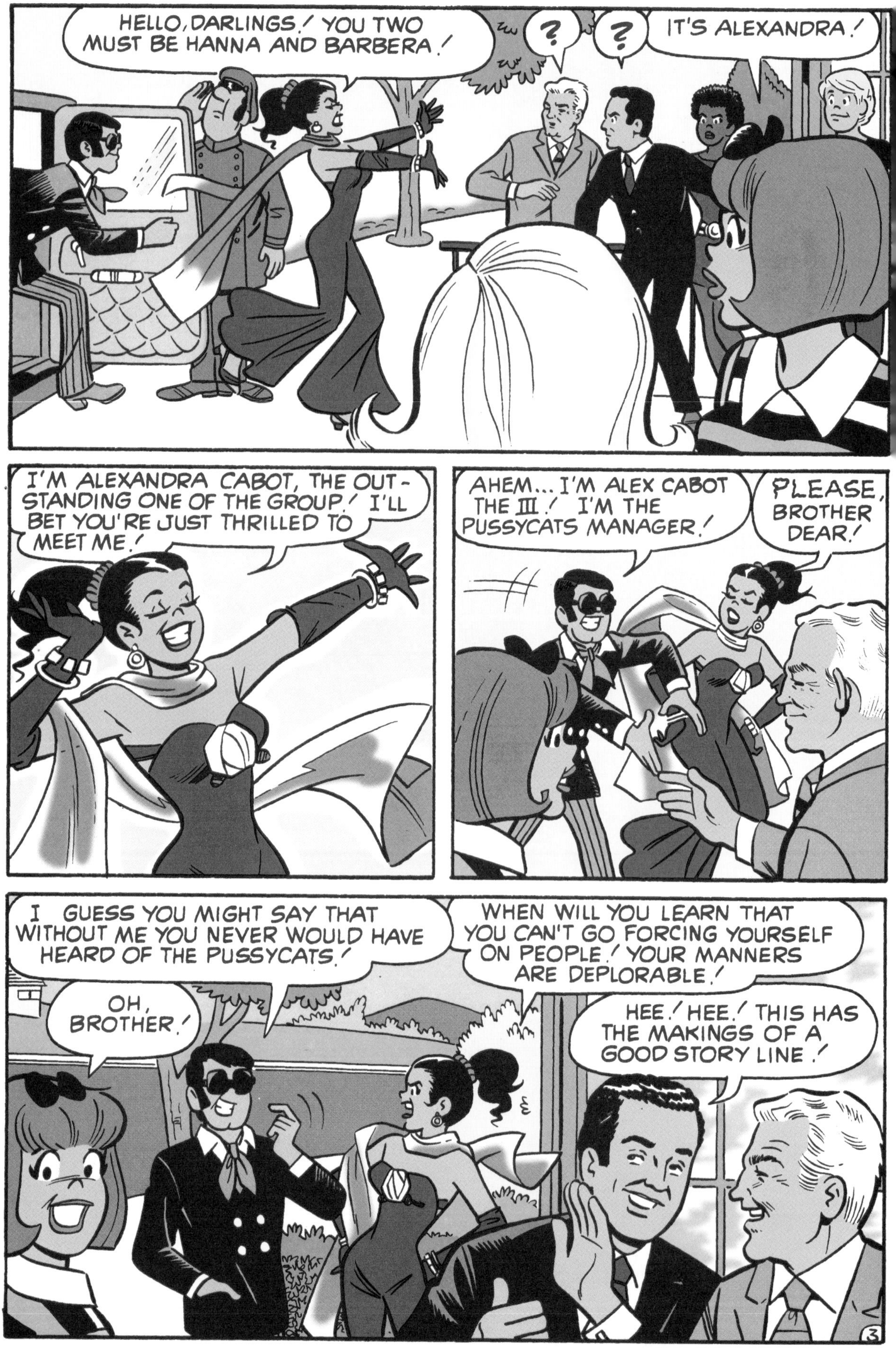
HELLO, DARLINGS! YOU TWO MUST BE HANNA AND BARBERA!
?
?
IT'S ALEXANDRA!
I'M ALEXANDRA CABOT, THE OUT-STANDING ONE OF THE GROUP! I'LL BET YOU'RE JUST THRILLED TO MEET ME!
AHEM... I'M ALEX CABOT THE III! I'M THE PUSSYCATS MANAGER!
PLEASE, BROTHER DEAR!
I GUESS YOU MIGHT SAY THAT WITHOUT ME YOU NEVER WOULD HAVE HEARD OF THE PUSSYCATS!
WHEN WILL YOU LEARN THAT YOU CAN'T GO FORCING YOURSELF ON PEOPLE! YOUR MANNERS ARE DEPLORABLE!
OH, BROTHER!
HEE! HEE! THIS HAS THE MAKINGS OF A GOOD STORY LINE!
3

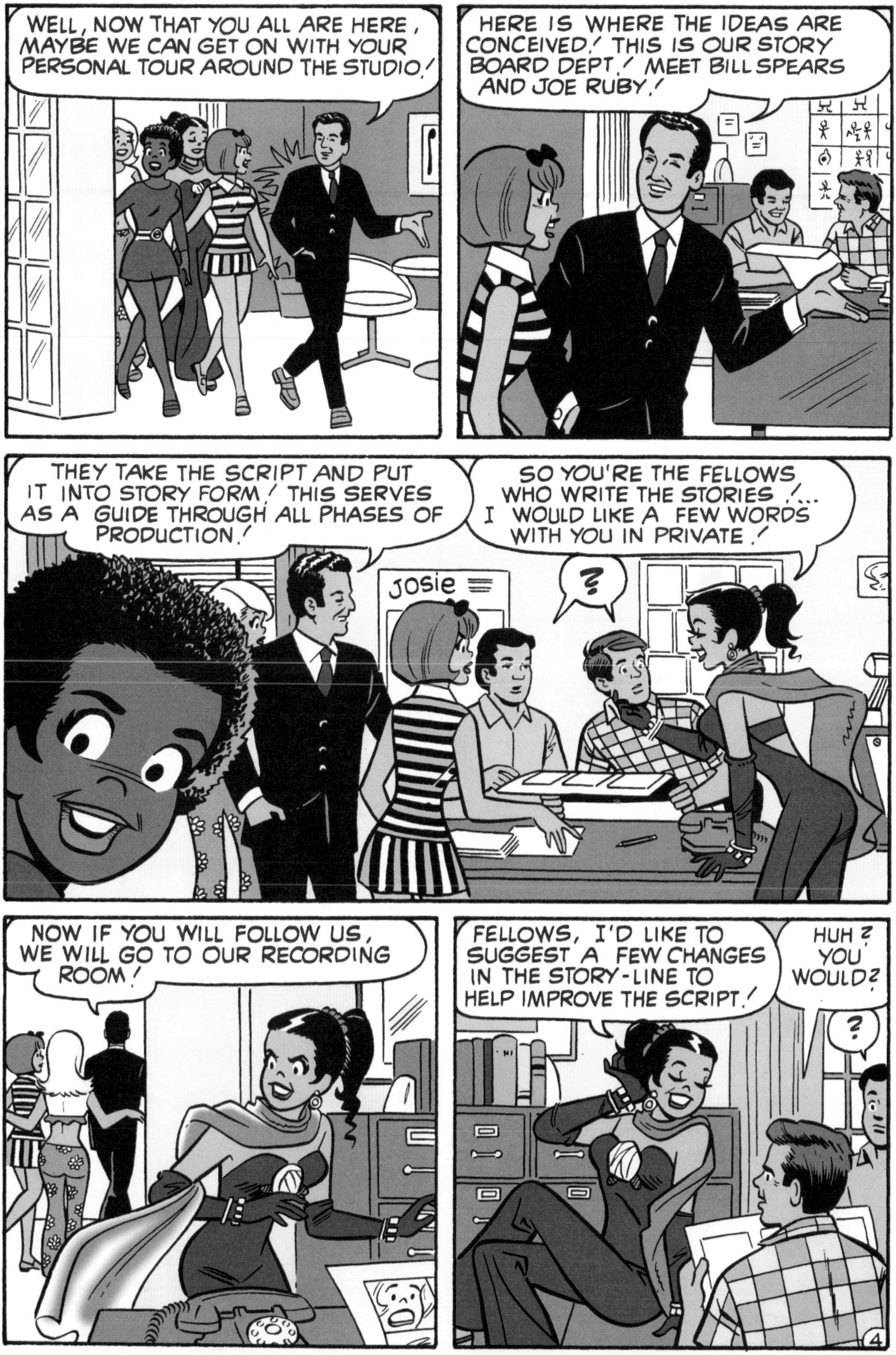
WELL, NOW THAT YOU ALL ARE HERE, MAYBE WE CAN GET ON WITH YOUR PERSONAL TOUR AROUND THE STUDIO!
HERE IS WHERE THE IDEAS ARE CONCEIVED! THIS IS OUR STORY BOARD DEPT.! MEET BILL SPEARS AND JOE RUBY!
THEY TAKE THE SCRIPT AND PUT IT INTO STORY FORM! THIS SERVES AS A GUIDE THROUGH ALL PHASES OF PRODUCTION!
SO YOU'RE THE FELLOWS WHO WRITE THE STORIES!... I WOULD LIKE A FEW WORDS WITH YOU IN PRIVATE!
?
JOSIE
NOW IF YOU WILL FOLLOW US, WE WILL GO TO OUR RECORDING ROOM!
FELLOWS, I'D LIKE TO SUGGEST A FEW CHANGES IN THE STORY-LINE TO HELP IMPROVE THE SCRIPT!
HUH? YOU WOULD?
?
4

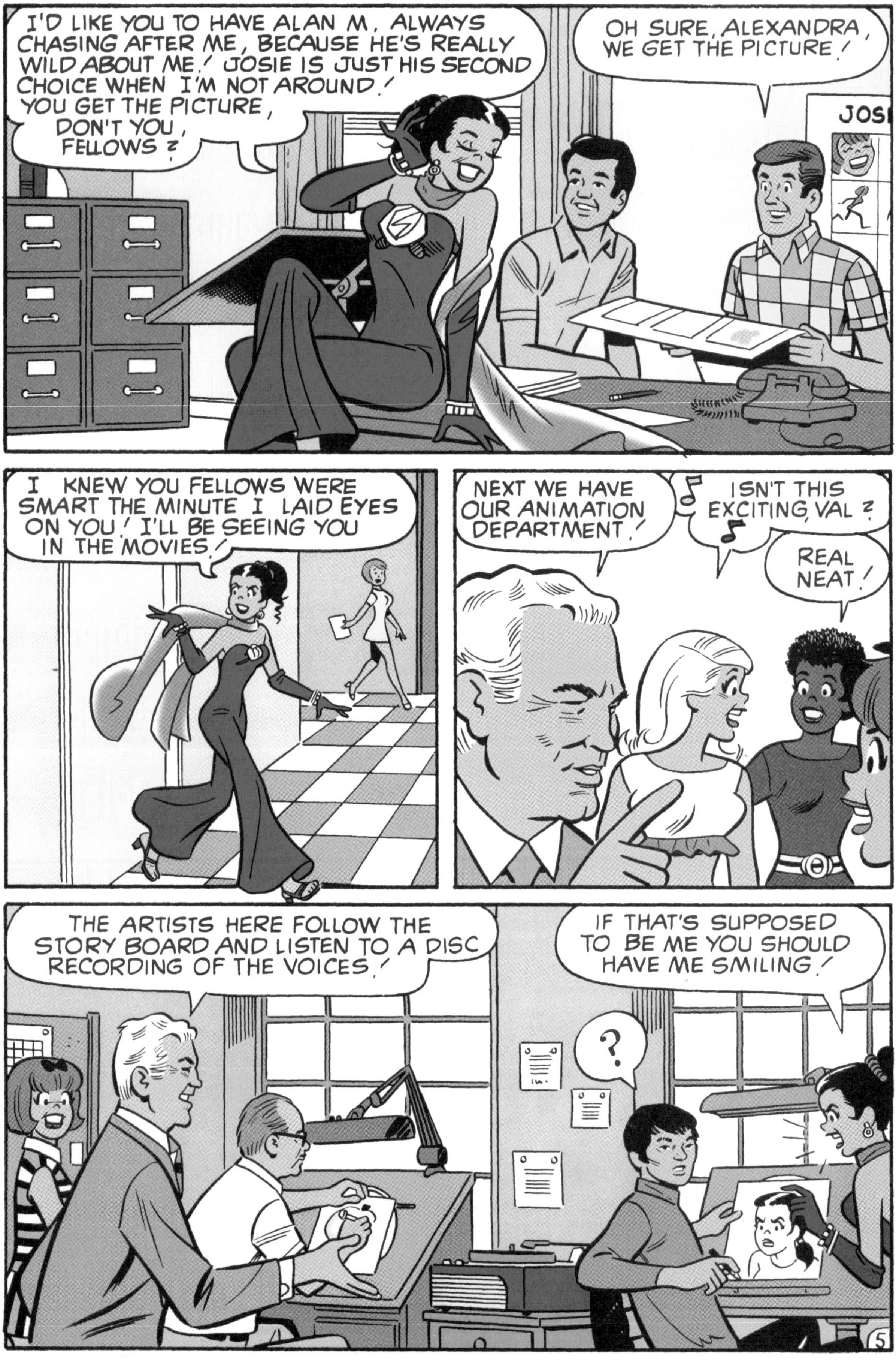
I'D LIKE YOU TO HAVE ALAN M. ALWAYS CHASING AFTER ME, BECAUSE HE'S REALLY WILD ABOUT ME! JOSIE IS JUST HIS SECOND CHOICE WHEN I'M NOT AROUND! YOU GET THE PICTURE, DON'T YOU, FELLOWS?
OH SURE, ALEXANDRA, WE GET THE PICTURE!
I KNEW YOU FELLOWS WERE SMART THE MINUTE I LAID EYES ON YOU! I'LL BE SEEING YOU IN THE MOVIES!
NEXT WE HAVE OUR ANIMATION DEPARTMENT!
ISN'T THIS EXCITING, VAL?
REAL NEAT!
THE ARTISTS HERE FOLLOW THE STORY BOARD AND LISTEN TO A DISC RECORDING OF THE VOICES!
?
IF THAT'S SUPPOSED TO BE ME YOU SHOULD HAVE ME SMILING!
5

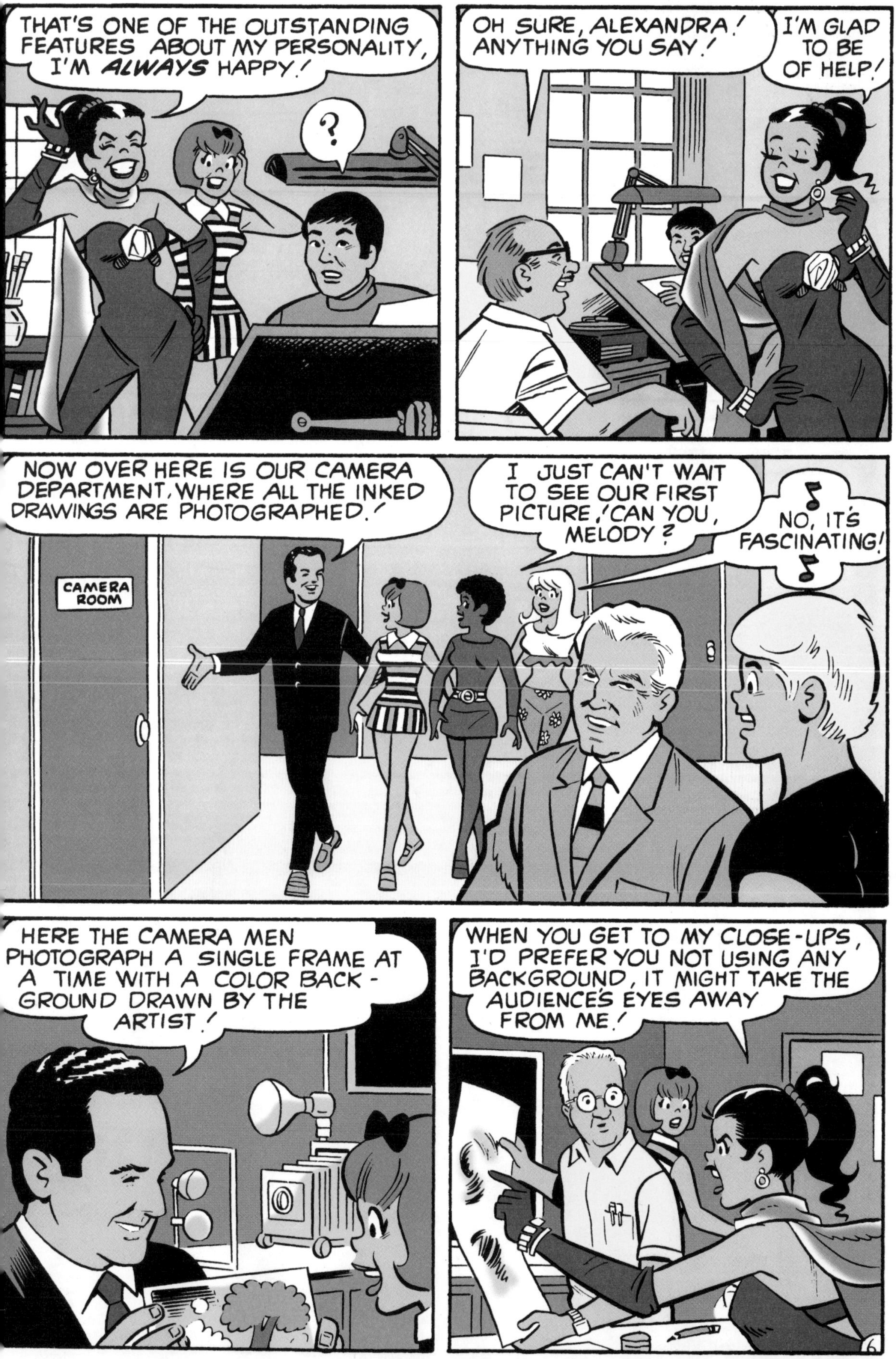
THAT'S ONE OF THE OUTSTANDING FEATURES ABOUT MY PERSONALITY, I'M ALWAYS HAPPY!
?
OH SURE, ALEXANDRA! ANYTHING YOU SAY!
I'M GLAD TO BE OF HELP!
NOW OVER HERE IS OUR CAMERA DEPARTMENT, WHERE ALL THE INKED DRAWINGS ARE PHOTOGRAPHED!
CAMERA ROOM
I JUST CAN'T WAIT TO SEE OUR FIRST PICTURE! CAN YOU, MELODY?
NO, IT'S FASCINATING!
HERE THE CAMERA MEN PHOTOGRAPH A SINGLE FRAME AT A TIME WITH A COLOR BACK-GROUND DRAWN BY THE ARTIST!
WHEN YOU GET TO MY CLOSE-UPS, I'D PREFER YOU NOT USING ANY BACKGROUND, IT MIGHT TAKE THE AUDIENCE'S EYES AWAY FROM ME!
6

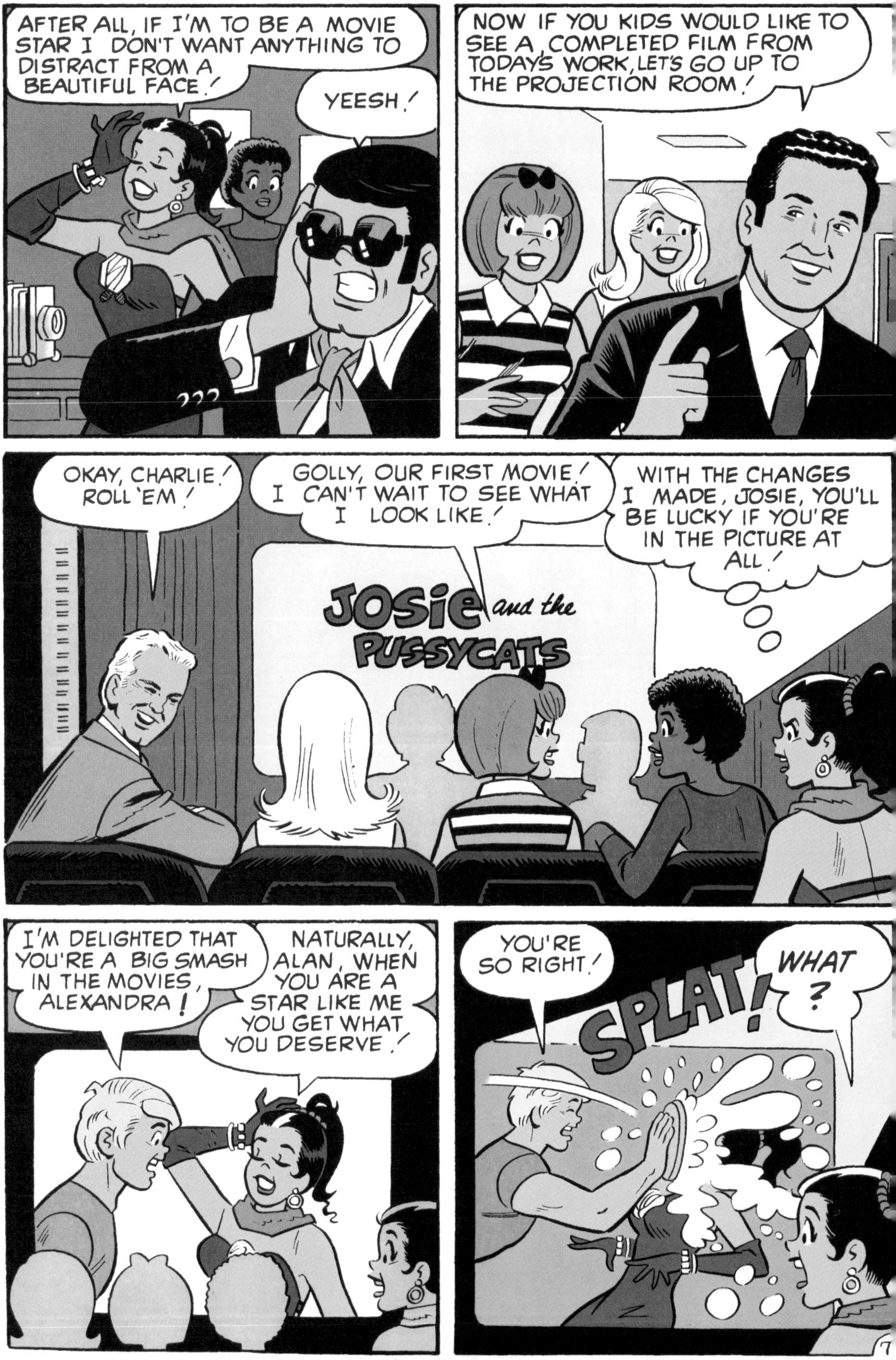
AFTER ALL, IF I'M TO BE A MOVIE STAR I DON'T WANT ANYTHING TO DISTRACT FROM A BEAUTIFUL FACE!
YEESH!
NOW IF YOU KIDS WOULD LIKE TO SEE A COMPLETED FILM FROM TODAY'S WORK, LET'S GO UP TO THE PROJECTION ROOM!
OKAY, CHARLIE! ROLL 'EM!
GOLLY, OUR FIRST MOVIE! I CAN'T WAIT TO SEE WHAT I LOOK LIKE!
WITH THE CHANGES I MADE, JOSIE, YOU'LL BE LUCKY IF YOU'RE IN THE PICTURE AT ALL!
JOSIE and the PUSSYCATS
I'M DELIGHTED THAT YOU'RE A BIG SMASH IN THE MOVIES, ALEXANDRA!
NATURALLY, ALAN, WHEN YOU ARE A STAR LIKE ME YOU GET WHAT YOU DESERVE!
YOU'RE SO RIGHT!
SPLAT!
WHAT?
7

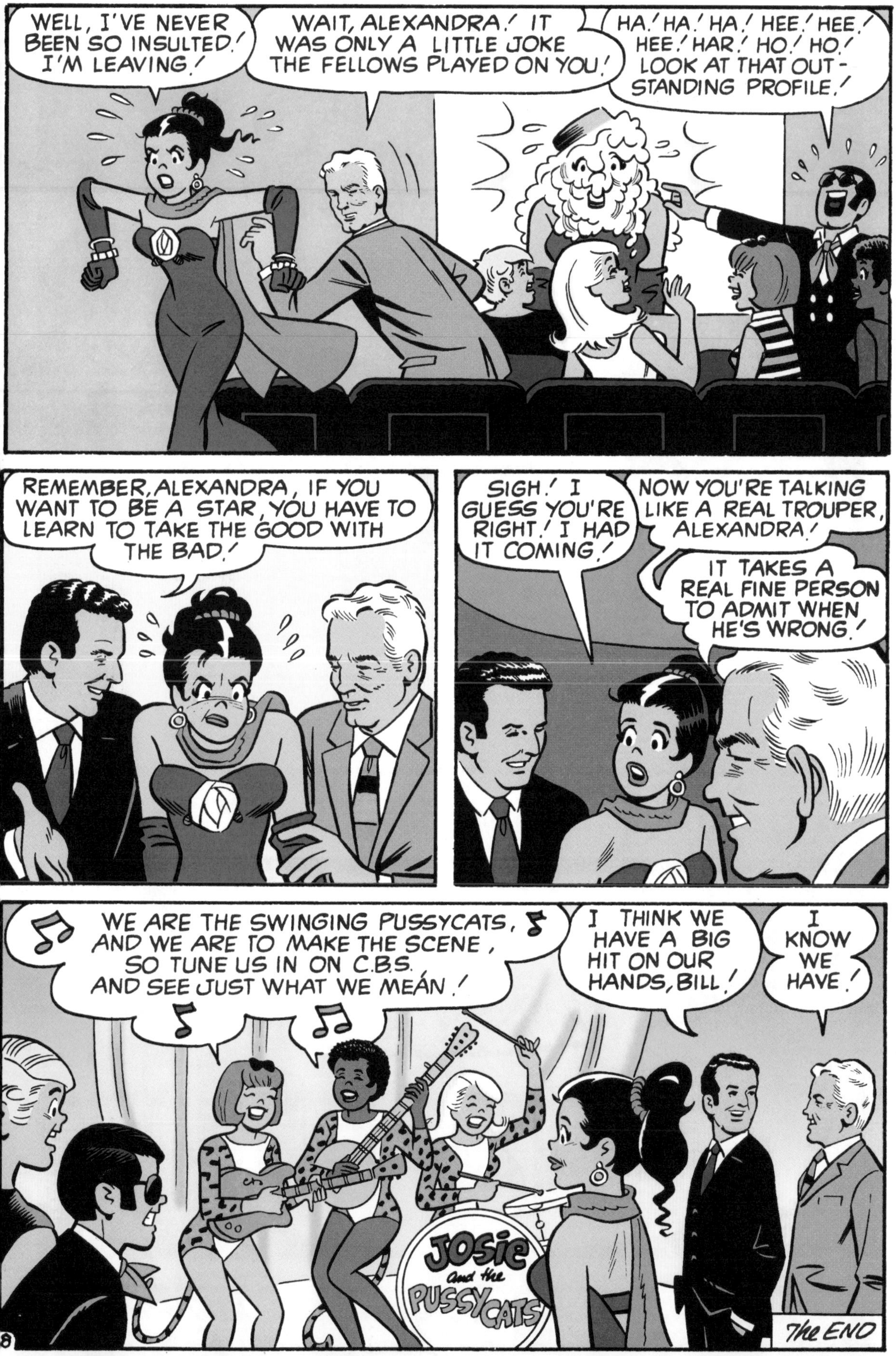
WELL, I'VE NEVER BEEN SO INSULTED! I'M LEAVING!
WAIT, ALEXANDRA! IT WAS ONLY A LITTLE JOKE THE FELLOWS PLAYED ON YOU!
HA! HA! HA! HEE! HEE! HEE! HAR! HO! HO! LOOK AT THAT OUT-STANDING PROFILE!
REMEMBER, ALEXANDRA, IF YOU WANT TO BE A STAR, YOU HAVE TO LEARN TO TAKE THE GOOD WITH THE BAD!
SIGH! I GUESS YOU'RE RIGHT! I HAD IT COMING!
NOW YOU'RE TALKING LIKE A REAL TROUPER, ALEXANDRA!
IT TAKES A REAL FINE PERSON TO ADMIT WHEN HE'S WRONG!
WE ARE THE SWINGING PUSSYCATS, AND WE ARE TO MAKE THE SCENE, SO TUNE US IN ON C.B.S. AND SEE JUST WHAT WE MEAN!
I THINK WE HAVE A BIG HIT ON OUR HANDS, BILL!
I KNOW WE HAVE!
JOSIE and the PUSSYCATS
The END

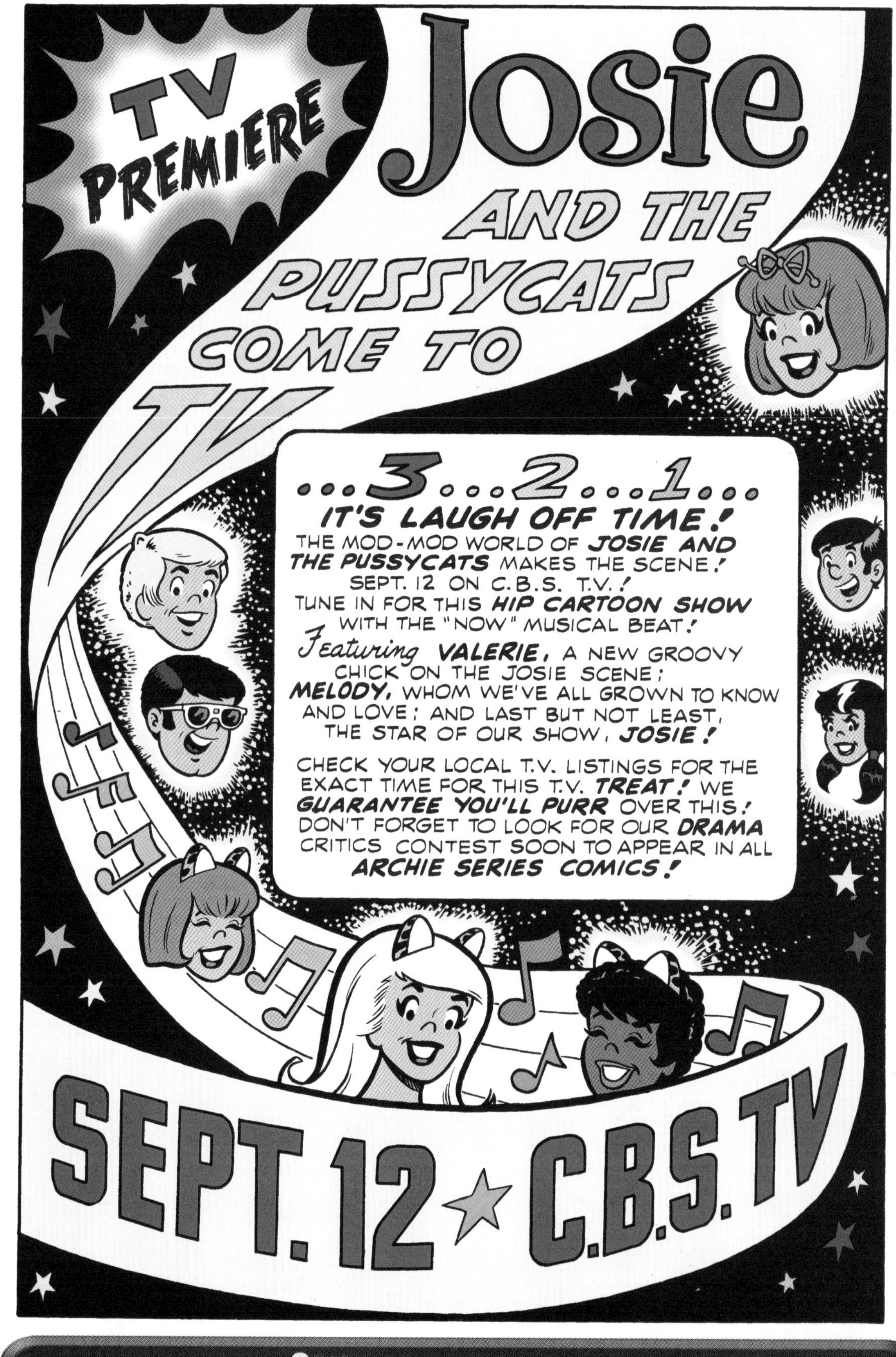
TV PREMIERE
Josie AND THE PUSSYCATS COME TO TV
...3...2...1...
IT'S LAUGH OFF TIME!
THE MOD-MOD WORLD OF JOSIE AND THE PUSSYCATS MAKES THE SCENE!
SEPT. 12 ON C.B.S. T.V.!
TUNE IN FOR THIS HIP CARTOON SHOW WITH THE "NOW" MUSICAL BEAT!
Featuring VALERIE, A NEW GROOVY CHICK ON THE JOSIE SCENE; MELODY, WHOM WE'VE ALL GROWN TO KNOW AND LOVE; AND LAST BUT NOT LEAST, THE STAR OF OUR SHOW, JOSIE!
CHECK YOUR LOCAL T.V. LISTINGS FOR THE EXACT TIME FOR THIS T.V. TREAT! WE GUARANTEE YOU'LL PURR OVER THIS! DON'T FORGET TO LOOK FOR OUR DRAMA CRITICS CONTEST SOON TO APPEAR IN ALL ARCHIE SERIES COMICS!
SEPT. 12 ★ C.B.S. TV

ORIGINALLY PRESENTED IN
JOSIE & THE PUSSYCATS #50, SEPTEMBER, 1970

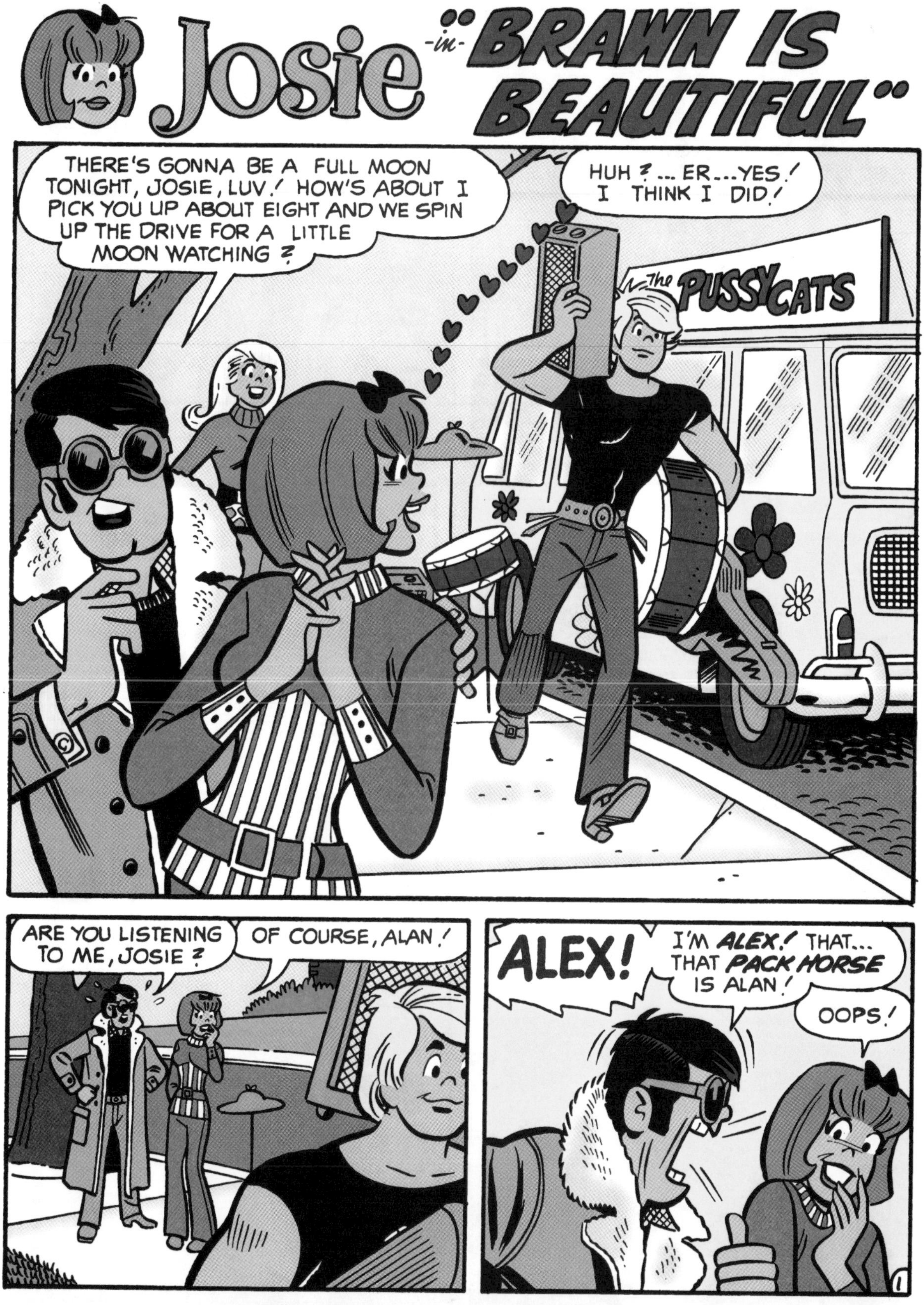
Josie -in- "BRAWN IS BEAUTIFUL"
THERE'S GONNA BE A FULL MOON TONIGHT, JOSIE, LUV! HOW'S ABOUT I PICK YOU UP ABOUT EIGHT AND WE SPIN UP THE DRIVE FOR A LITTLE MOON WATCHING?
HUH?... ER...YES! I THINK I DID!
The PUSSYCATS
ARE YOU LISTENING TO ME, JOSIE?
OF COURSE, ALAN!
ALEX!
I'M ALEX! THAT... THAT PACK HORSE IS ALAN!
OOPS!
1

ORIGINALLY PRESENTED IN
JOSIE & THE PUSSYCATS #53, FEBRUARY, 1971

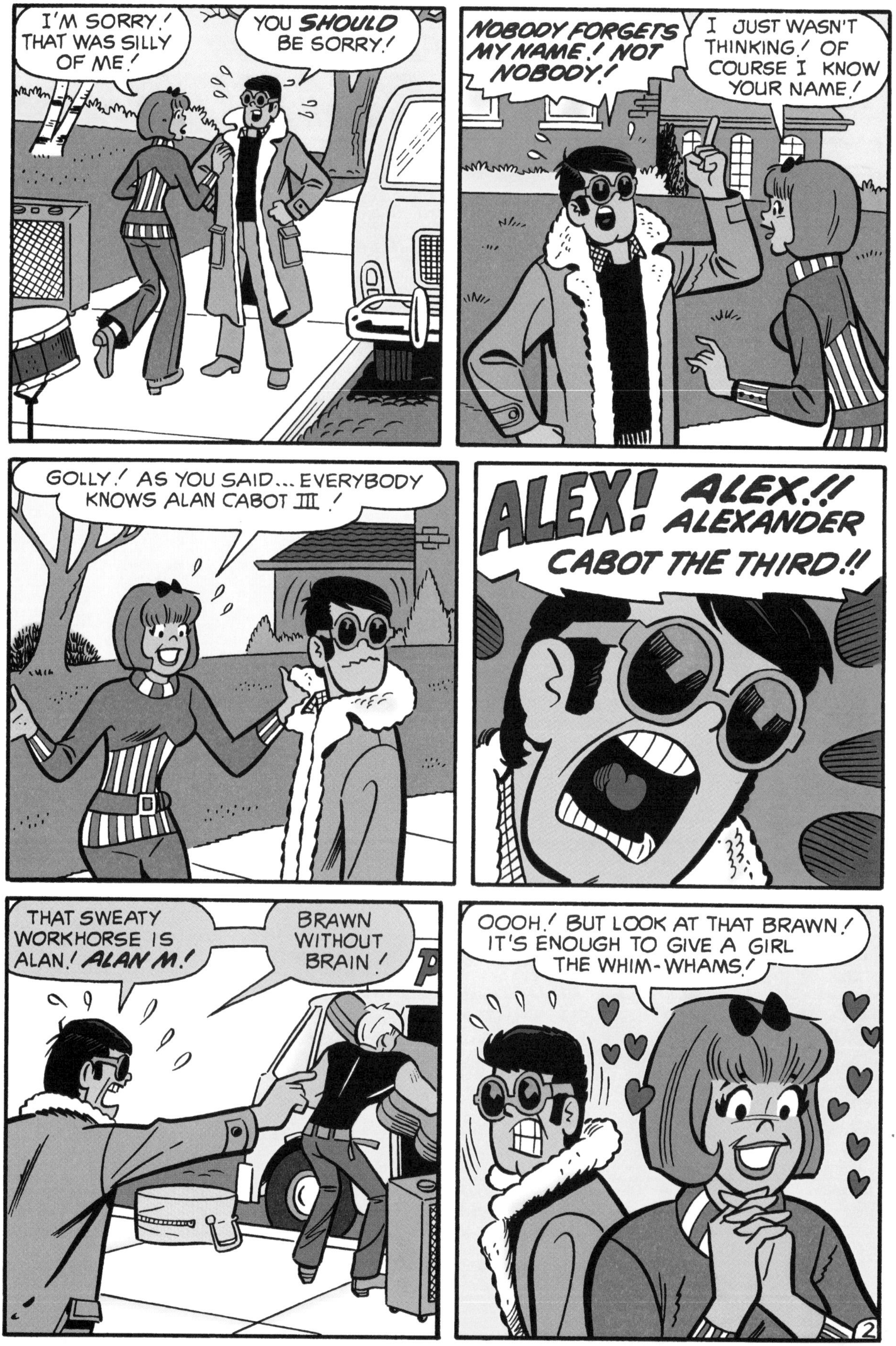
I'M SORRY! THAT WAS SILLY OF ME!
YOU **SHOULD** BE SORRY!
NOBODY FORGETS MY NAME! NOT NOBODY!
I JUST WASN'T THINKING! OF COURSE I KNOW YOUR NAME!
GOLLY! AS YOU SAID... EVERYBODY KNOWS ALAN CABOT III!
ALEX! ALEX!! ALEXANDER CABOT THE THIRD!!
THAT SWEATY WORKHORSE IS ALAN! ALAN M!
BRAWN WITHOUT BRAIN!
OOOH! BUT LOOK AT THAT BRAWN! IT'S ENOUGH TO GIVE A GIRL THE WHIM-WHAMS!
2

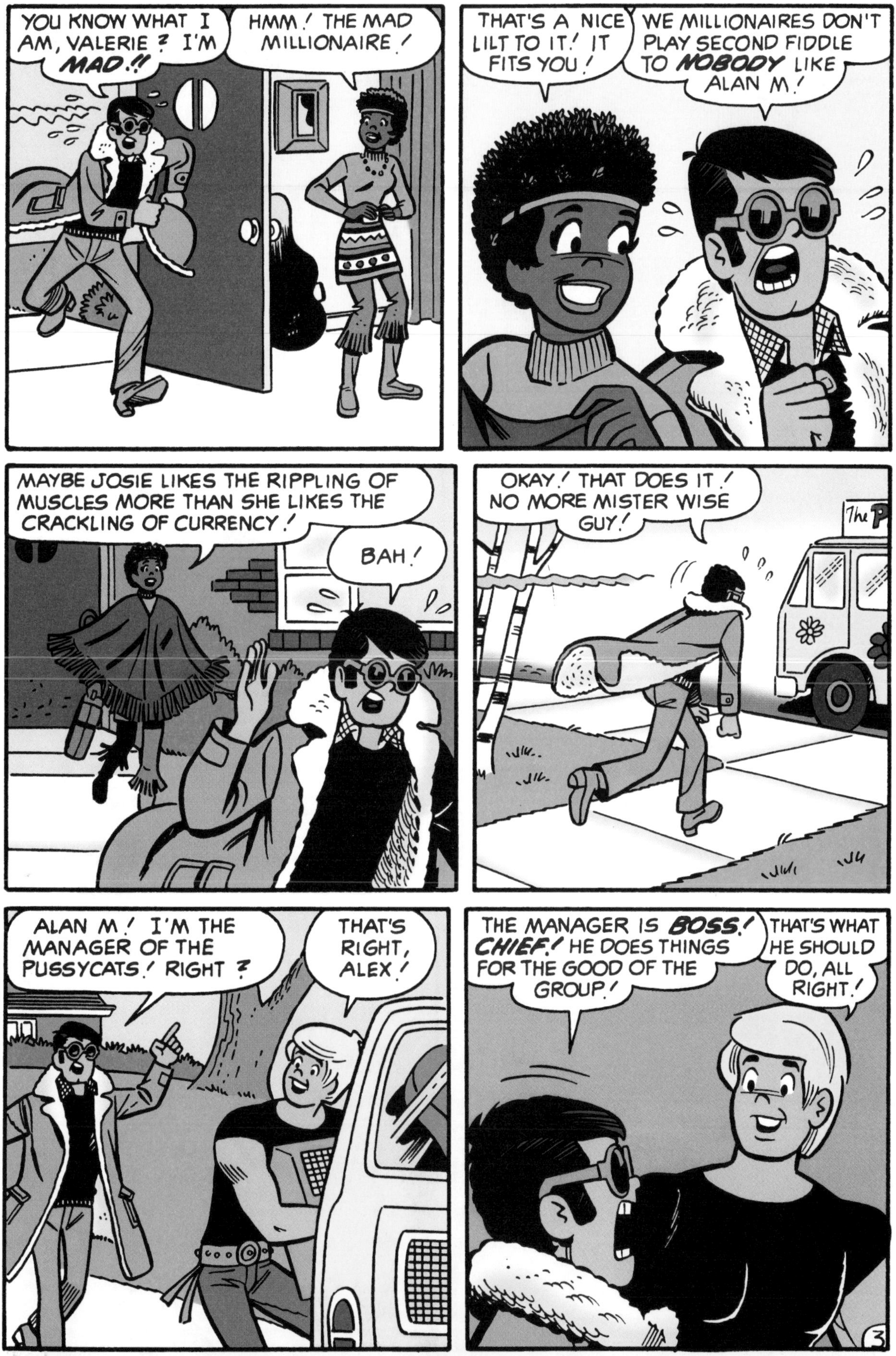
YOU KNOW WHAT I AM, VALERIE? I'M MAD!!
HMM! THE MAD MILLIONAIRE!
THAT'S A NICE LILT TO IT! IT FITS YOU!
WE MILLIONAIRES DON'T PLAY SECOND FIDDLE TO NOBODY LIKE ALAN M!
MAYBE JOSIE LIKES THE RIPPLING OF MUSCLES MORE THAN SHE LIKES THE CRACKLING OF CURRENCY!
BAH!
OKAY! THAT DOES IT! NO MORE MISTER WISE GUY!
The P
ALAN M! I'M THE MANAGER OF THE PUSSYCATS! RIGHT?
THAT'S RIGHT, ALEX!
THE MANAGER IS BOSS! CHIEF! HE DOES THINGS FOR THE GOOD OF THE GROUP!
THAT'S WHAT HE SHOULD DO, ALL RIGHT!
3

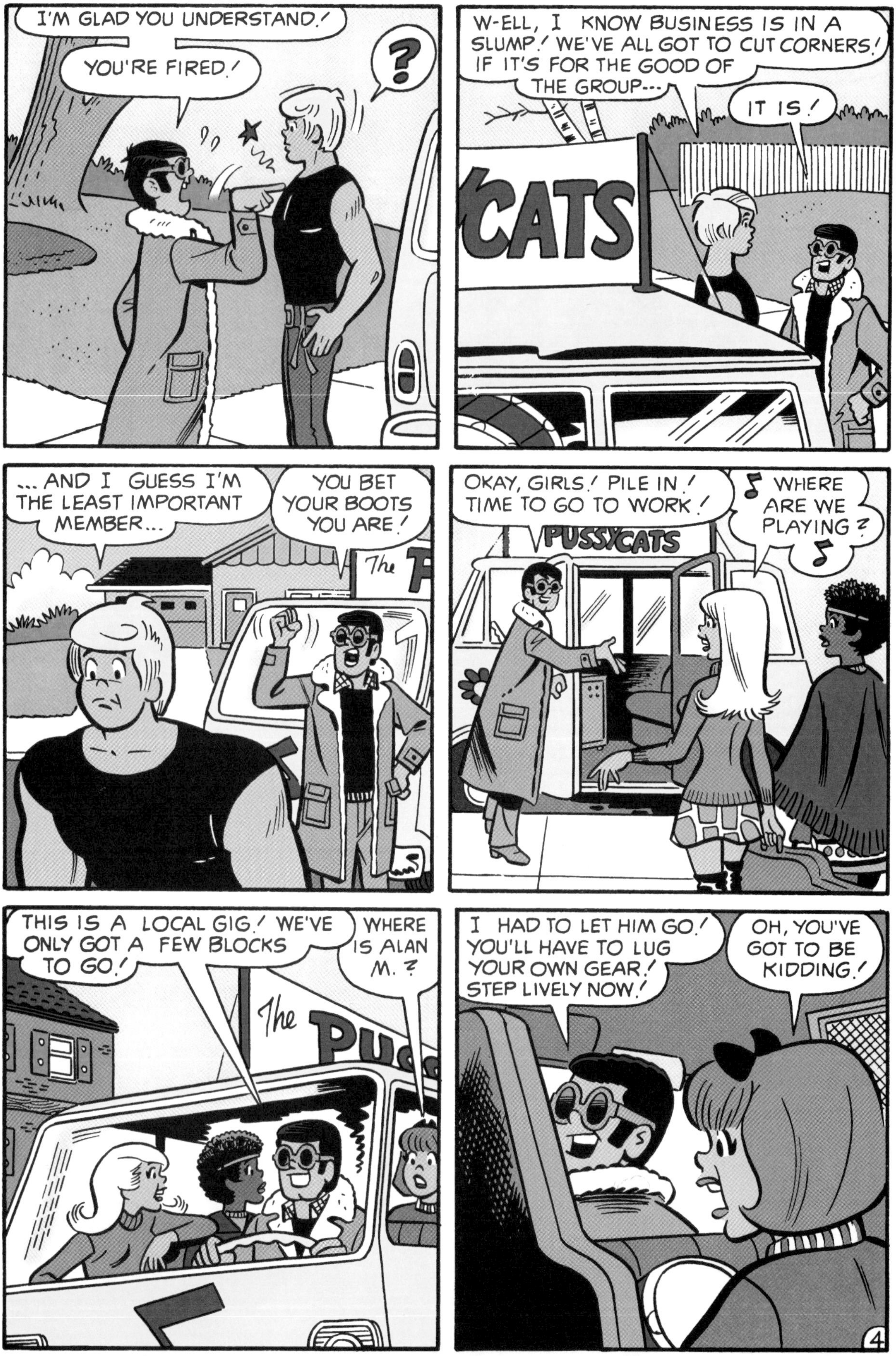
I'M GLAD YOU UNDERSTAND!
YOU'RE FIRED!
?
W-ELL, I KNOW BUSINESS IS IN A SLUMP! WE'VE ALL GOT TO CUT CORNERS! IF IT'S FOR THE GOOD OF THE GROUP---
IT IS!
CATS
... AND I GUESS I'M THE LEAST IMPORTANT MEMBER...
YOU BET YOUR BOOTS YOU ARE!
The
OKAY, GIRLS! PILE IN! TIME TO GO TO WORK!
WHERE ARE WE PLAYING?
PUSSYCATS
THIS IS A LOCAL GIG! WE'VE ONLY GOT A FEW BLOCKS TO GO!
WHERE IS ALAN M.?
The
I HAD TO LET HIM GO! YOU'LL HAVE TO LUG YOUR OWN GEAR! STEP LIVELY NOW!
OH, YOU'VE GOT TO BE KIDDING!
4

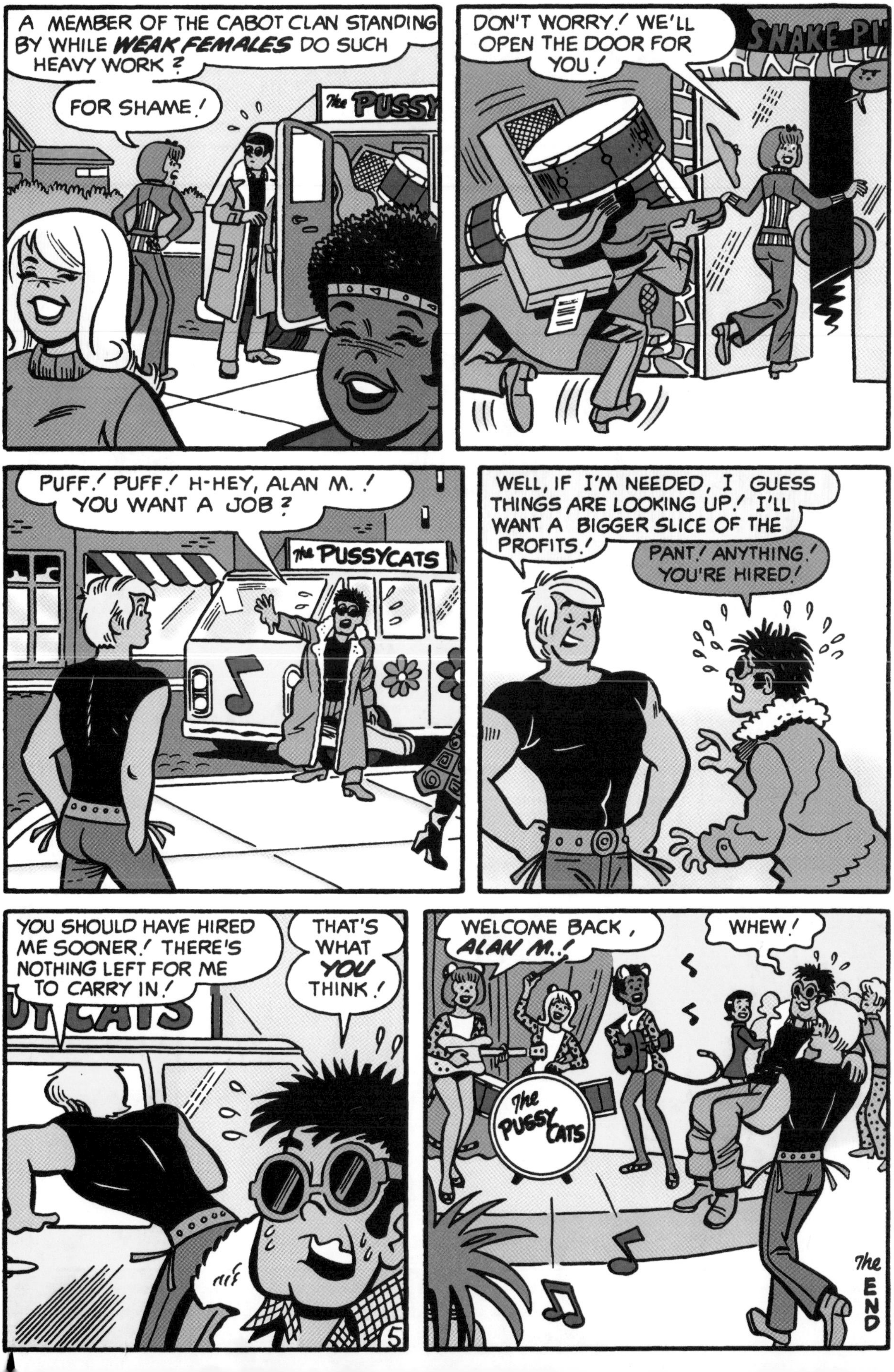
A MEMBER OF THE CABOT CLAN STANDING BY WHILE WEAK FEMALES DO SUCH HEAVY WORK?
FOR SHAME!
The PUSSY
DON'T WORRY! WE'LL OPEN THE DOOR FOR YOU!
SNAKE PI
PUFF! PUFF! H-HEY, ALAN M.! YOU WANT A JOB?
The PUSSYCATS
WELL, IF I'M NEEDED, I GUESS THINGS ARE LOOKING UP! I'LL WANT A BIGGER SLICE OF THE PROFITS!
PANT! ANYTHING! YOU'RE HIRED!
YOU SHOULD HAVE HIRED ME SOONER! THERE'S NOTHING LEFT FOR ME TO CARRY IN!
THAT'S WHAT YOU THINK!
WELCOME BACK, ALAN M.!
WHEW!
The PUSSYCATS
The END

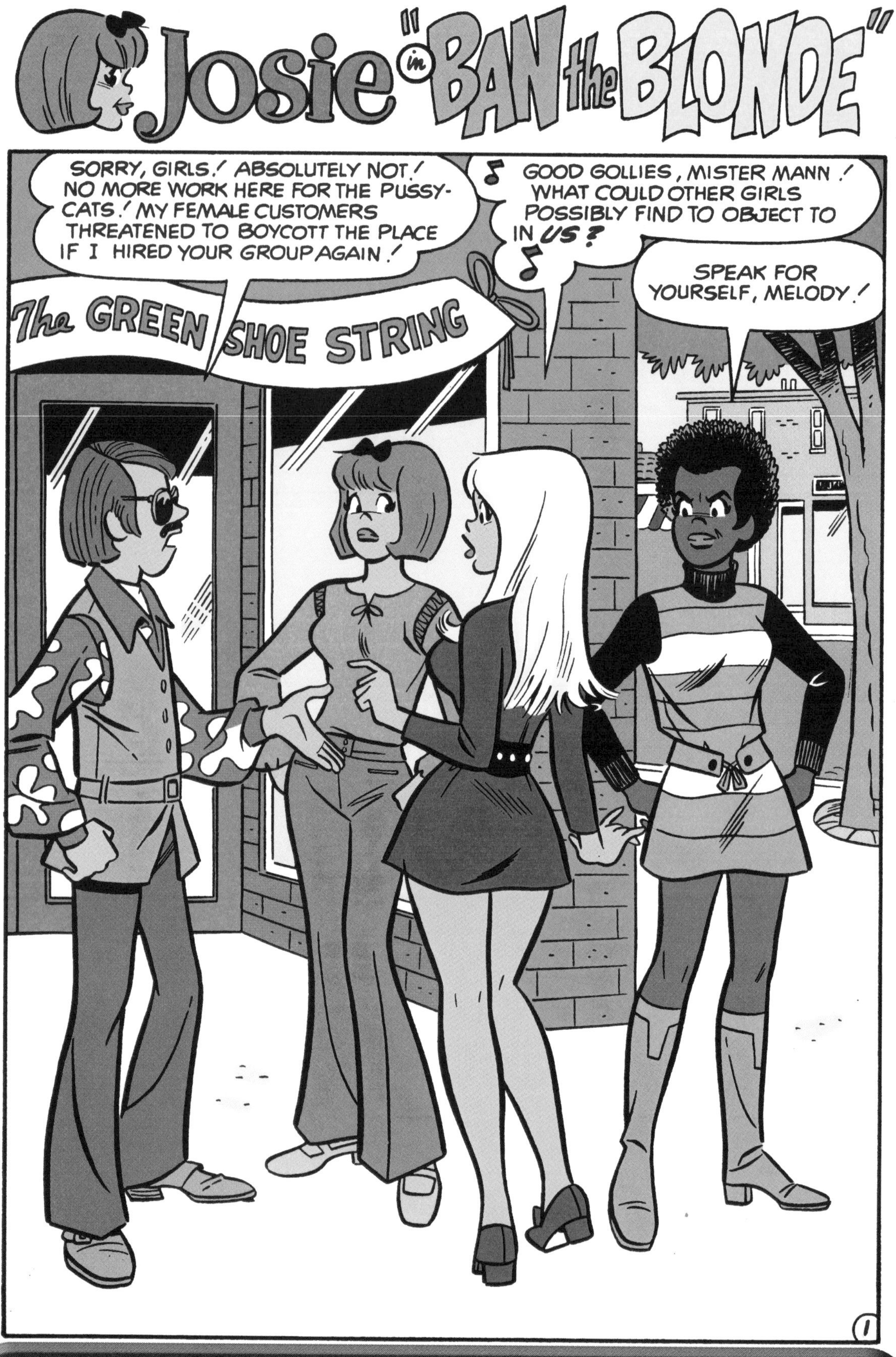
Josie in "BAN the BLONDE"
SORRY, GIRLS! ABSOLUTELY NOT! NO MORE WORK HERE FOR THE PUSSY-CATS! MY FEMALE CUSTOMERS THREATENED TO BOYCOTT THE PLACE IF I HIRED YOUR GROUP AGAIN!
GOOD GOLLIES, MISTER MANN! WHAT COULD OTHER GIRLS POSSIBLY FIND TO OBJECT TO IN US?
SPEAK FOR YOURSELF, MELODY!
The GREEN SHOE STRING
1

ORIGINALLY PRESENTED IN
JOSIE & THE PUSSYCATS #55, JUNE, 1971

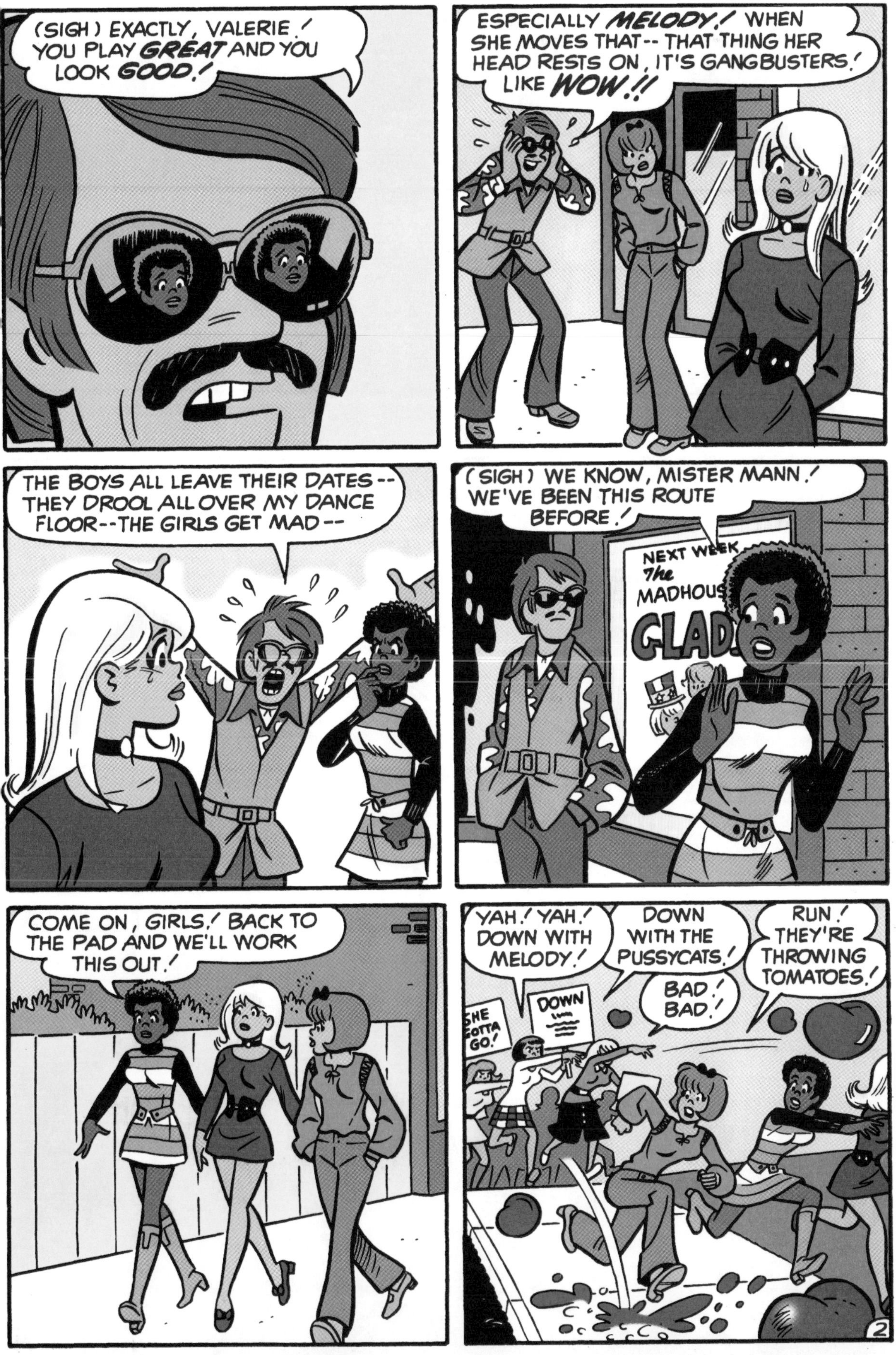
(SIGH) EXACTLY, VALERIE! YOU PLAY GREAT AND YOU LOOK GOOD!
ESPECIALLY MELODY! WHEN SHE MOVES THAT-- THAT THING HER HEAD RESTS ON, IT'S GANGBUSTERS! LIKE WOW!!
THE BOYS ALL LEAVE THEIR DATES-- THEY DROOL ALL OVER MY DANCE FLOOR--THE GIRLS GET MAD--
(SIGH) WE KNOW, MISTER MANN! WE'VE BEEN THIS ROUTE BEFORE!
NEXT WEEK
The
MADHOUS
GLAD
COME ON, GIRLS! BACK TO THE PAD AND WE'LL WORK THIS OUT!
YAH! YAH! DOWN WITH MELODY!
DOWN WITH THE PUSSYCATS!
BAD! BAD!
RUN! THEY'RE THROWING TOMATOES!
DOWN
SHE GOTTA GO!
2

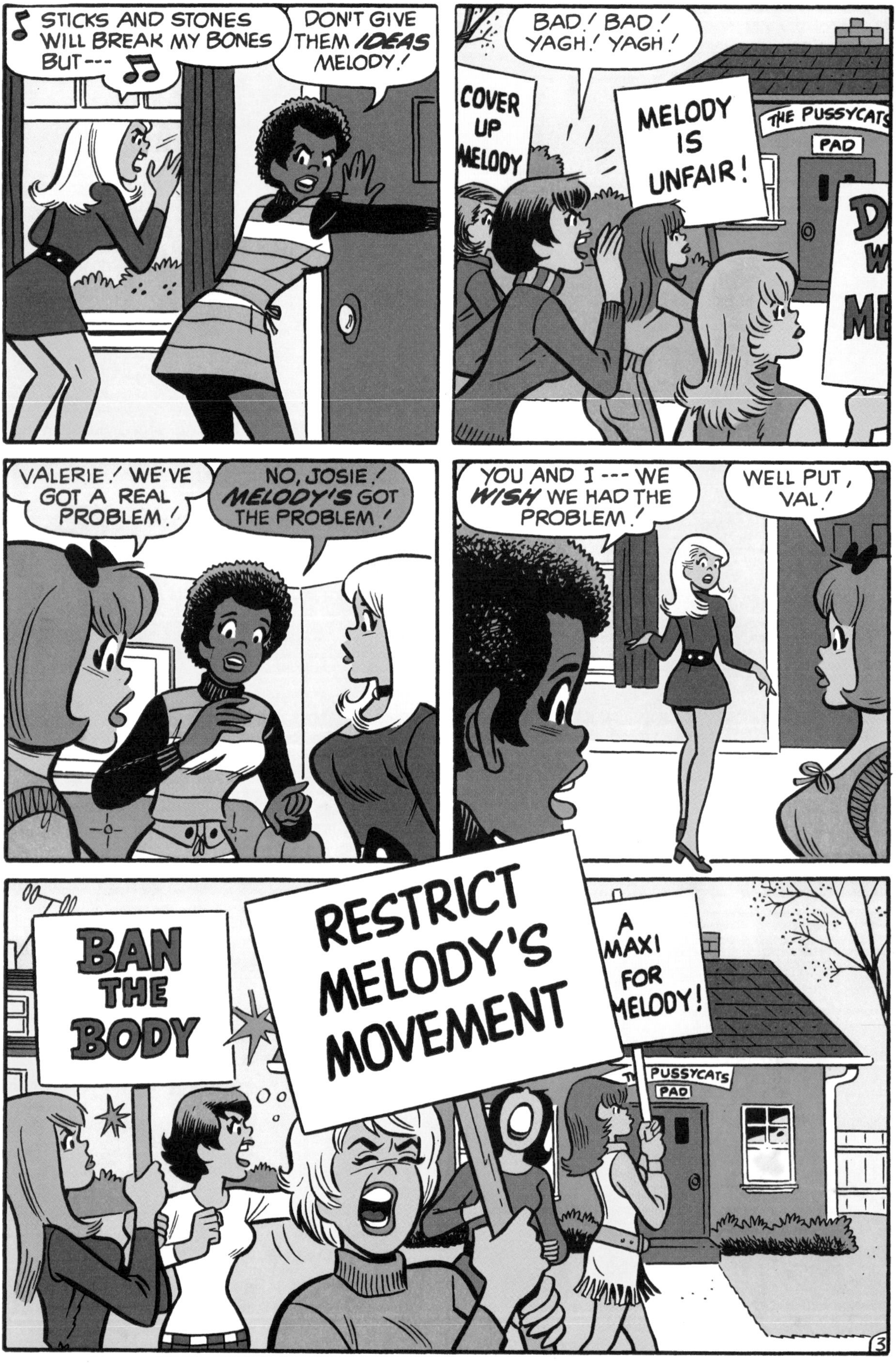
STICKS AND STONES WILL BREAK MY BONES BUT---
DON'T GIVE THEM IDEAS MELODY!
BAD! BAD! YAGH! YAGH!
COVER UP MELODY
MELODY IS UNFAIR!
THE PUSSYCATS PAD
VALERIE! WE'VE GOT A REAL PROBLEM!
NO, JOSIE! MELODY'S GOT THE PROBLEM!
YOU AND I --- WE WISH WE HAD THE PROBLEM!
WELL PUT, VAL!
BAN THE BODY
RESTRICT MELODY'S MOVEMENT
A MAXI FOR MELODY!
PUSSYCATS PAD
3

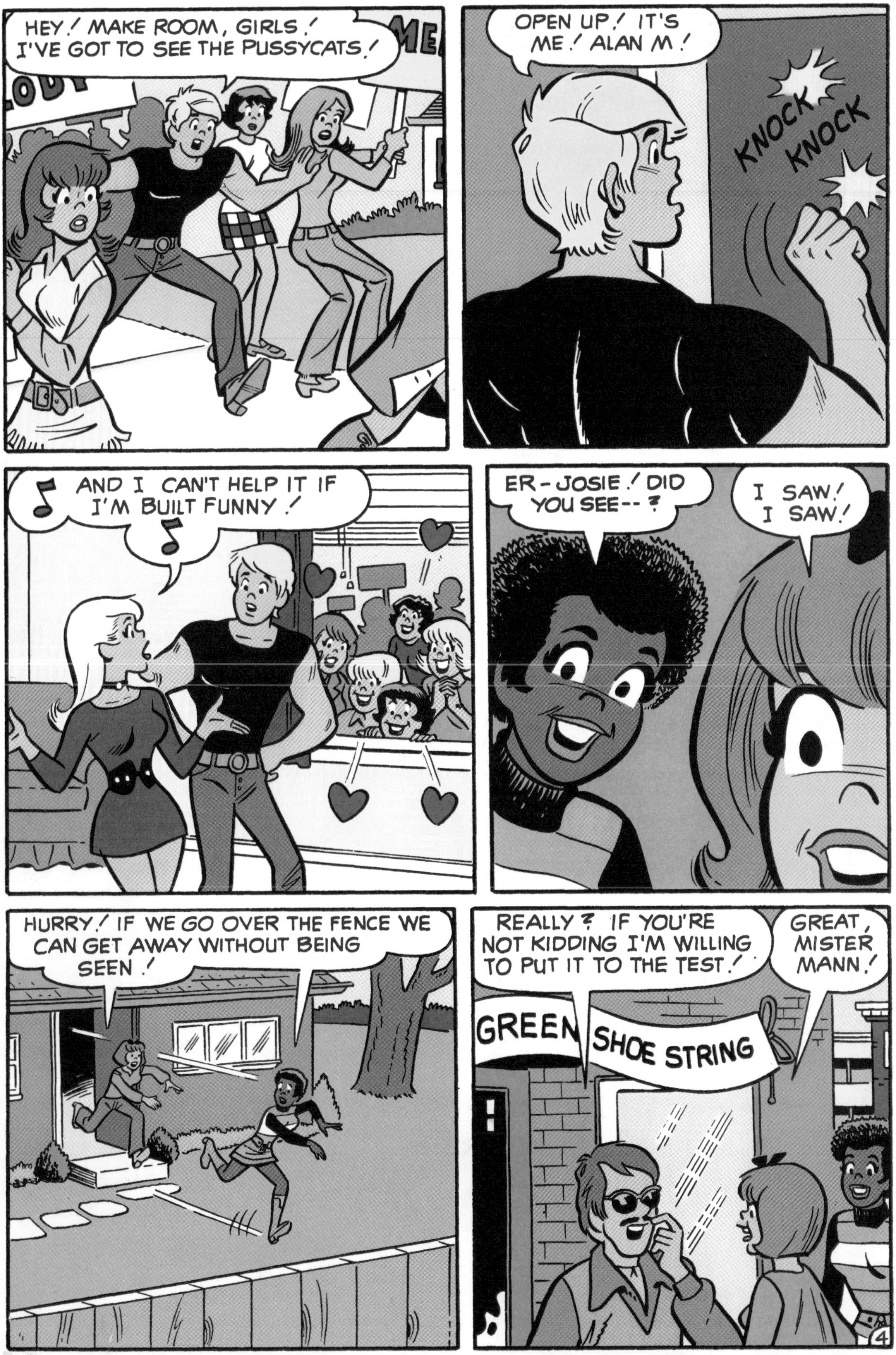
HEY! MAKE ROOM, GIRLS! I'VE GOT TO SEE THE PUSSYCATS!
OPEN UP! IT'S ME! ALAN M!
KNOCK KNOCK
AND I CAN'T HELP IT IF I'M BUILT FUNNY!
ER-JOSIE! DID YOU SEE--?
I SAW! I SAW!
HURRY! IF WE GO OVER THE FENCE WE CAN GET AWAY WITHOUT BEING SEEN!
REALLY? IF YOU'RE NOT KIDDING I'M WILLING TO PUT IT TO THE TEST!
GREAT, MISTER MANN!
GREEN
SHOE STRING
4

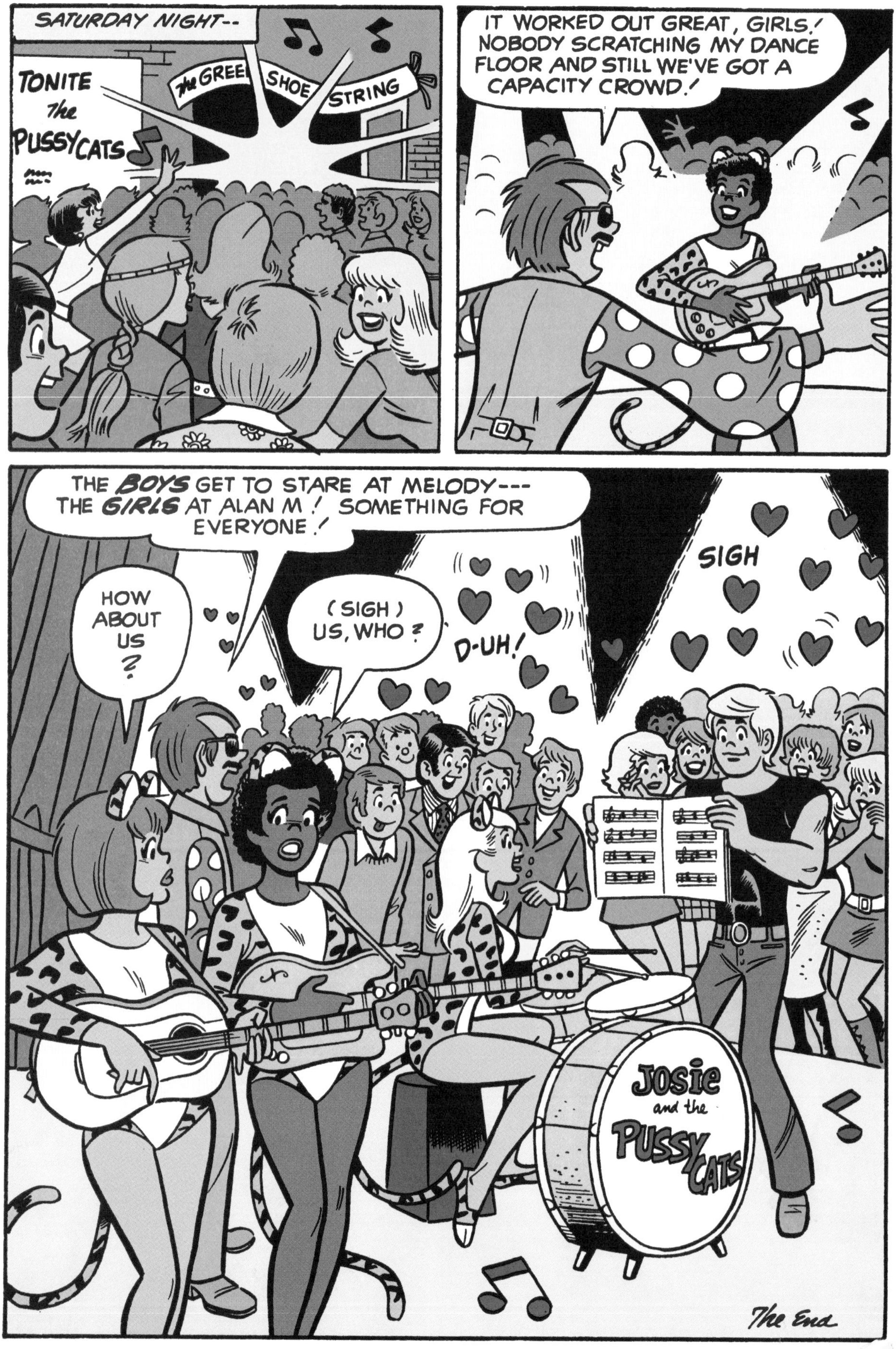
SATURDAY NIGHT--
TONITE The PUSSYCATS
The GREEN SHOE STRING
IT WORKED OUT GREAT, GIRLS! NOBODY SCRATCHING MY DANCE FLOOR AND STILL WE'VE GOT A CAPACITY CROWD!
THE BOYS GET TO STARE AT MELODY--- THE GIRLS AT ALAN M! SOMETHING FOR EVERYONE!
HOW ABOUT US ?
(SIGH) US, WHO ?
D-UH!
SIGH
JOSIE and the PUSSYCATS
The End

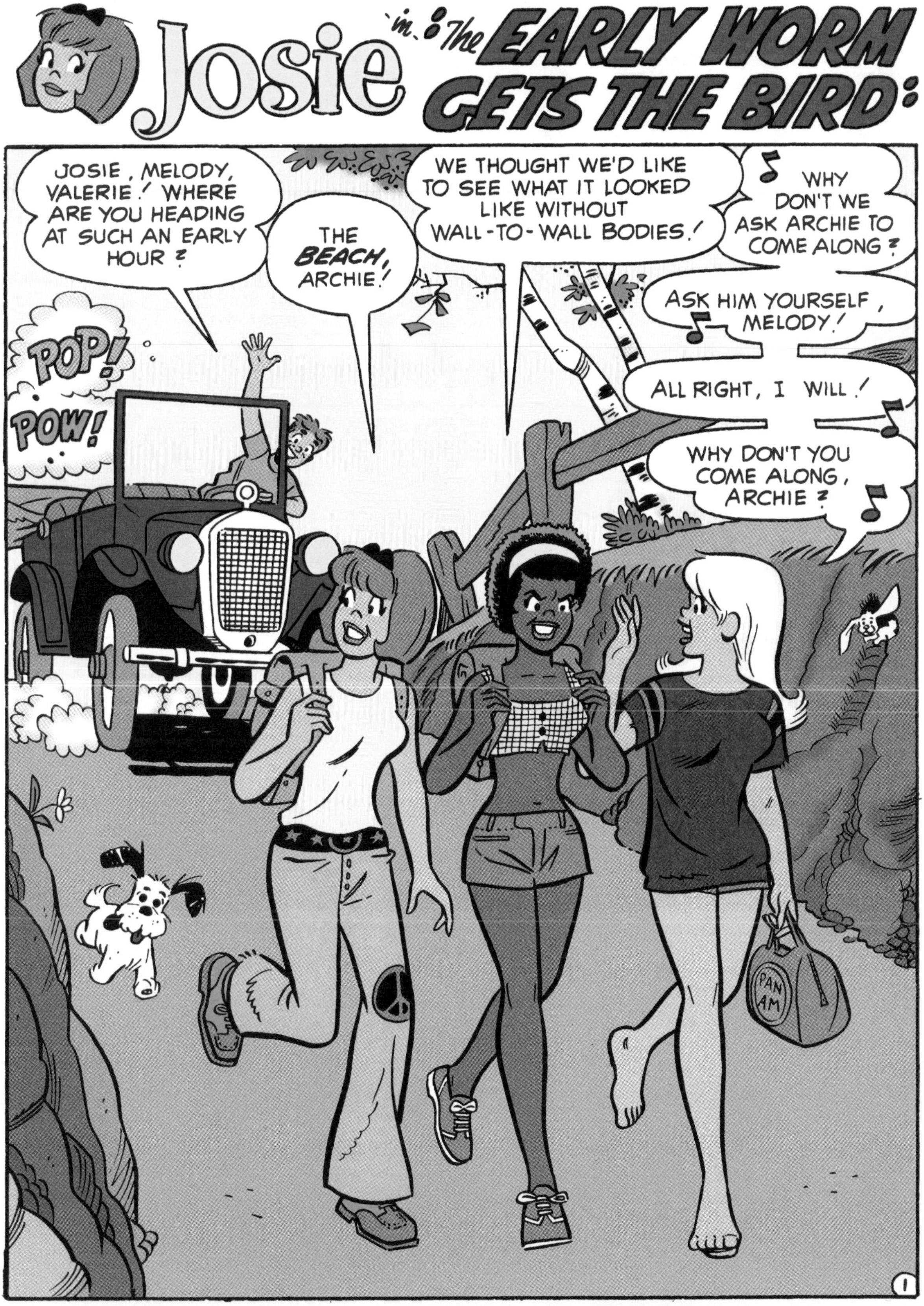
Josie in: The EARLY WORM GETS THE BIRD:
JOSIE, MELODY, VALERIE! WHERE ARE YOU HEADING AT SUCH AN EARLY HOUR?
THE BEACH, ARCHIE!
WE THOUGHT WE'D LIKE TO SEE WHAT IT LOOKED LIKE WITHOUT WALL-TO-WALL BODIES!
WHY DON'T WE ASK ARCHIE TO COME ALONG?
ASK HIM YOURSELF, MELODY!
ALL RIGHT, I WILL!
WHY DON'T YOU COME ALONG, ARCHIE?
POP!
POW!
PAN AM
1

ORIGINALLY PRESENTED IN
JOSIE & THE PUSSYCATS #56, AUGUST, 1971

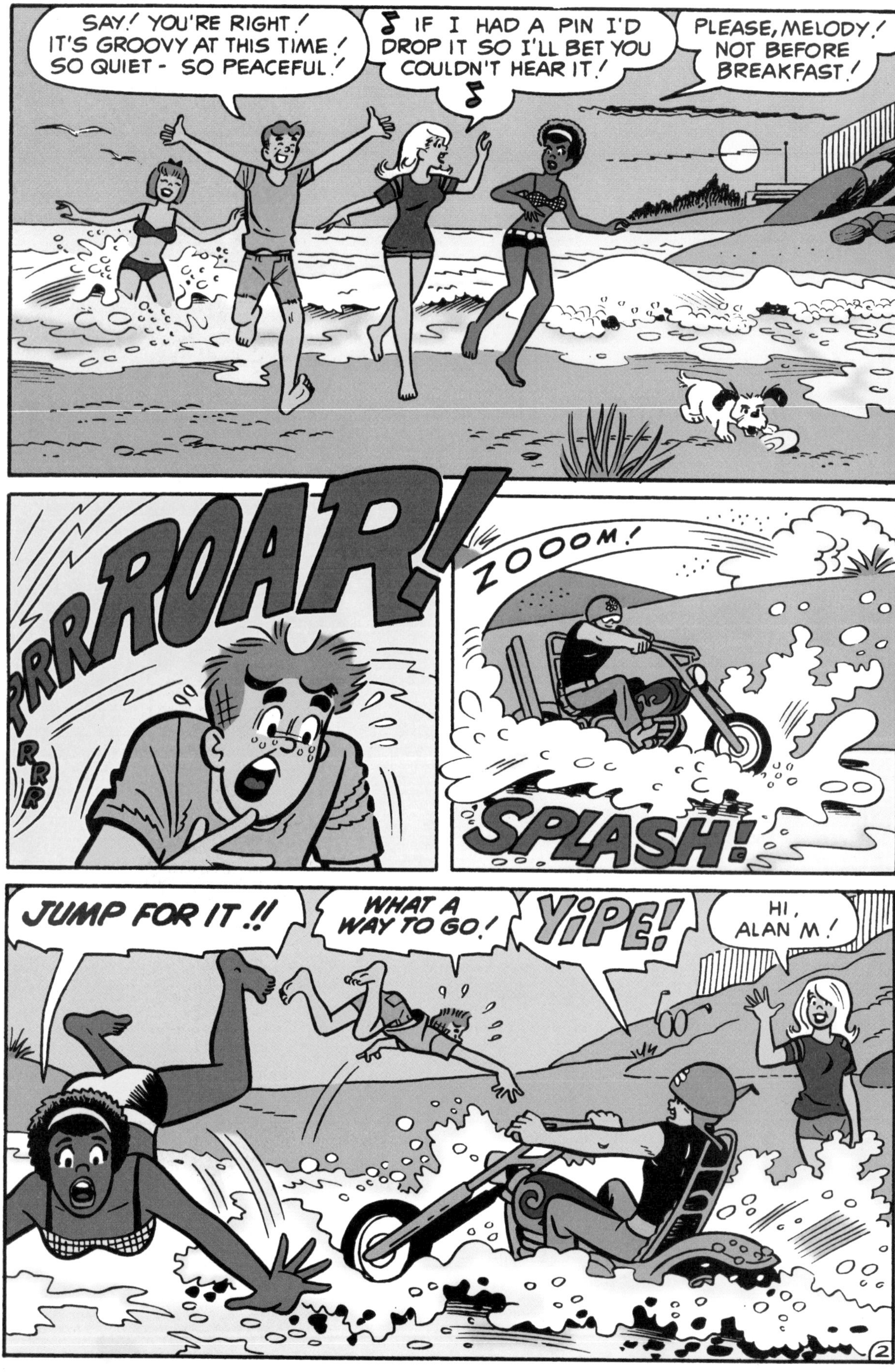
SAY! YOU'RE RIGHT! IT'S GROOVY AT THIS TIME! SO QUIET - SO PEACEFUL!
♪ IF I HAD A PIN I'D DROP IT SO I'LL BET YOU COULDN'T HEAR IT! ♪
PLEASE, MELODY! NOT BEFORE BREAKFAST!
RRRROAR! RRR
ZOOOM!
SPLASH!
JUMP FOR IT!!
WHAT A WAY TO GO!
YIPE!
HI, ALAN M!
2

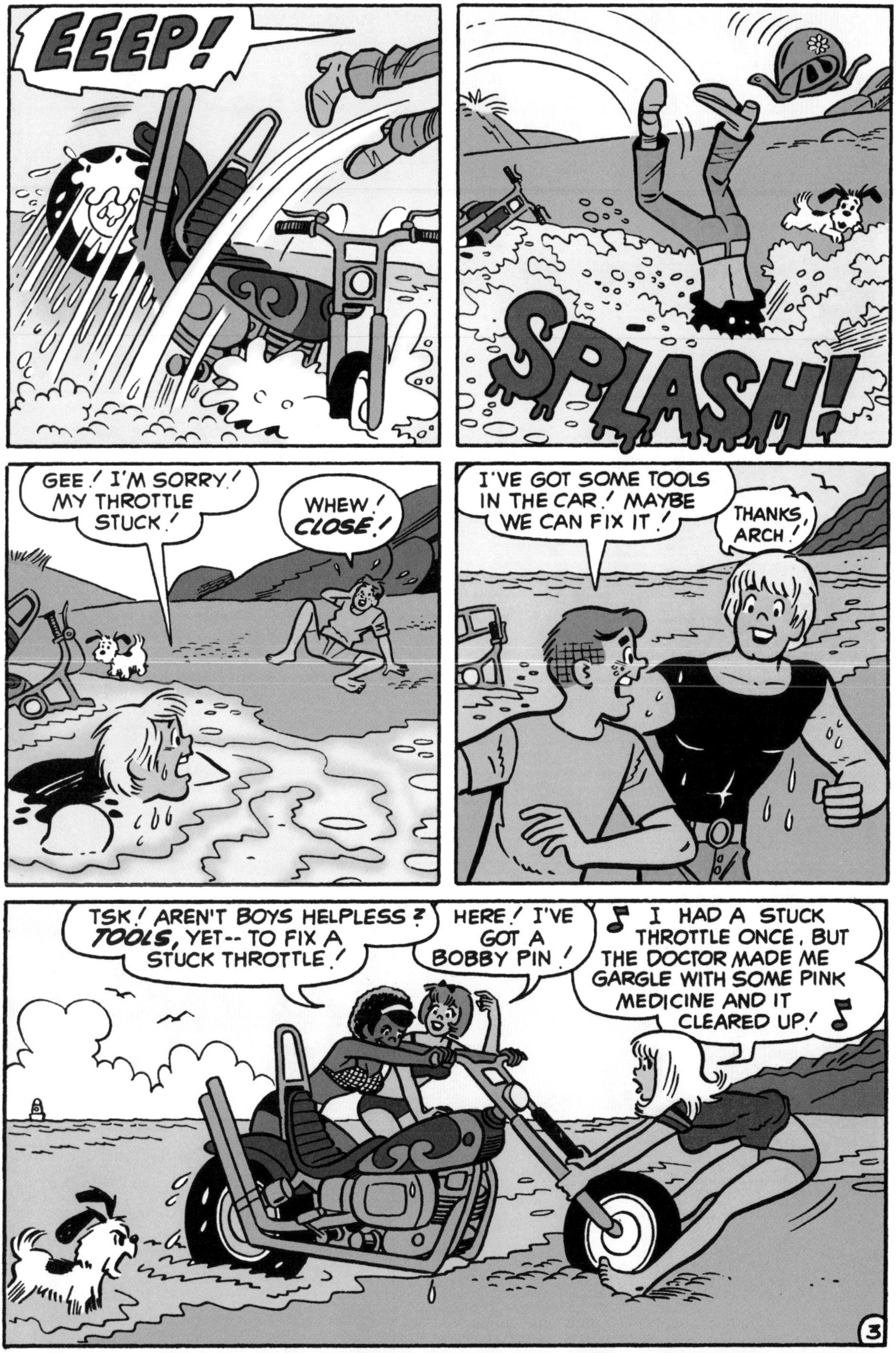
EEEP!
SPLASH!
GEE! I'M SORRY! MY THROTTLE STUCK!
WHEW! CLOSE!
I'VE GOT SOME TOOLS IN THE CAR! MAYBE WE CAN FIX IT!
THANKS, ARCH!
TSK! AREN'T BOYS HELPLESS? TOOLS, YET-- TO FIX A STUCK THROTTLE!
HERE! I'VE GOT A BOBBY PIN!
♪ I HAD A STUCK THROTTLE ONCE, BUT THE DOCTOR MADE ME GARGLE WITH SOME PINK MEDICINE AND IT CLEARED UP! ♪
3

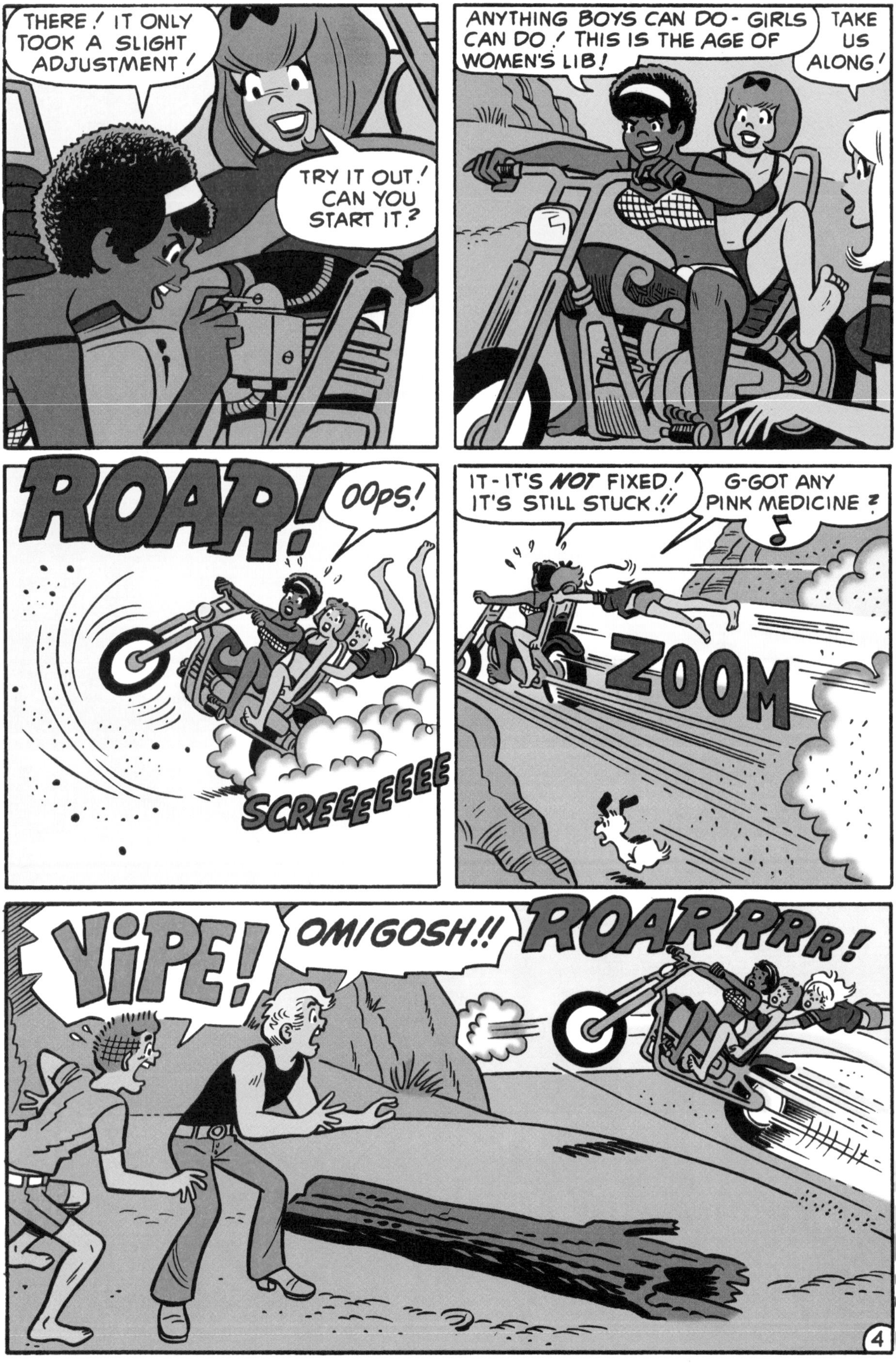
THERE! IT ONLY TOOK A SLIGHT ADJUSTMENT!
TRY IT OUT! CAN YOU START IT?
ANYTHING BOYS CAN DO- GIRLS CAN DO! THIS IS THE AGE OF WOMEN'S LIB!
TAKE US ALONG!
ROAR!
OOps!
SCREEEEEEEE
IT-IT'S NOT FIXED! IT'S STILL STUCK.!!
G-GOT ANY PINK MEDICINE?
ZOOM
YIPE!
OMIGOSH!!
ROARRRRR!
4

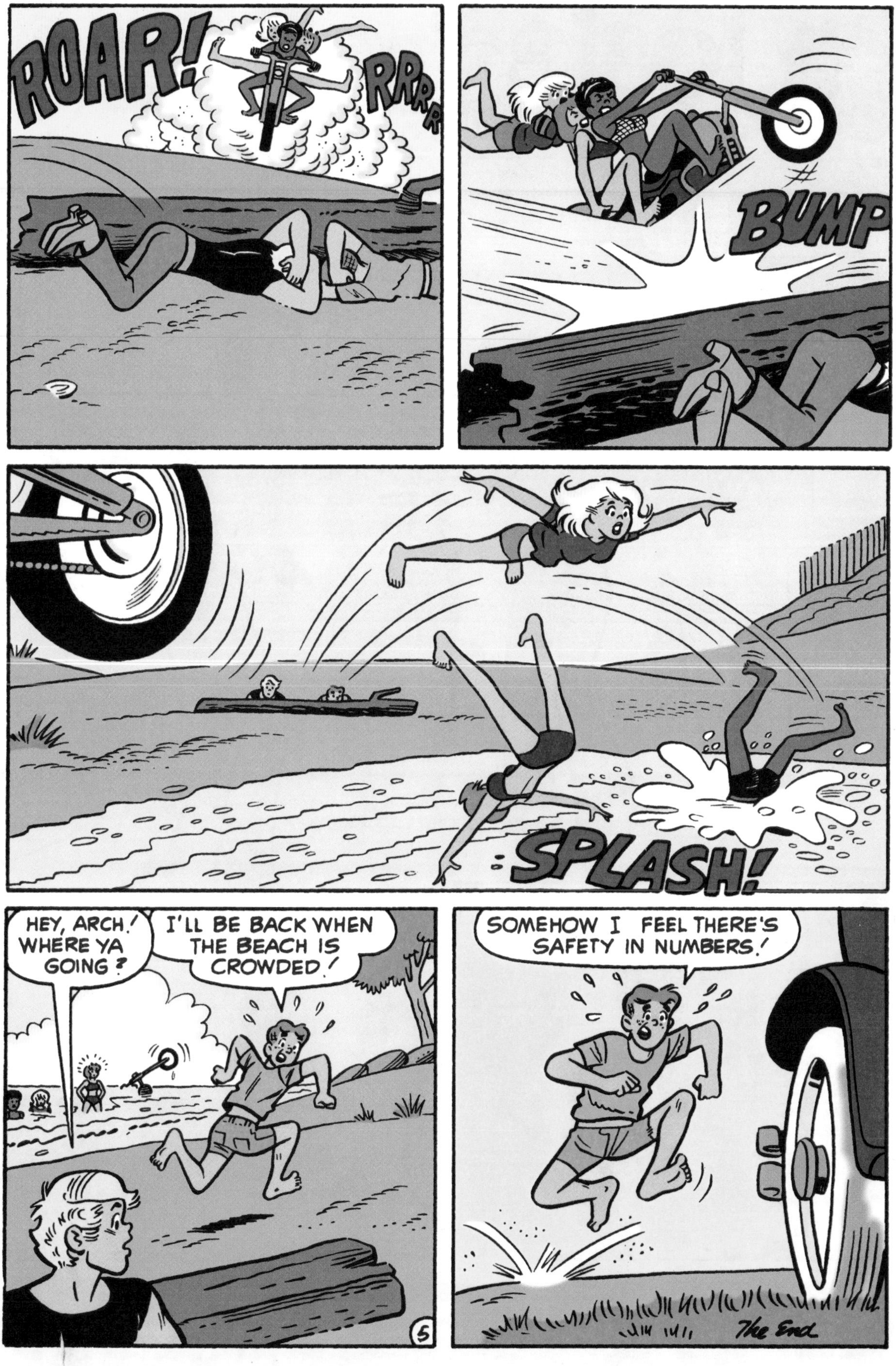
ROAR!
RRRR
BUMP
SPLASH!
HEY, ARCH! WHERE YA GOING?
I'LL BE BACK WHEN THE BEACH IS CROWDED!
5
SOMEHOW I FEEL THERE'S SAFETY IN NUMBERS!
The End

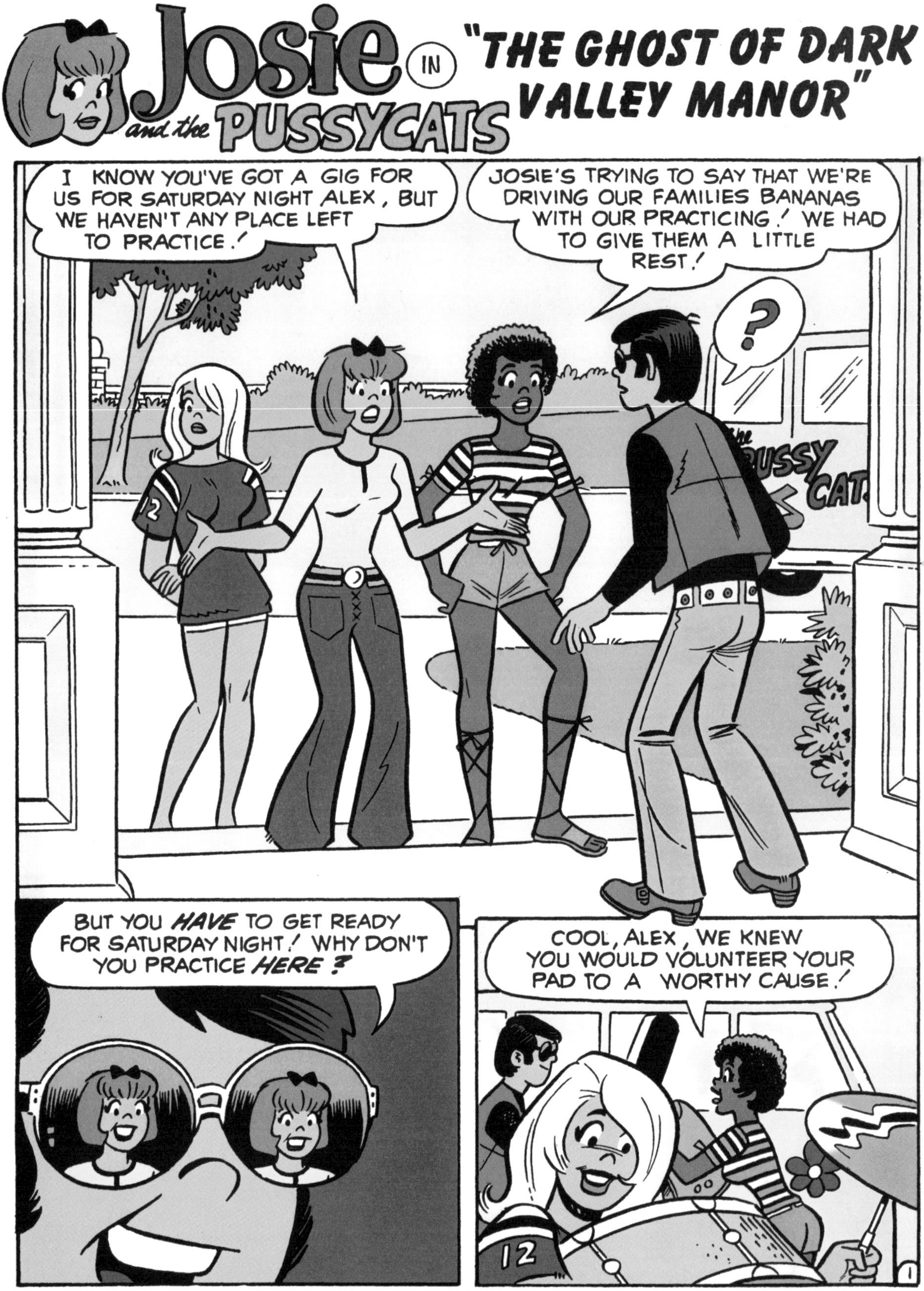
Josie and the PUSSYCATS
IN
"THE GHOST OF DARK VALLEY MANOR"
I KNOW YOU'VE GOT A GIG FOR US FOR SATURDAY NIGHT ALEX, BUT WE HAVEN'T ANY PLACE LEFT TO PRACTICE!
JOSIE'S TRYING TO SAY THAT WE'RE DRIVING OUR FAMILIES BANANAS WITH OUR PRACTICING! WE HAD TO GIVE THEM A LITTLE REST!
?
BUT YOU HAVE TO GET READY FOR SATURDAY NIGHT! WHY DON'T YOU PRACTICE HERE?
COOL, ALEX, WE KNEW YOU WOULD VOLUNTEER YOUR PAD TO A WORTHY CAUSE!
1

ORIGINALLY PRESENTED IN
JOSIE & THE PUSSYCATS #57, SEPTEMBER, 1971

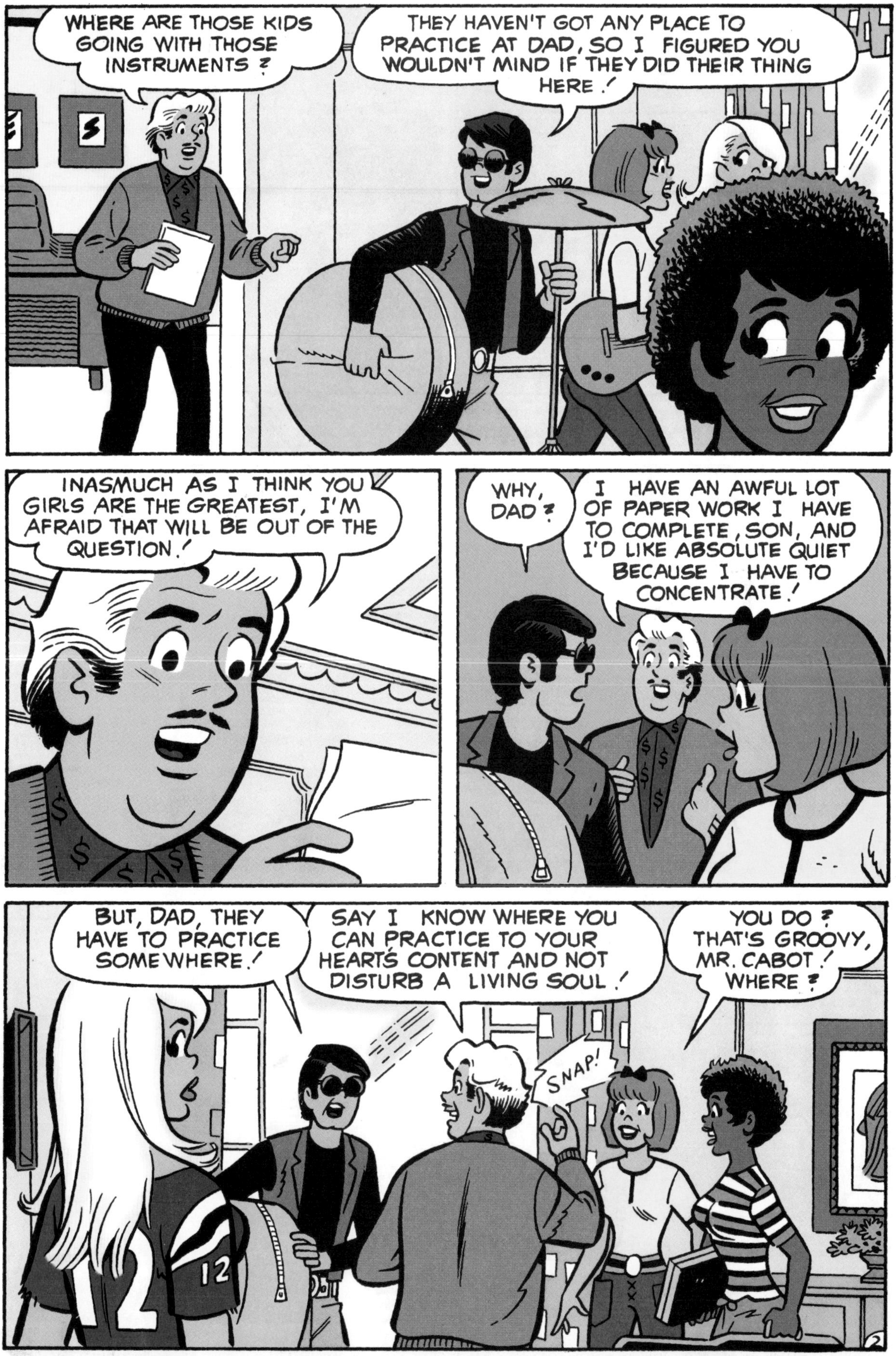
WHERE ARE THOSE KIDS GOING WITH THOSE INSTRUMENTS?
THEY HAVEN'T GOT ANY PLACE TO PRACTICE AT DAD, SO I FIGURED YOU WOULDN'T MIND IF THEY DID THEIR THING HERE!
INASMUCH AS I THINK YOU GIRLS ARE THE GREATEST, I'M AFRAID THAT WILL BE OUT OF THE QUESTION!
WHY, DAD?
I HAVE AN AWFUL LOT OF PAPER WORK I HAVE TO COMPLETE, SON, AND I'D LIKE ABSOLUTE QUIET BECAUSE I HAVE TO CONCENTRATE!
BUT, DAD, THEY HAVE TO PRACTICE SOMEWHERE!
SAY I KNOW WHERE YOU CAN PRACTICE TO YOUR HEART'S CONTENT AND NOT DISTURB A LIVING SOUL!
YOU DO? THAT'S GROOVY, MR. CABOT! WHERE?
SNAP!
12
12
2

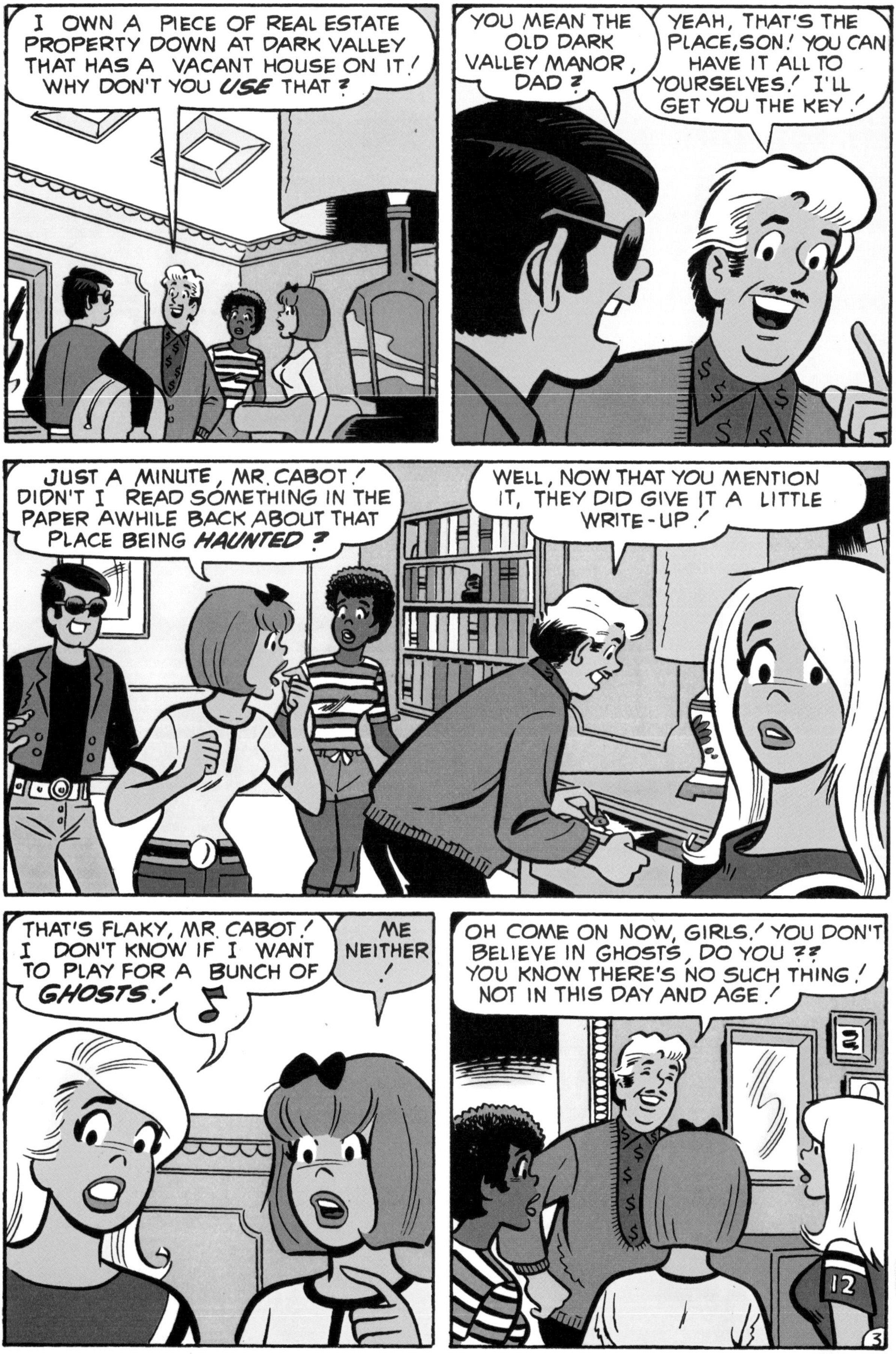
I OWN A PIECE OF REAL ESTATE PROPERTY DOWN AT DARK VALLEY THAT HAS A VACANT HOUSE ON IT! WHY DON'T YOU USE THAT?
YOU MEAN THE OLD DARK VALLEY MANOR, DAD?
YEAH, THAT'S THE PLACE, SON! YOU CAN HAVE IT ALL TO YOURSELVES! I'LL GET YOU THE KEY!
JUST A MINUTE, MR. CABOT! DIDN'T I READ SOMETHING IN THE PAPER AWHILE BACK ABOUT THAT PLACE BEING HAUNTED?
WELL, NOW THAT YOU MENTION IT, THEY DID GIVE IT A LITTLE WRITE-UP!
THAT'S FLAKY, MR. CABOT! I DON'T KNOW IF I WANT TO PLAY FOR A BUNCH OF GHOSTS!
ME NEITHER!
OH COME ON NOW, GIRLS! YOU DON'T BELIEVE IN GHOSTS, DO YOU?? YOU KNOW THERE'S NO SUCH THING! NOT IN THIS DAY AND AGE!
12
3

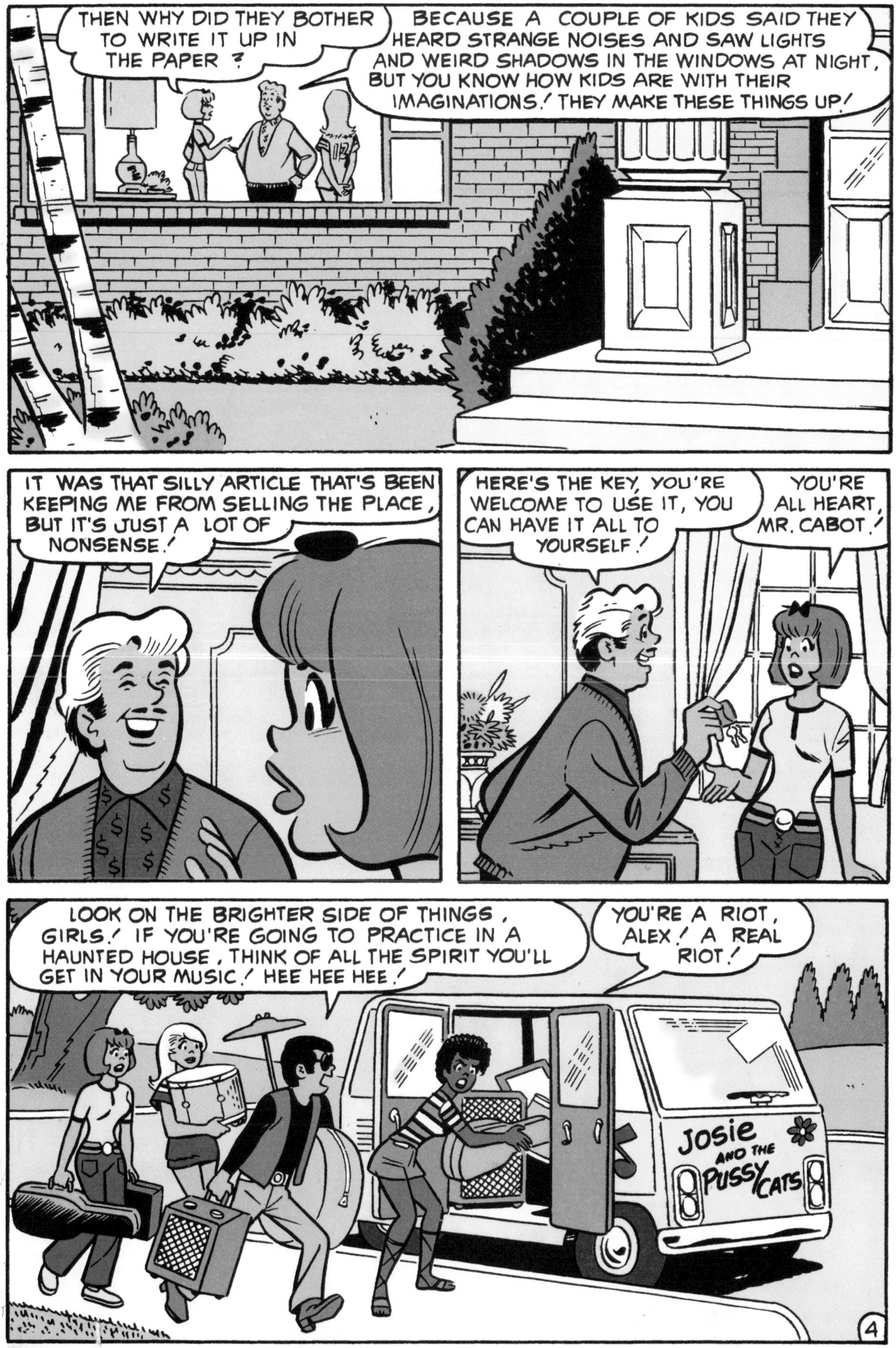
THEN WHY DID THEY BOTHER TO WRITE IT UP IN THE PAPER ?
BECAUSE A COUPLE OF KIDS SAID THEY HEARD STRANGE NOISES AND SAW LIGHTS AND WEIRD SHADOWS IN THE WINDOWS AT NIGHT, BUT YOU KNOW HOW KIDS ARE WITH THEIR IMAGINATIONS! THEY MAKE THESE THINGS UP!
IT WAS THAT SILLY ARTICLE THAT'S BEEN KEEPING ME FROM SELLING THE PLACE, BUT IT'S JUST A LOT OF NONSENSE!
HERE'S THE KEY, YOU'RE WELCOME TO USE IT, YOU CAN HAVE IT ALL TO YOURSELF!
YOU'RE ALL HEART, MR. CABOT!
LOOK ON THE BRIGHTER SIDE OF THINGS, GIRLS! IF YOU'RE GOING TO PRACTICE IN A HAUNTED HOUSE, THINK OF ALL THE SPIRIT YOU'LL GET IN YOUR MUSIC! HEE HEE HEE!
YOU'RE A RIOT, ALEX! A REAL RIOT!
Josie AND THE PUSSYCATS
4

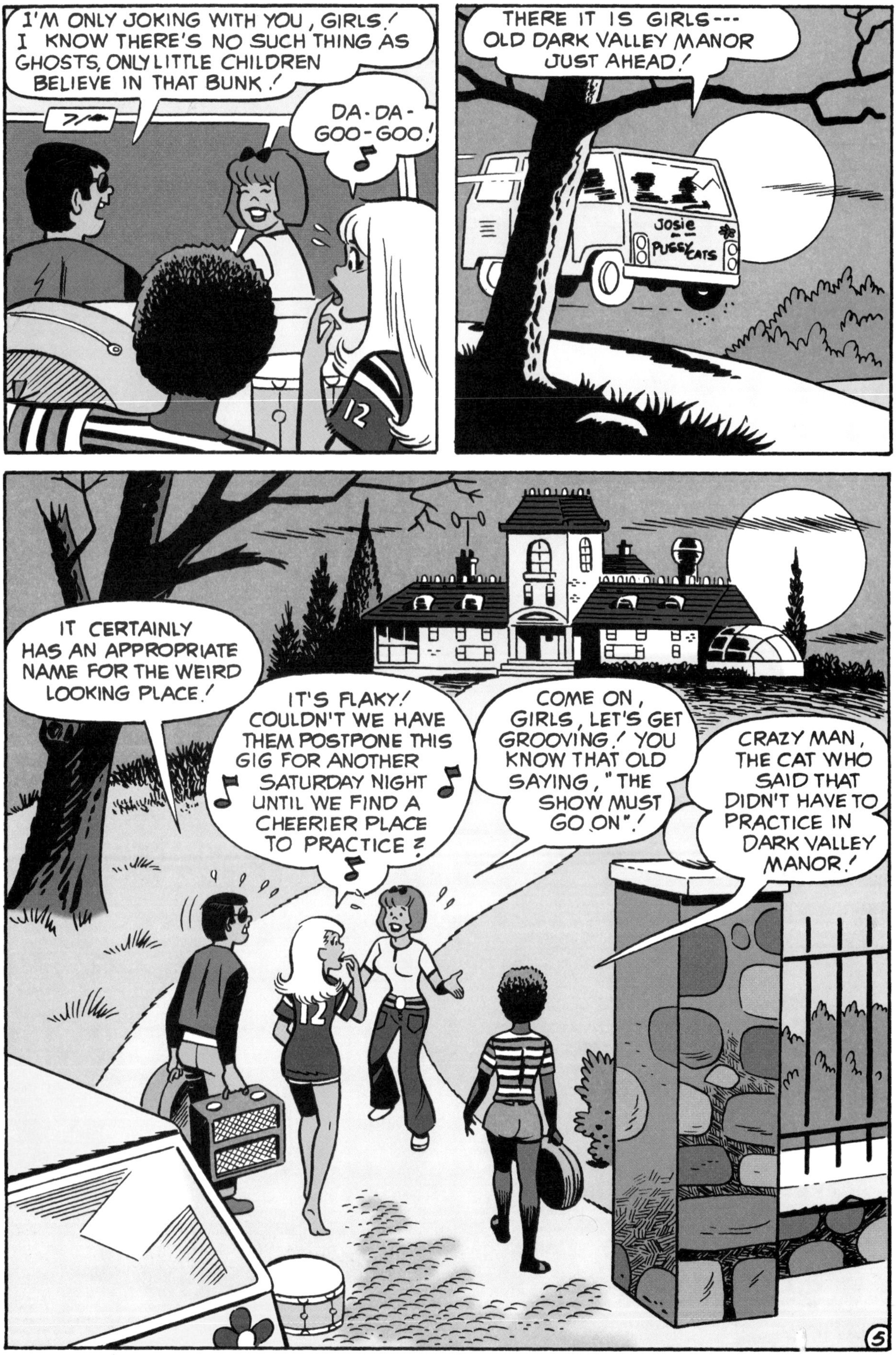
I'M ONLY JOKING WITH YOU, GIRLS! I KNOW THERE'S NO SUCH THING AS GHOSTS, ONLY LITTLE CHILDREN BELIEVE IN THAT BUNK!
DA-DA-GOO-GOO!
THERE IT IS GIRLS--- OLD DARK VALLEY MANOR JUST AHEAD!
JOSIE PUSSYCATS
IT CERTAINLY HAS AN APPROPRIATE NAME FOR THE WEIRD LOOKING PLACE!
IT'S FLAKY! COULDN'T WE HAVE THEM POSTPONE THIS GIG FOR ANOTHER SATURDAY NIGHT UNTIL WE FIND A CHEERIER PLACE TO PRACTICE?
COME ON, GIRLS, LET'S GET GROOVING! YOU KNOW THAT OLD SAYING, "THE SHOW MUST GO ON"!
CRAZY MAN, THE CAT WHO SAID THAT DIDN'T HAVE TO PRACTICE IN DARK VALLEY MANOR!
12
5

Josie and the PUSSYCATS IN "THE GHOST OF DARK VALLEY MANOR"

COME ON NOW, MELODY, YOU'RE NOT WITH IT --- YOU'RE WAY OFF THE BEAT!

I CAN'T HELP IT, GIRLS! I HAVE THE STRANGEST FEELING THAT SOMETHING IS WATCHING US!

ME TOO!

THIS PLACE GIVES ME THE CREEPS!

THAT'S SILLY, GIRLS, THERE'S NO ONE IN THIS PLACE BUT US!

THUMP! THUMP! THUMP!

?

6

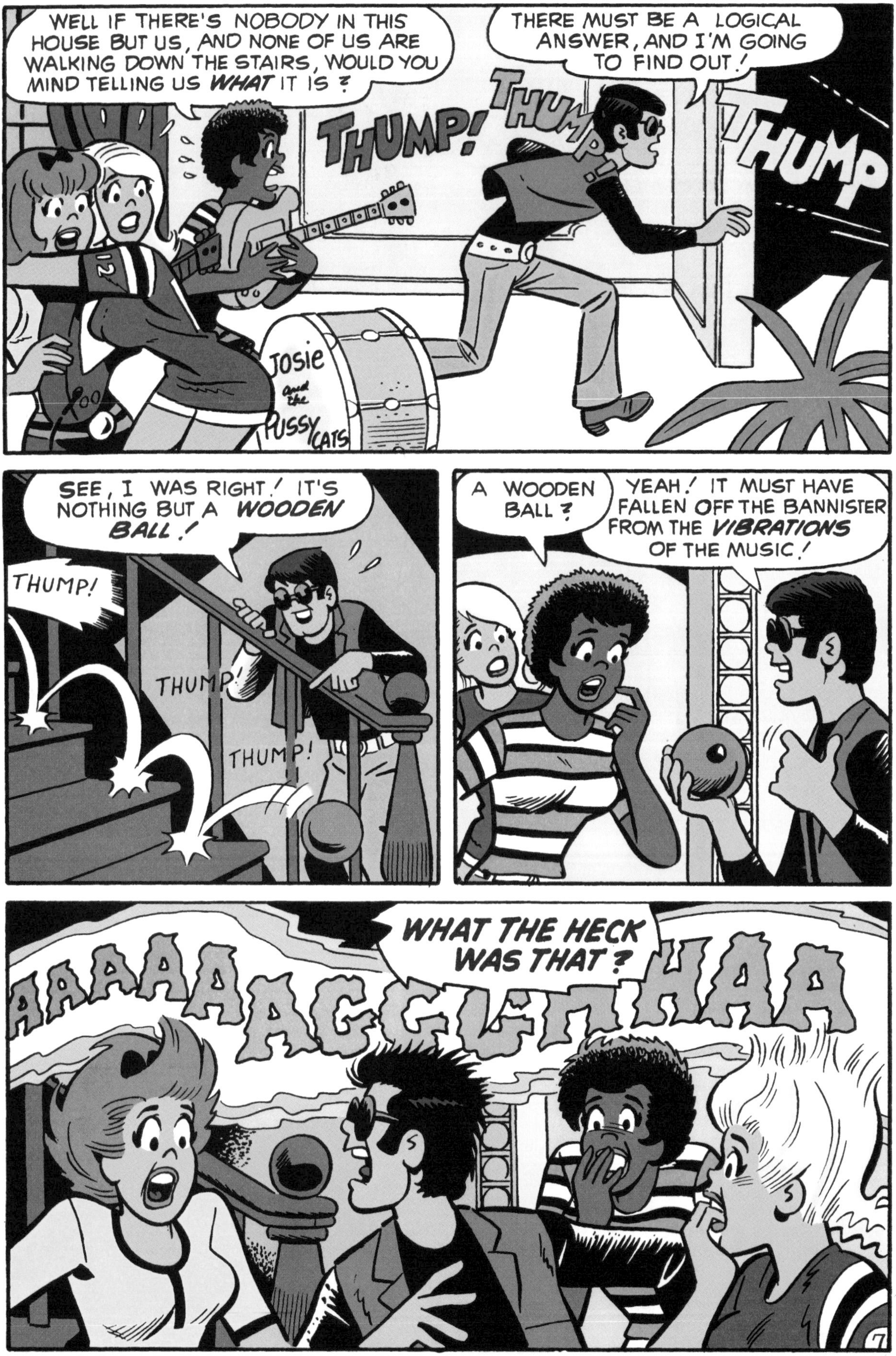
WELL IF THERE'S NOBODY IN THIS HOUSE BUT US, AND NONE OF US ARE WALKING DOWN THE STAIRS, WOULD YOU MIND TELLING US WHAT IT IS?
THERE MUST BE A LOGICAL ANSWER, AND I'M GOING TO FIND OUT!
THUMP!
THUMP!
THUMP
12
Josie and the Pussycats
SEE, I WAS RIGHT! IT'S NOTHING BUT A WOODEN BALL!
THUMP!
THUMP!
THUMP!
A WOODEN BALL?
YEAH! IT MUST HAVE FALLEN OFF THE BANNISTER FROM THE VIBRATIONS OF THE MUSIC!
WHAT THE HECK WAS THAT?
AAAAAAGGGHHAA
7

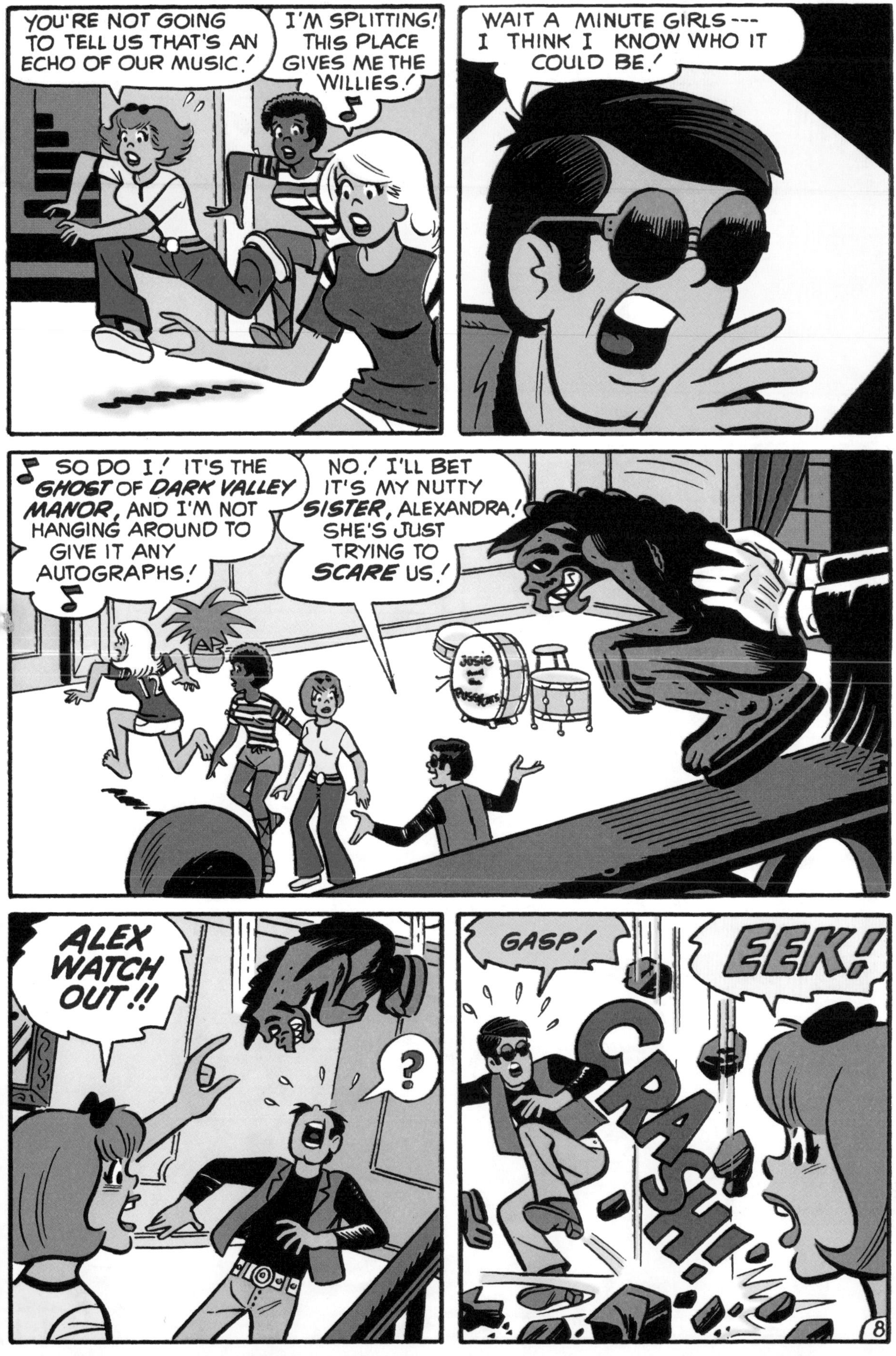
YOU'RE NOT GOING TO TELL US THAT'S AN ECHO OF OUR MUSIC!
I'M SPLITTING! THIS PLACE GIVES ME THE WILLIES!
WAIT A MINUTE GIRLS --- I THINK I KNOW WHO IT COULD BE!
SO DO I! IT'S THE GHOST OF DARK VALLEY MANOR, AND I'M NOT HANGING AROUND TO GIVE IT ANY AUTOGRAPHS!
NO! I'LL BET IT'S MY NUTTY SISTER, ALEXANDRA! SHE'S JUST TRYING TO SCARE US!
Josie and the Pussycats
ALEX WATCH OUT!!
?
GASP!
EEK!
CRASH!
8

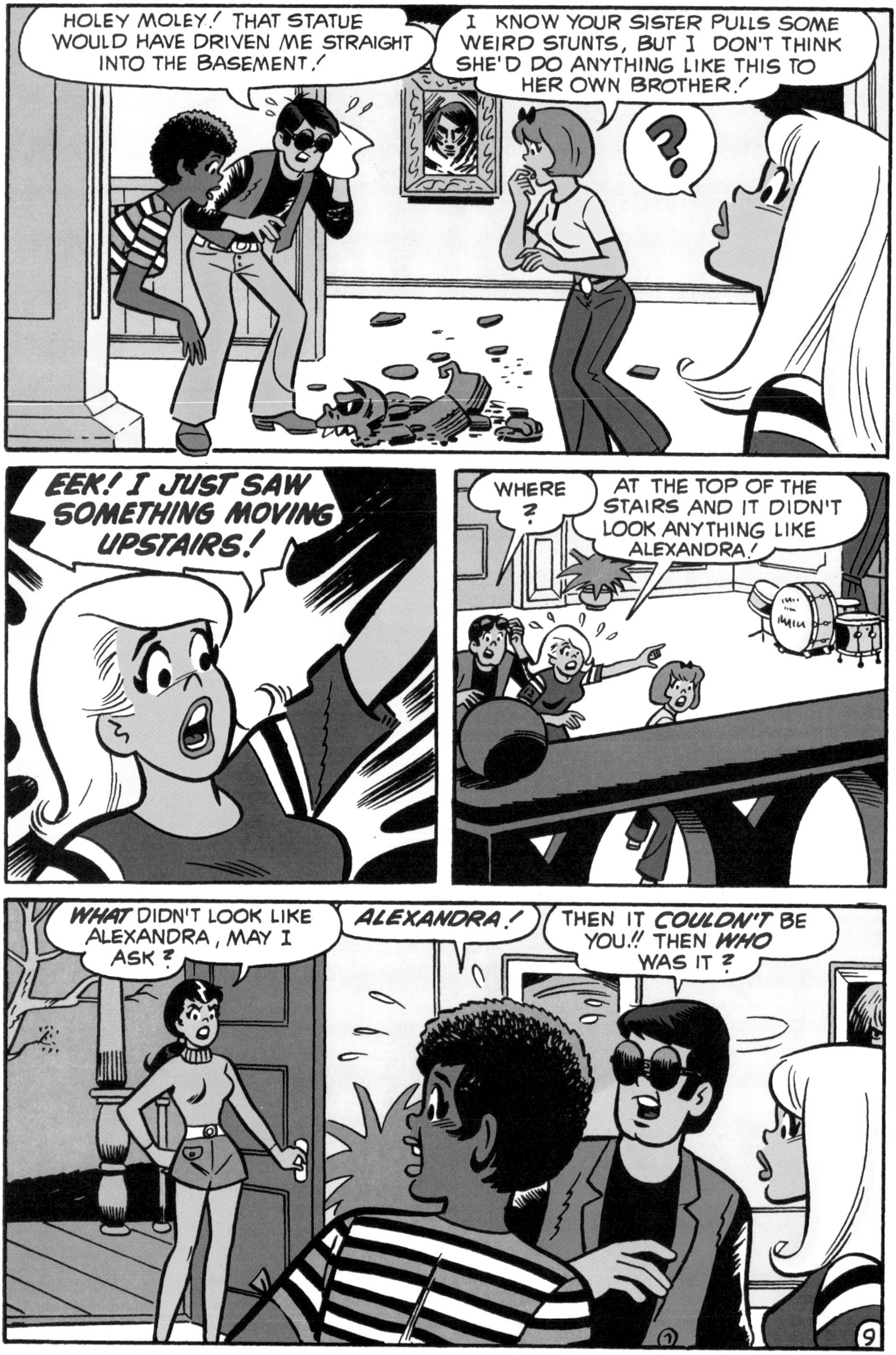
HOLEY MOLEY! THAT STATUE WOULD HAVE DRIVEN ME STRAIGHT INTO THE BASEMENT!
I KNOW YOUR SISTER PULLS SOME WEIRD STUNTS, BUT I DON'T THINK SHE'D DO ANYTHING LIKE THIS TO HER OWN BROTHER!
?
EEK! I JUST SAW SOMETHING MOVING UPSTAIRS!
WHERE ?
AT THE TOP OF THE STAIRS AND IT DIDN'T LOOK ANYTHING LIKE ALEXANDRA!
WHAT DIDN'T LOOK LIKE ALEXANDRA, MAY I ASK ?
ALEXANDRA!
THEN IT COULDN'T BE YOU!! THEN WHO WAS IT ?
9

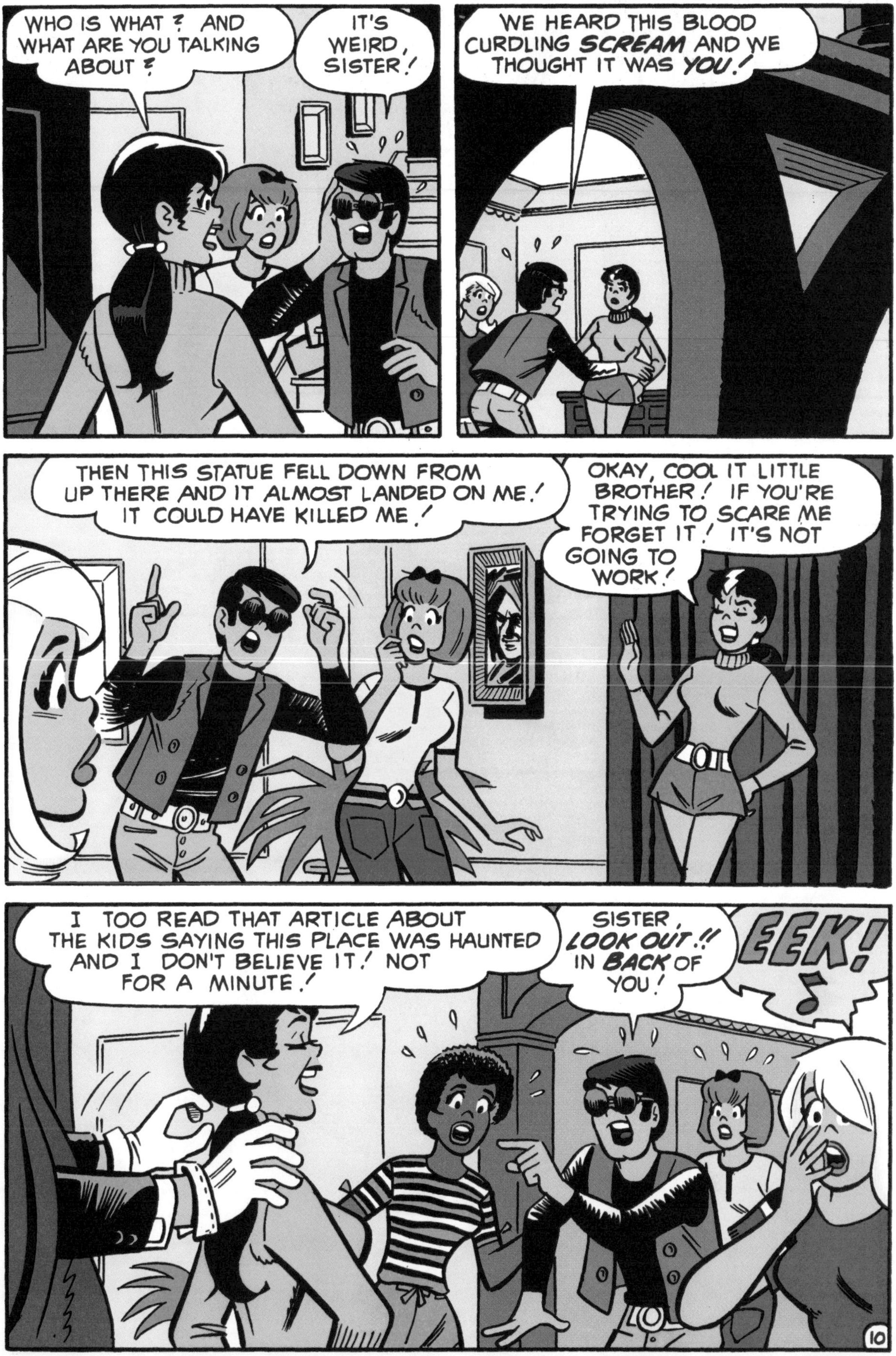
WHO IS WHAT ? AND WHAT ARE YOU TALKING ABOUT ?
IT'S WEIRD, SISTER!
WE HEARD THIS BLOOD CURDLING SCREAM AND WE THOUGHT IT WAS YOU!
THEN THIS STATUE FELL DOWN FROM UP THERE AND IT ALMOST LANDED ON ME! IT COULD HAVE KILLED ME!
OKAY, COOL IT LITTLE BROTHER! IF YOU'RE TRYING TO SCARE ME FORGET IT! IT'S NOT GOING TO WORK!
I TOO READ THAT ARTICLE ABOUT THE KIDS SAYING THIS PLACE WAS HAUNTED AND I DON'T BELIEVE IT! NOT FOR A MINUTE!
SISTER, LOOK OUT!! IN BACK OF YOU!
EEK!
10

Josie and the Pussycats -in- "THE GHOST OF DARK VALLEY MANOR"

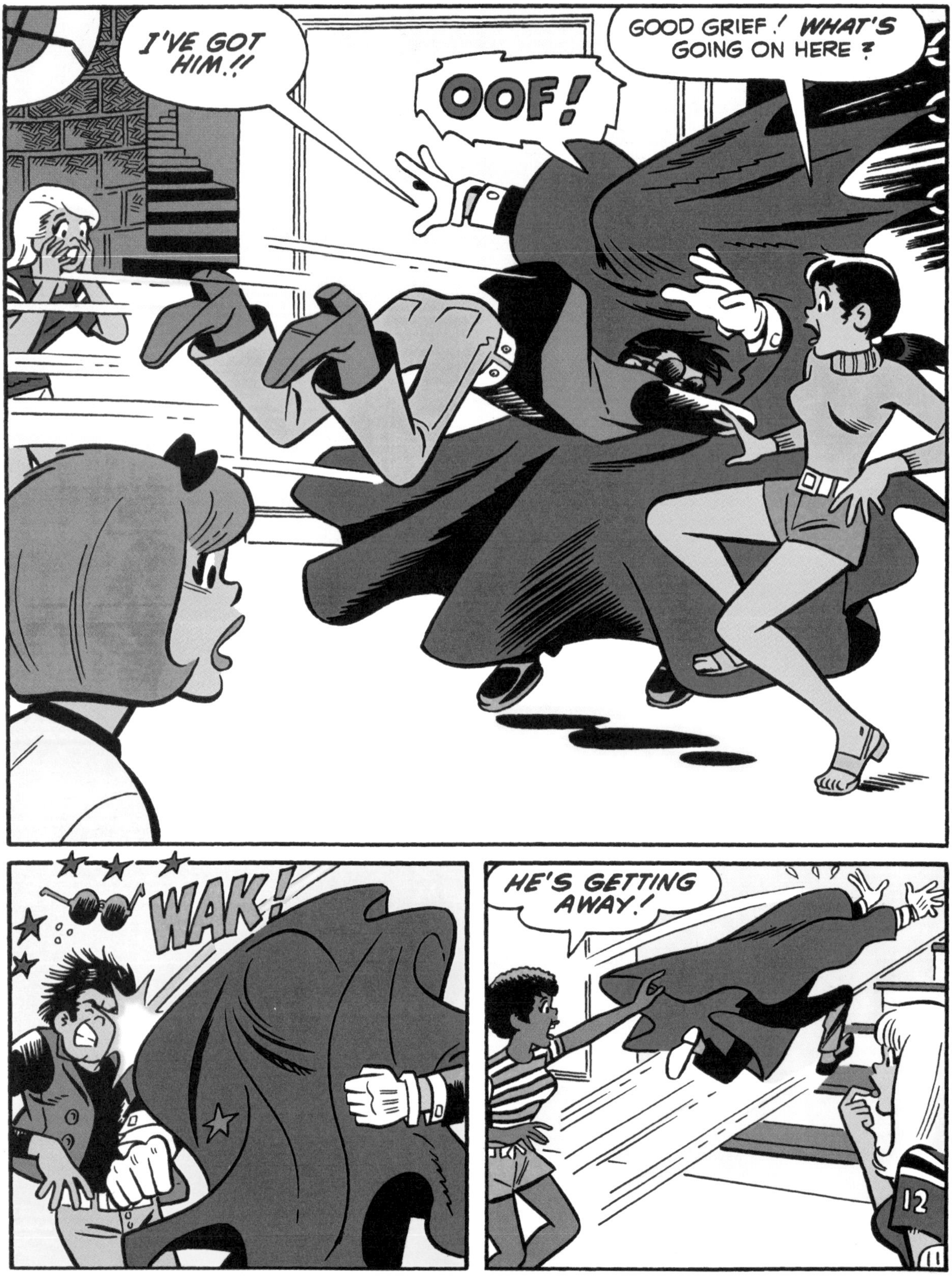
I'VE GOT HIM.!!
OOF!
GOOD GRIEF! WHAT'S GOING ON HERE?
WAK!
HE'S GETTING AWAY.!
12

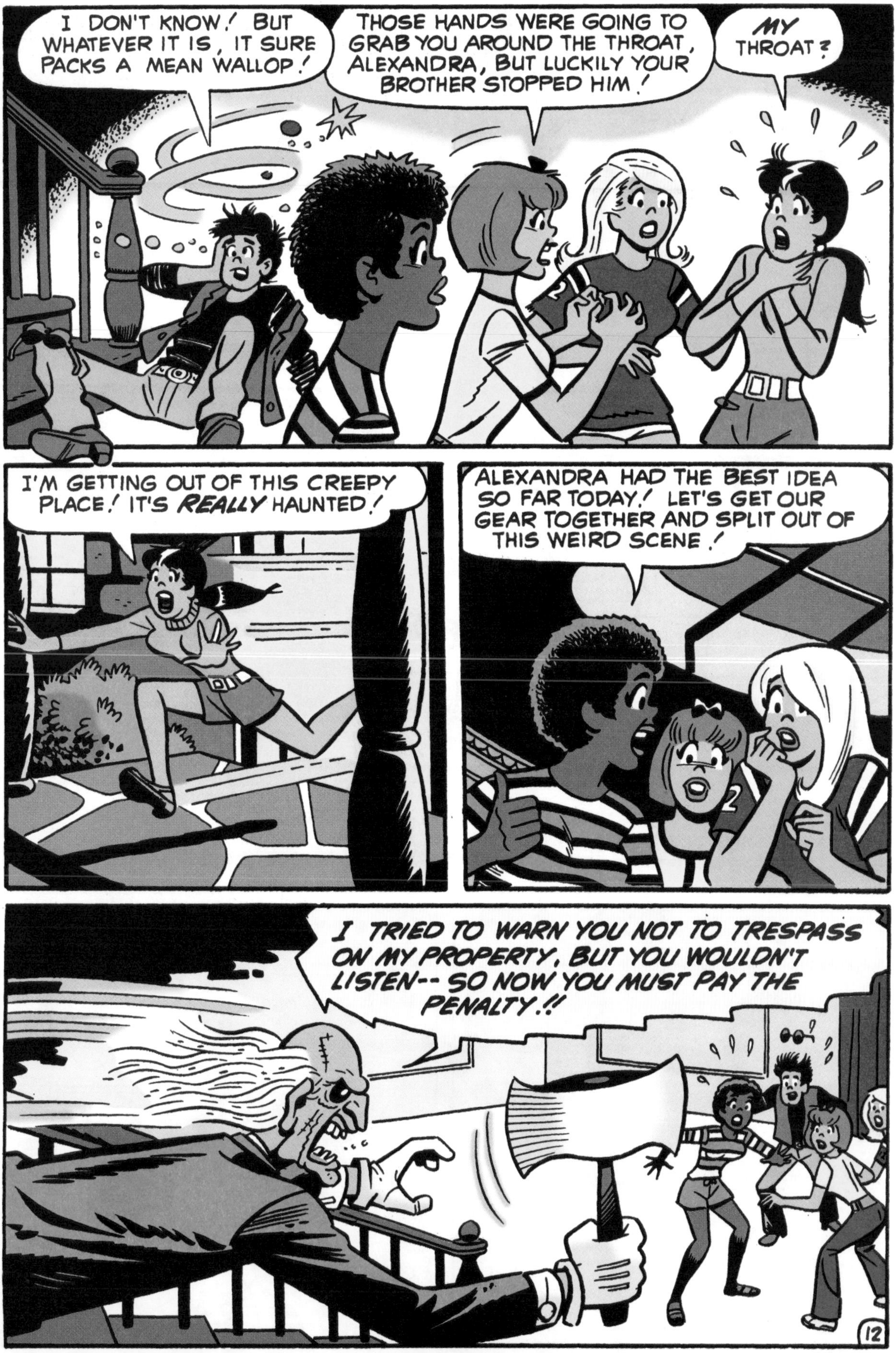
I DON'T KNOW! BUT WHATEVER IT IS, IT SURE PACKS A MEAN WALLOP!
THOSE HANDS WERE GOING TO GRAB YOU AROUND THE THROAT, ALEXANDRA, BUT LUCKILY YOUR BROTHER STOPPED HIM!
MY THROAT?
I'M GETTING OUT OF THIS CREEPY PLACE! IT'S REALLY HAUNTED!
ALEXANDRA HAD THE BEST IDEA SO FAR TODAY! LET'S GET OUR GEAR TOGETHER AND SPLIT OUT OF THIS WEIRD SCENE!
I TRIED TO WARN YOU NOT TO TRESPASS ON MY PROPERTY, BUT YOU WOULDN'T LISTEN-- SO NOW YOU MUST PAY THE PENALTY!!
12

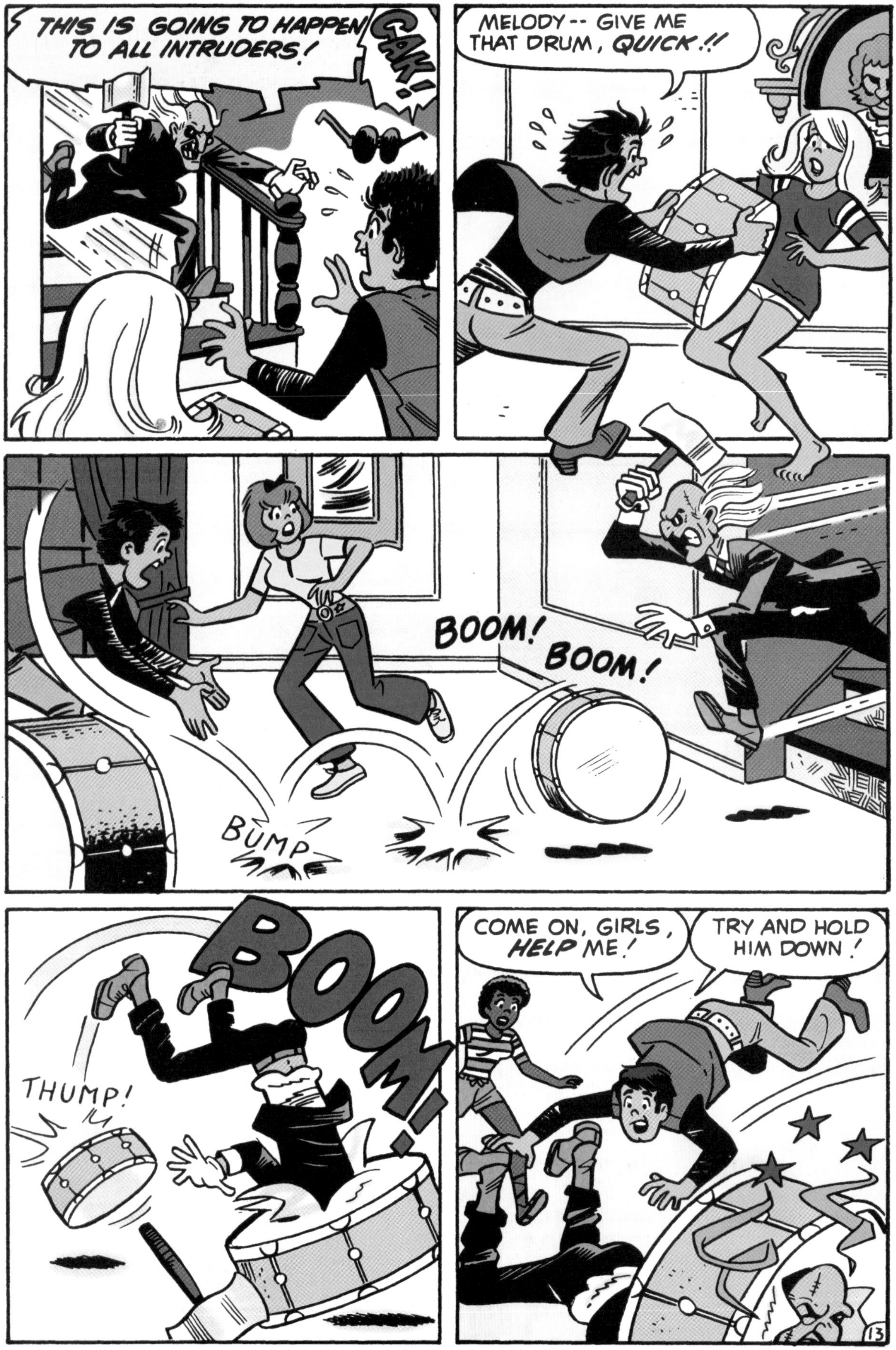
THIS IS GOING TO HAPPEN TO ALL INTRUDERS!
CHAK!
MELODY -- GIVE ME THAT DRUM, QUICK!!
BOOM!
BOOM!
BUMP
BOOM!
THUMP!
COME ON, GIRLS, HELP ME!
TRY AND HOLD HIM DOWN!
13

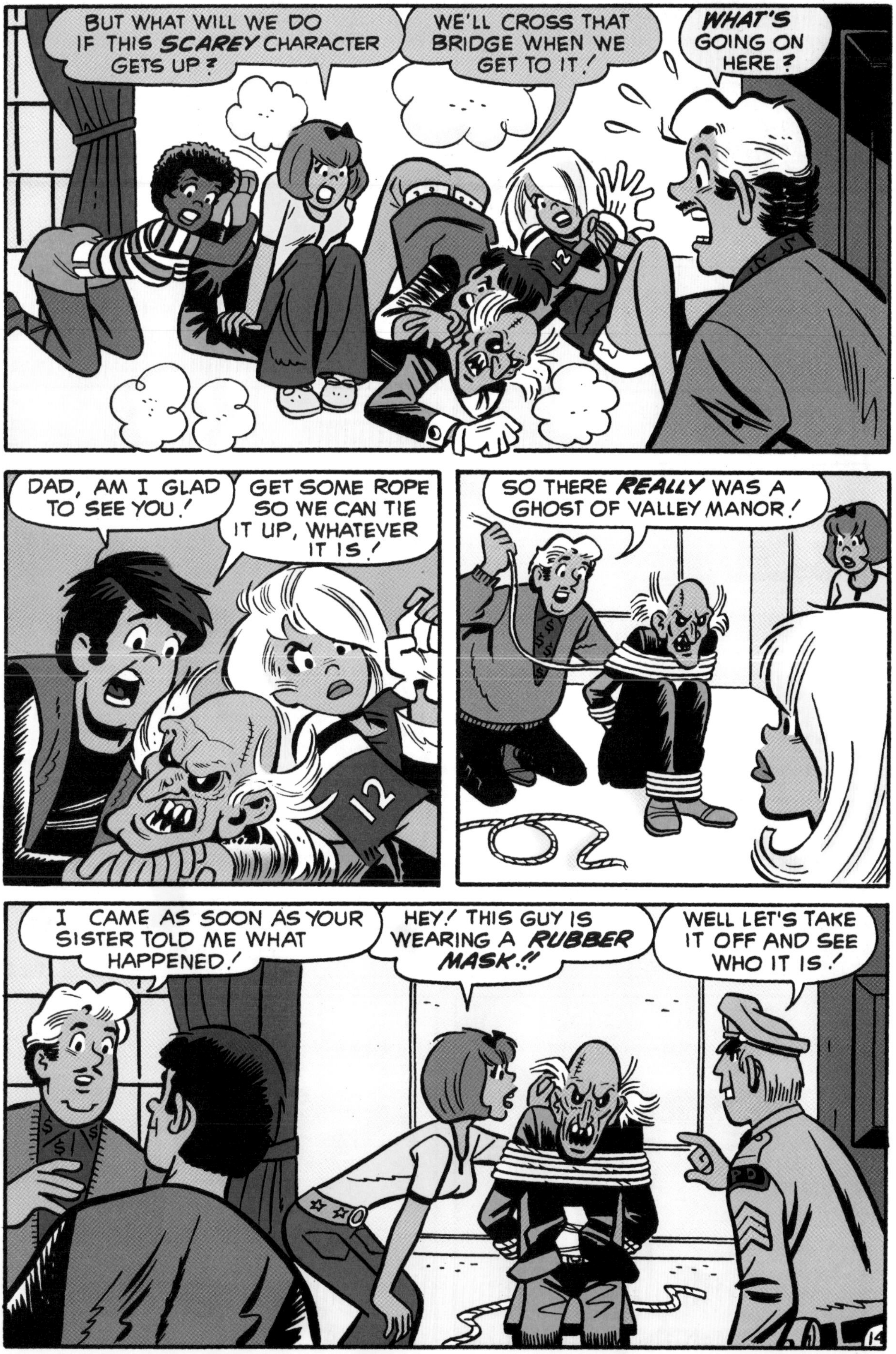
BUT WHAT WILL WE DO IF THIS SCAREY CHARACTER GETS UP?
WE'LL CROSS THAT BRIDGE WHEN WE GET TO IT!
WHAT'S GOING ON HERE?
DAD, AM I GLAD TO SEE YOU!
GET SOME ROPE SO WE CAN TIE IT UP, WHATEVER IT IS!
12
SO THERE REALLY WAS A GHOST OF VALLEY MANOR!
I CAME AS SOON AS YOUR SISTER TOLD ME WHAT HAPPENED!
HEY! THIS GUY IS WEARING A RUBBER MASK!!
WELL LET'S TAKE IT OFF AND SEE WHO IT IS!
PD
14

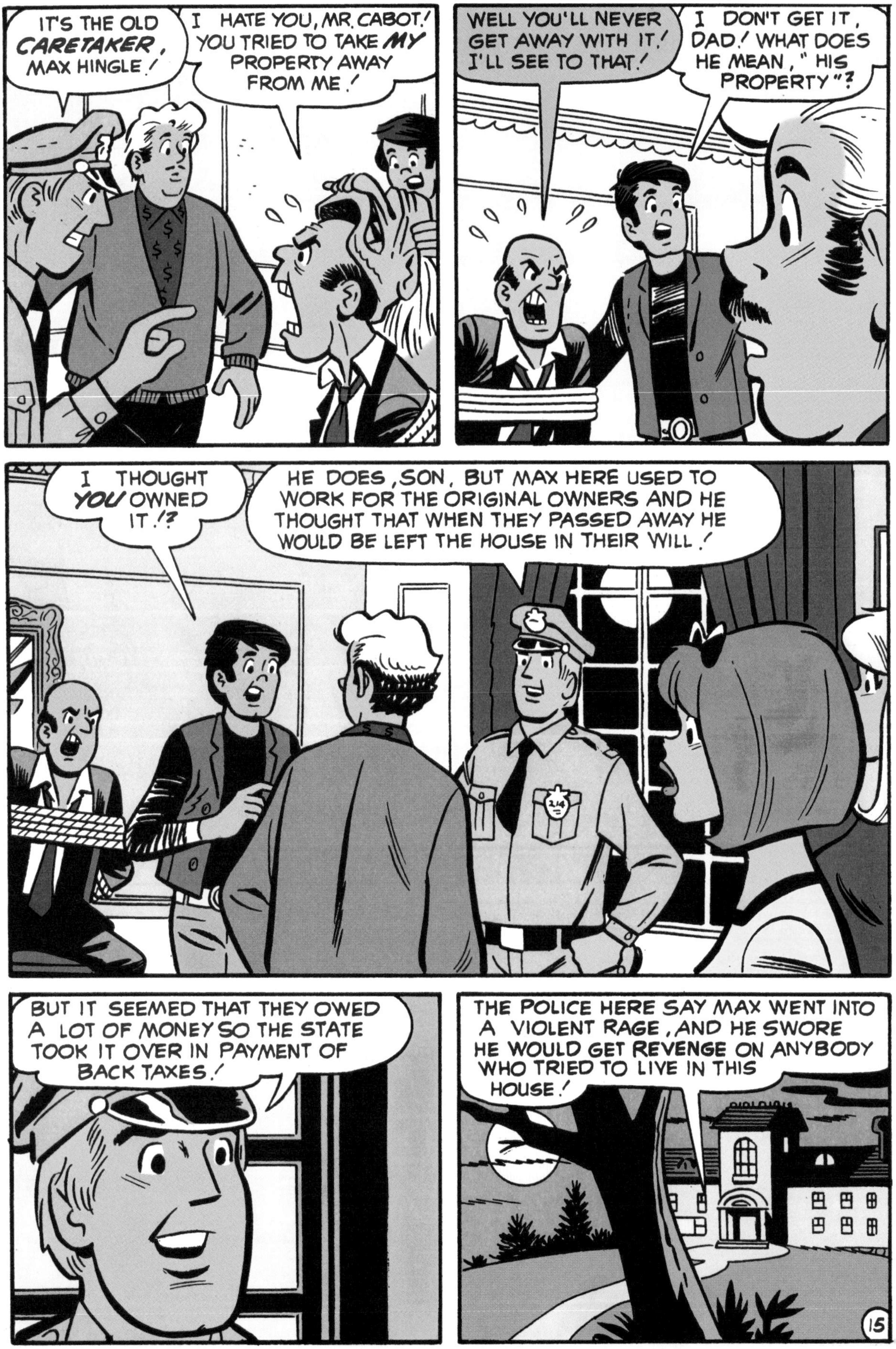
IT'S THE OLD CARETAKER, MAX HINGLE!
I HATE YOU, MR. CABOT! YOU TRIED TO TAKE MY PROPERTY AWAY FROM ME!
WELL YOU'LL NEVER GET AWAY WITH IT! I'LL SEE TO THAT!
I DON'T GET IT, DAD! WHAT DOES HE MEAN, "HIS PROPERTY"?
I THOUGHT YOU OWNED IT!?
HE DOES, SON, BUT MAX HERE USED TO WORK FOR THE ORIGINAL OWNERS AND HE THOUGHT THAT WHEN THEY PASSED AWAY HE WOULD BE LEFT THE HOUSE IN THEIR WILL!
BUT IT SEEMED THAT THEY OWED A LOT OF MONEY SO THE STATE TOOK IT OVER IN PAYMENT OF BACK TAXES!
THE POLICE HERE SAY MAX WENT INTO A VIOLENT RAGE, AND HE SWORE HE WOULD GET REVENGE ON ANYBODY WHO TRIED TO LIVE IN THIS HOUSE!
15

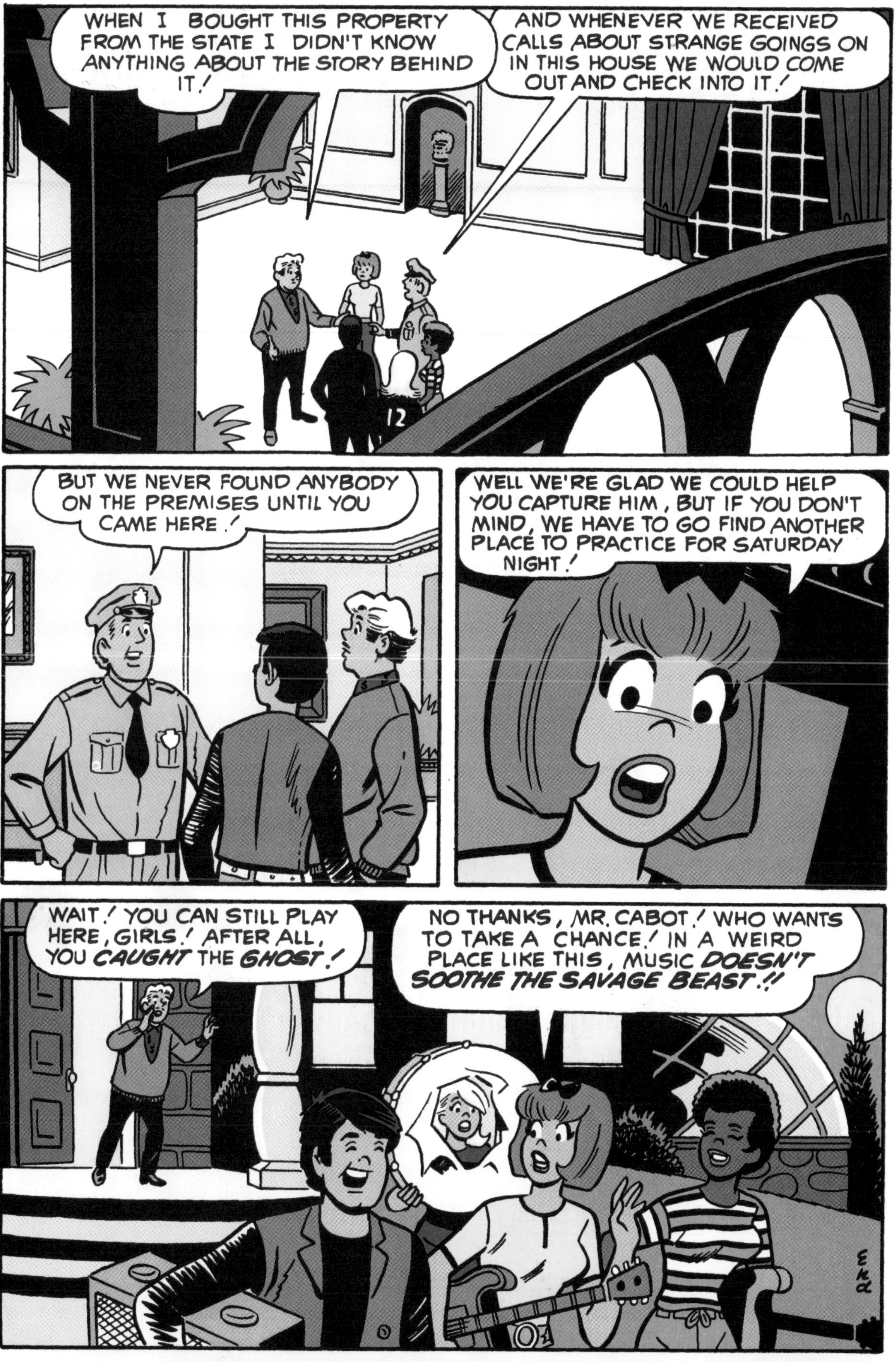
WHEN I BOUGHT THIS PROPERTY FROM THE STATE I DIDN'T KNOW ANYTHING ABOUT THE STORY BEHIND IT!
AND WHENEVER WE RECEIVED CALLS ABOUT STRANGE GOINGS ON IN THIS HOUSE WE WOULD COME OUT AND CHECK INTO IT!
12
BUT WE NEVER FOUND ANYBODY ON THE PREMISES UNTIL YOU CAME HERE!
WELL WE'RE GLAD WE COULD HELP YOU CAPTURE HIM, BUT IF YOU DON'T MIND, WE HAVE TO GO FIND ANOTHER PLACE TO PRACTICE FOR SATURDAY NIGHT!
WAIT! YOU CAN STILL PLAY HERE, GIRLS! AFTER ALL, YOU CAUGHT THE GHOST!
NO THANKS, MR. CABOT! WHO WANTS TO TAKE A CHANCE! IN A WEIRD PLACE LIKE THIS, MUSIC DOESN'T SOOTHE THE SAVAGE BEAST!!

Josie in UP UP AND AWAY!!

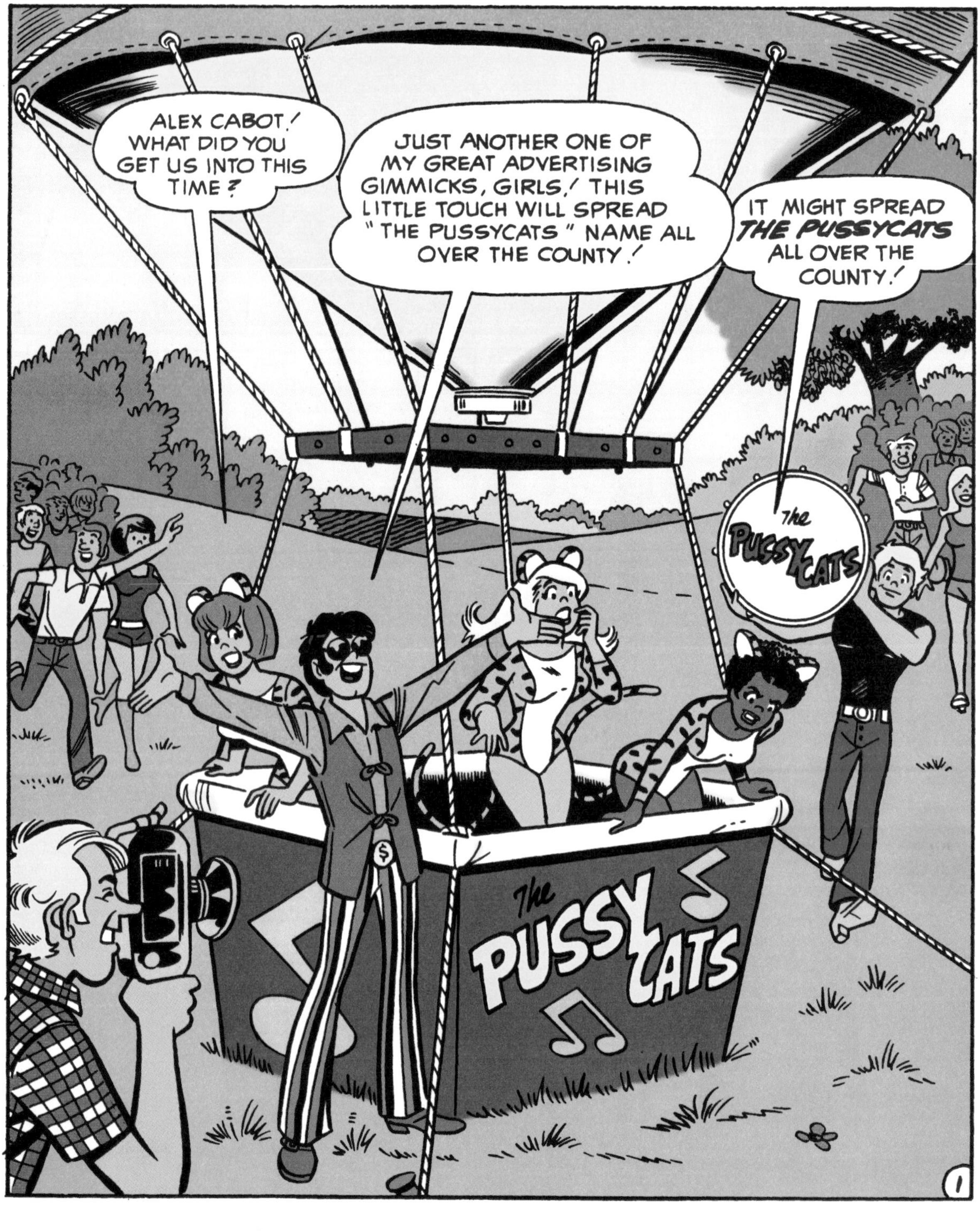
ALEX CABOT! WHAT DID YOU GET US INTO THIS TIME?
JUST ANOTHER ONE OF MY GREAT ADVERTISING GIMMICKS, GIRLS! THIS LITTLE TOUCH WILL SPREAD "THE PUSSYCATS" NAME ALL OVER THE COUNTY!
IT MIGHT SPREAD THE PUSSYCATS ALL OVER THE COUNTY!
The PUSSYCATS
The PUSSY CATS
1

ORIGINALLY PRESENTED IN
JOSIE & THE PUSSYCATS #58, OCTOBER, 1971

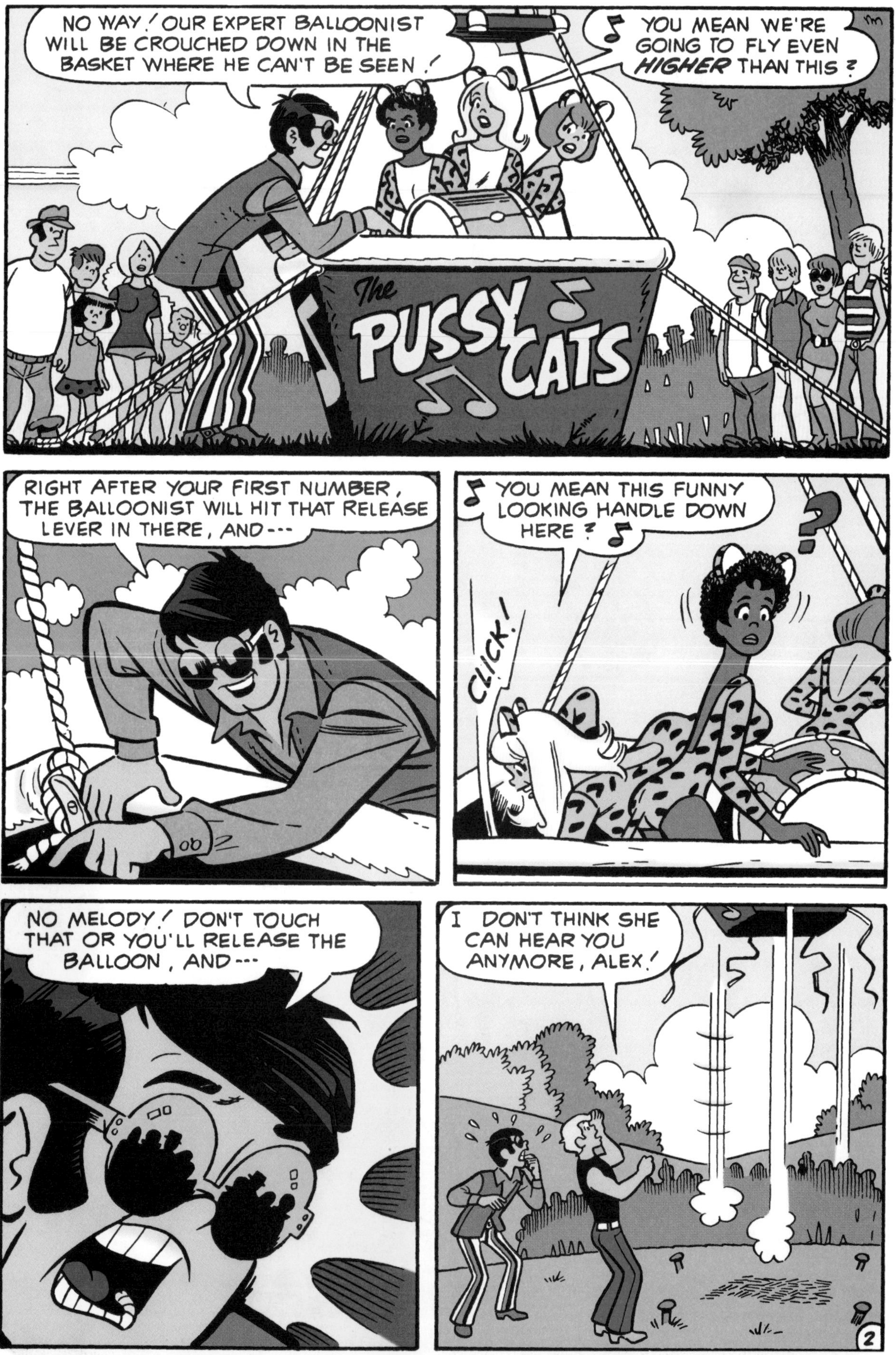
NO WAY! OUR EXPERT BALLOONIST WILL BE CROUCHED DOWN IN THE BASKET WHERE HE CAN'T BE SEEN!
YOU MEAN WE'RE GOING TO FLY EVEN HIGHER THAN THIS?
The PUSSY CATS
RIGHT AFTER YOUR FIRST NUMBER, THE BALLOONIST WILL HIT THAT RELEASE LEVER IN THERE, AND---
YOU MEAN THIS FUNNY LOOKING HANDLE DOWN HERE?
CLICK!
NO MELODY! DON'T TOUCH THAT OR YOU'LL RELEASE THE BALLOON, AND---
I DON'T THINK SHE CAN HEAR YOU ANYMORE, ALEX!
2

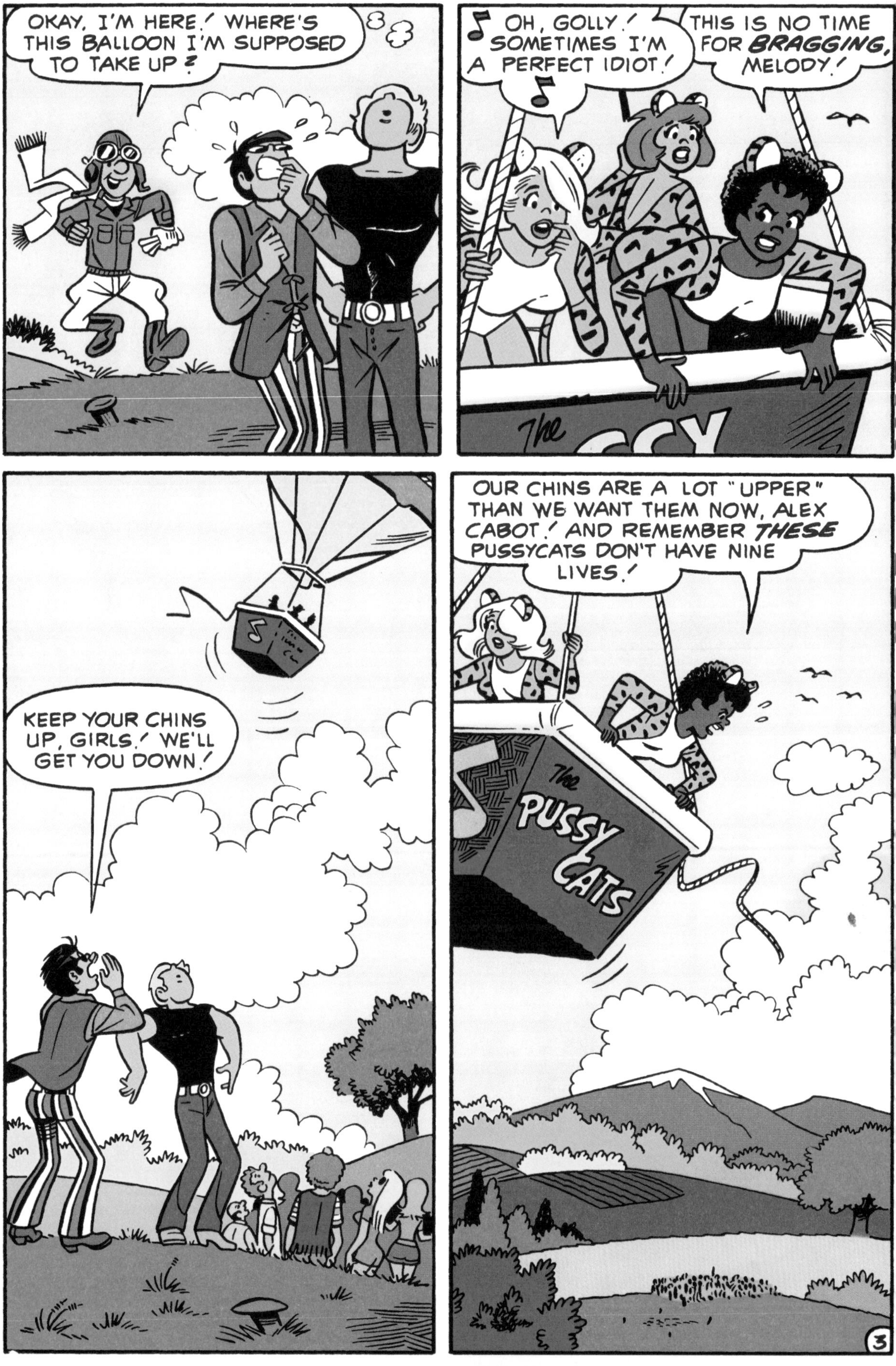
OKAY, I'M HERE! WHERE'S THIS BALLOON I'M SUPPOSED TO TAKE UP?
OH, GOLLY! SOMETIMES I'M A PERFECT IDIOT!
THIS IS NO TIME FOR BRAGGING, MELODY!
The
KEEP YOUR CHINS UP, GIRLS! WE'LL GET YOU DOWN!
OUR CHINS ARE A LOT "UPPER" THAN WE WANT THEM NOW, ALEX CABOT! AND REMEMBER THESE PUSSYCATS DON'T HAVE NINE LIVES!
The PUSSY CATS
3

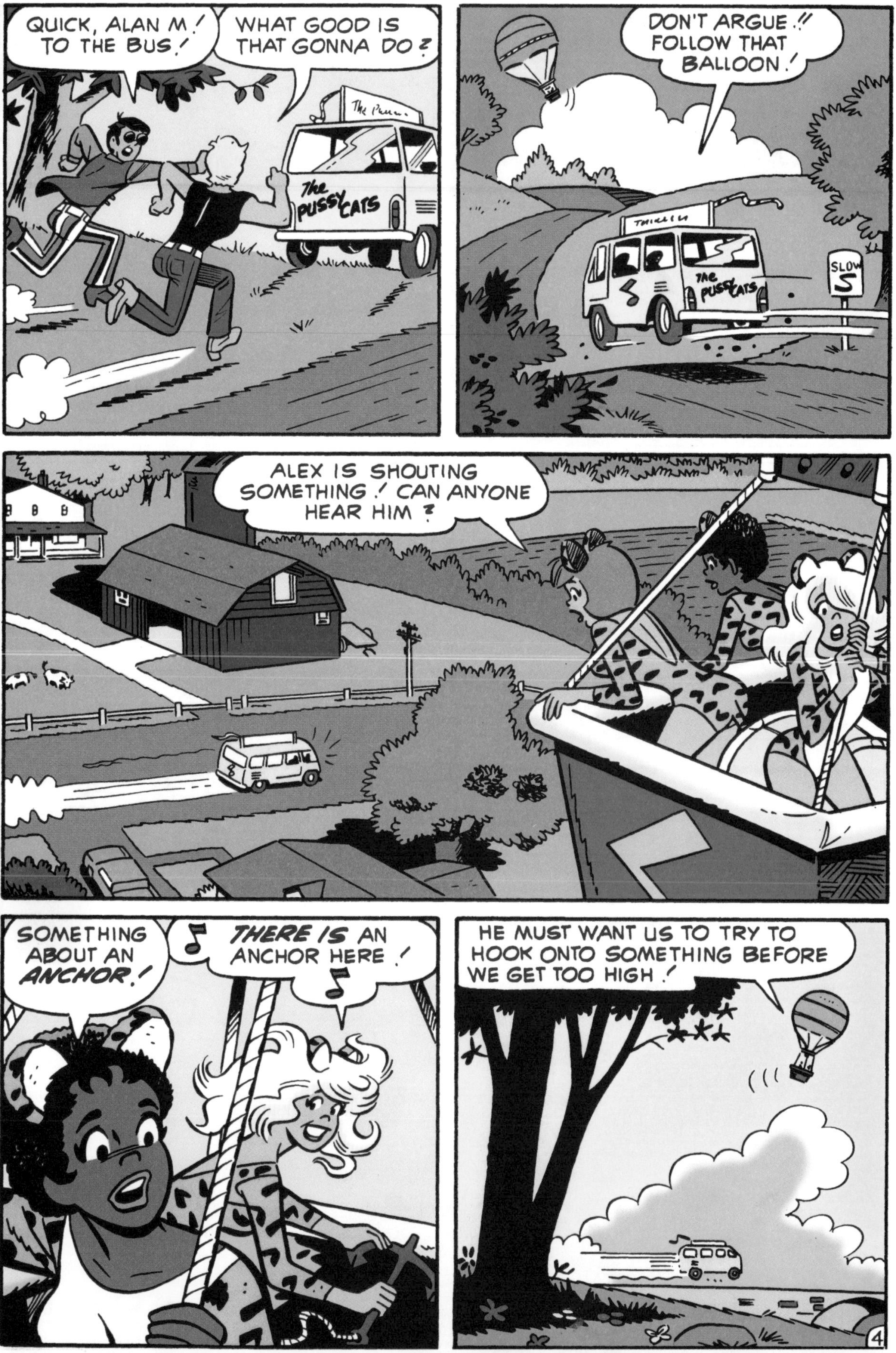
QUICK, ALAN M! TO THE BUS!
WHAT GOOD IS THAT GONNA DO?
The PUSSYCATS
DON'T ARGUE!! FOLLOW THAT BALLOON!
SLOW
ALEX IS SHOUTING SOMETHING! CAN ANYONE HEAR HIM?
SOMETHING ABOUT AN ANCHOR!
THERE IS AN ANCHOR HERE!
HE MUST WANT US TO TRY TO HOOK ONTO SOMETHING BEFORE WE GET TOO HIGH!
4

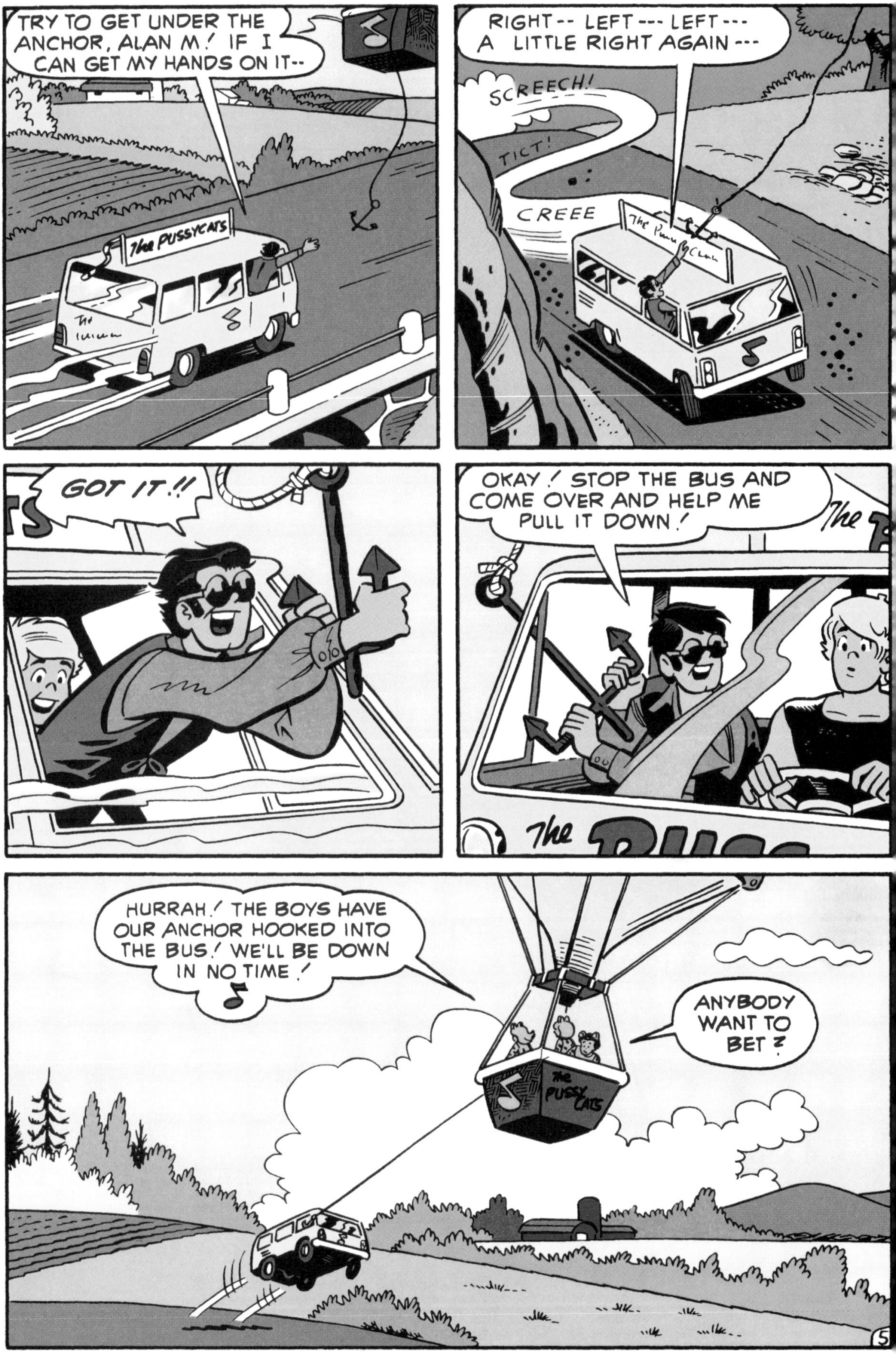
TRY TO GET UNDER THE ANCHOR, ALAN M! IF I CAN GET MY HANDS ON IT--
The PUSSYCATS
RIGHT -- LEFT --- LEFT --- A LITTLE RIGHT AGAIN ---
SCREECH!
TICT!
CREEE
GOT IT!!
OKAY! STOP THE BUS AND COME OVER AND HELP ME PULL IT DOWN!
HURRAH! THE BOYS HAVE OUR ANCHOR HOOKED INTO THE BUS! WE'LL BE DOWN IN NO TIME!
ANYBODY WANT TO BET?
The PUSSY CATS
5

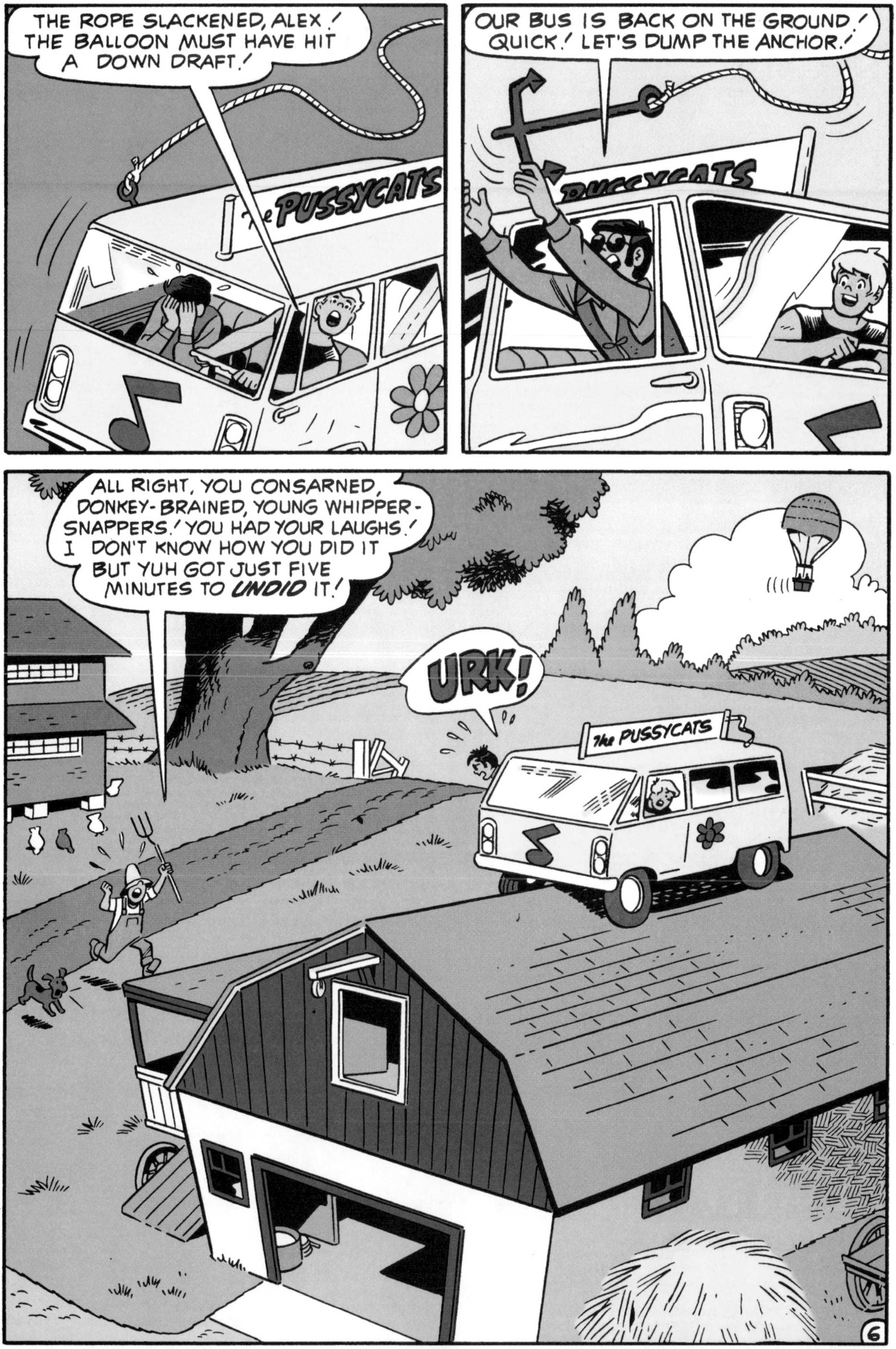
THE ROPE SLACKENED, ALEX! THE BALLOON MUST HAVE HIT A DOWN DRAFT!
The PUSSYCATS
OUR BUS IS BACK ON THE GROUND! QUICK! LET'S DUMP THE ANCHOR!
PUSSYCATS
ALL RIGHT, YOU CONSARNED, DONKEY-BRAINED, YOUNG WHIPPER-SNAPPERS! YOU HAD YOUR LAUGHS! I DON'T KNOW HOW YOU DID IT BUT YUH GOT JUST FIVE MINUTES TO UNDID IT!
URK!
The PUSSYCATS
6

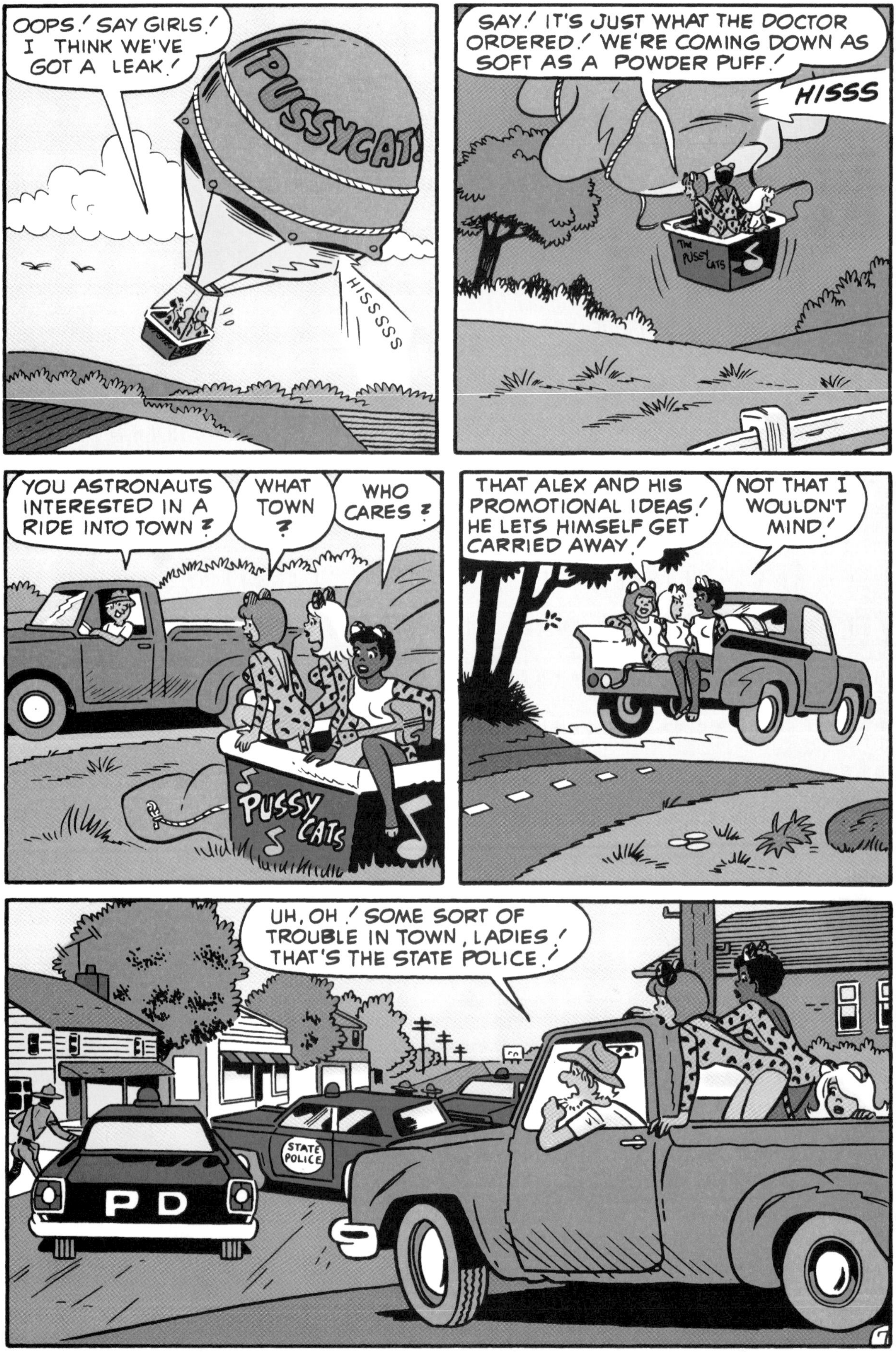
OOPS! SAY GIRLS! I THINK WE'VE GOT A LEAK!
PUSSYCATS
HISSSSS
SAY! IT'S JUST WHAT THE DOCTOR ORDERED! WE'RE COMING DOWN AS SOFT AS A POWDER PUFF!
HISSS
THE PUSSY CATS
YOU ASTRONAUTS INTERESTED IN A RIDE INTO TOWN?
WHAT TOWN?
WHO CARES?
PUSSY CATS
THAT ALEX AND HIS PROMOTIONAL IDEAS! HE LETS HIMSELF GET CARRIED AWAY!
NOT THAT I WOULDN'T MIND!
UH, OH! SOME SORT OF TROUBLE IN TOWN, LADIES! THAT'S THE STATE POLICE!
STATE POLICE
P D
7

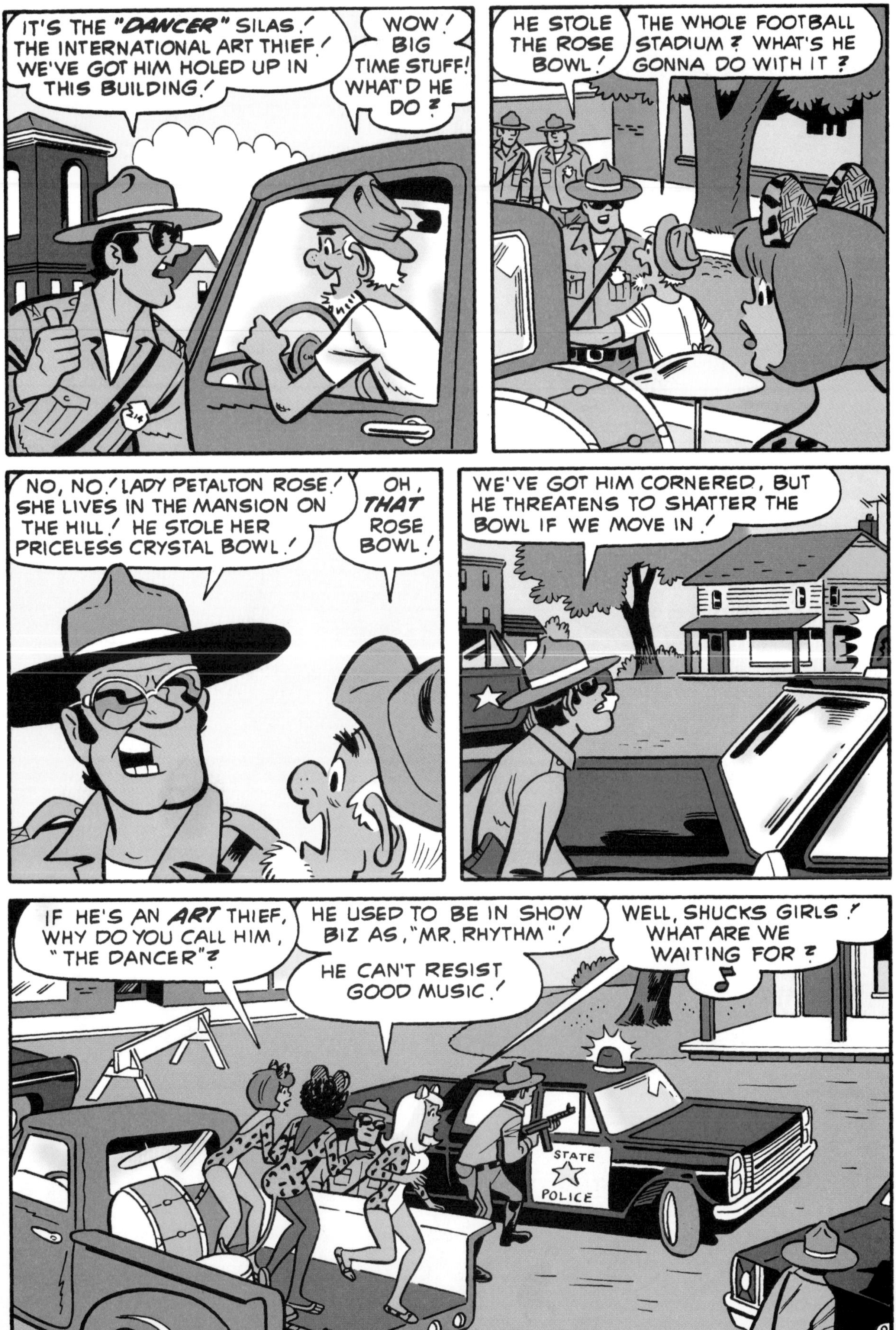
IT'S THE "DANCER" SILAS! THE INTERNATIONAL ART THIEF! WE'VE GOT HIM HOLED UP IN THIS BUILDING!
WOW! BIG TIME STUFF! WHAT'D HE DO?
HE STOLE THE ROSE BOWL!
THE WHOLE FOOTBALL STADIUM? WHAT'S HE GONNA DO WITH IT?
NO, NO! LADY PETALTON ROSE! SHE LIVES IN THE MANSION ON THE HILL! HE STOLE HER PRICELESS CRYSTAL BOWL!
OH, THAT ROSE BOWL!
WE'VE GOT HIM CORNERED, BUT HE THREATENS TO SHATTER THE BOWL IF WE MOVE IN!
IF HE'S AN ART THIEF, WHY DO YOU CALL HIM, "THE DANCER"?
HE USED TO BE IN SHOW BIZ AS, "MR. RHYTHM"!
HE CAN'T RESIST GOOD MUSIC!
WELL, SHUCKS GIRLS! WHAT ARE WE WAITING FOR?
STATE POLICE
8

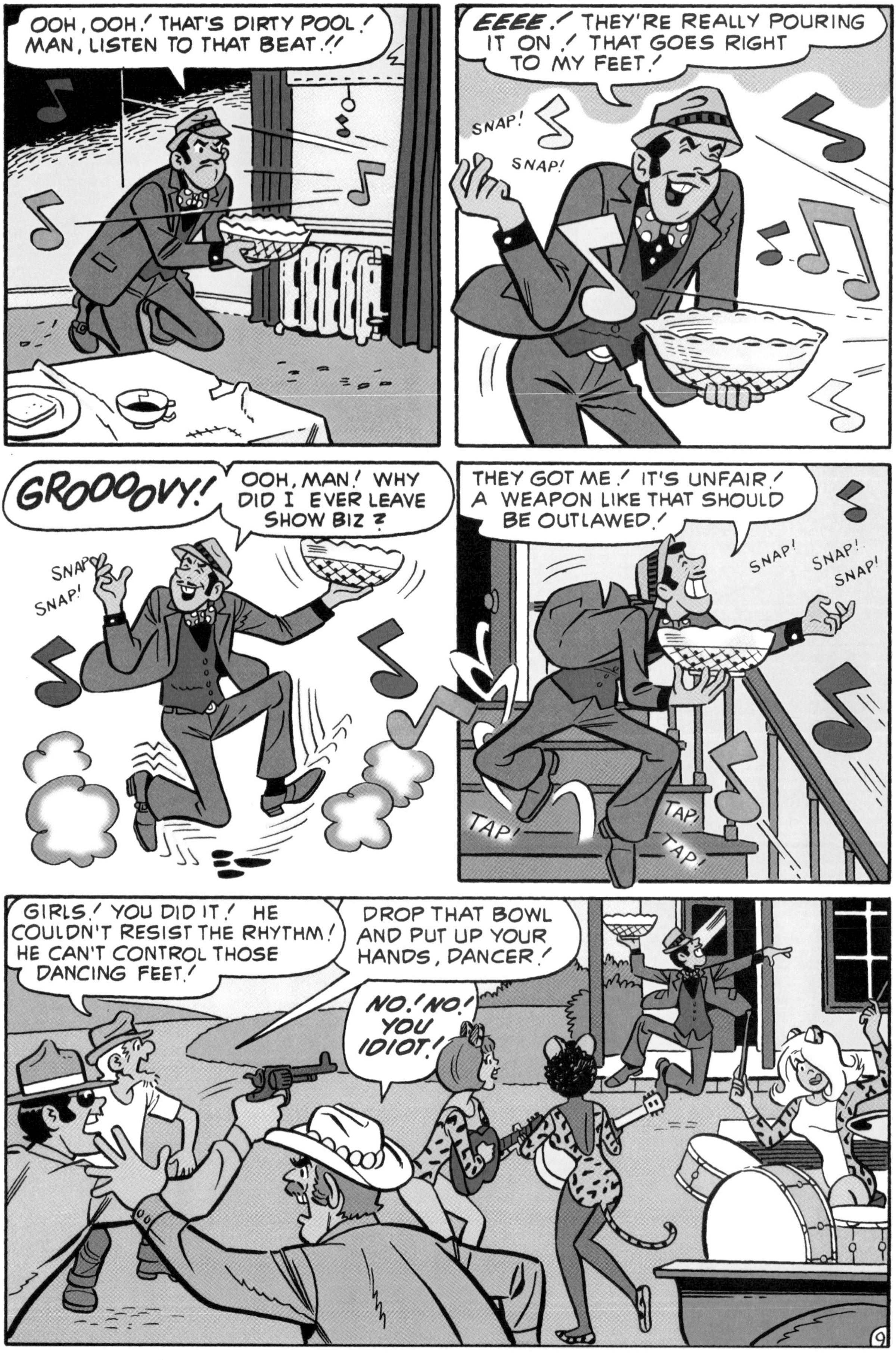
OOH, OOH.! THAT'S DIRTY POOL! MAN, LISTEN TO THAT BEAT!!
EEEE.! THEY'RE REALLY POURING IT ON! THAT GOES RIGHT TO MY FEET!
SNAP!
SNAP!
GROOOOVY!
OOH, MAN! WHY DID I EVER LEAVE SHOW BIZ?
SNAP!
SNAP!
THEY GOT ME! IT'S UNFAIR! A WEAPON LIKE THAT SHOULD BE OUTLAWED!
SNAP!
SNAP!
SNAP!
TAP!
TAP!
TAP!
GIRLS! YOU DID IT! HE COULDN'T RESIST THE RHYTHM! HE CAN'T CONTROL THOSE DANCING FEET!
DROP THAT BOWL AND PUT UP YOUR HANDS, DANCER!
NO.! NO! YOU IDIOT!
9

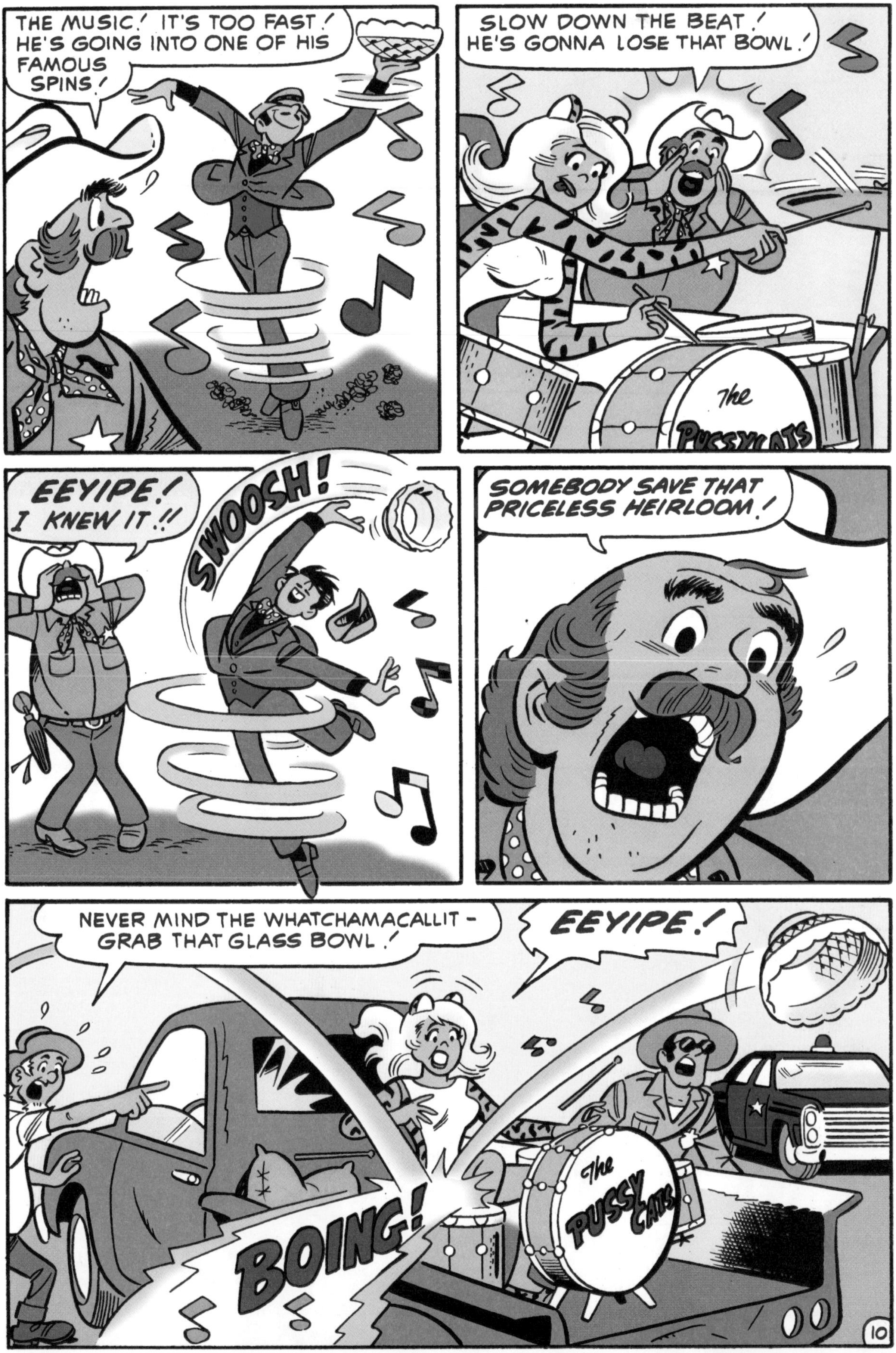
THE MUSIC! IT'S TOO FAST! HE'S GOING INTO ONE OF HIS FAMOUS SPINS!
SLOW DOWN THE BEAT! HE'S GONNA LOSE THAT BOWL!
The PUSSYCATS
EEYIPE! I KNEW IT!!
SWOOSH!
SOMEBODY SAVE THAT PRICELESS HEIRLOOM!
NEVER MIND THE WHATCHAMACALLIT - GRAB THAT GLASS BOWL!
EEYIPE!
BOING!
The PUSSYCATS
10

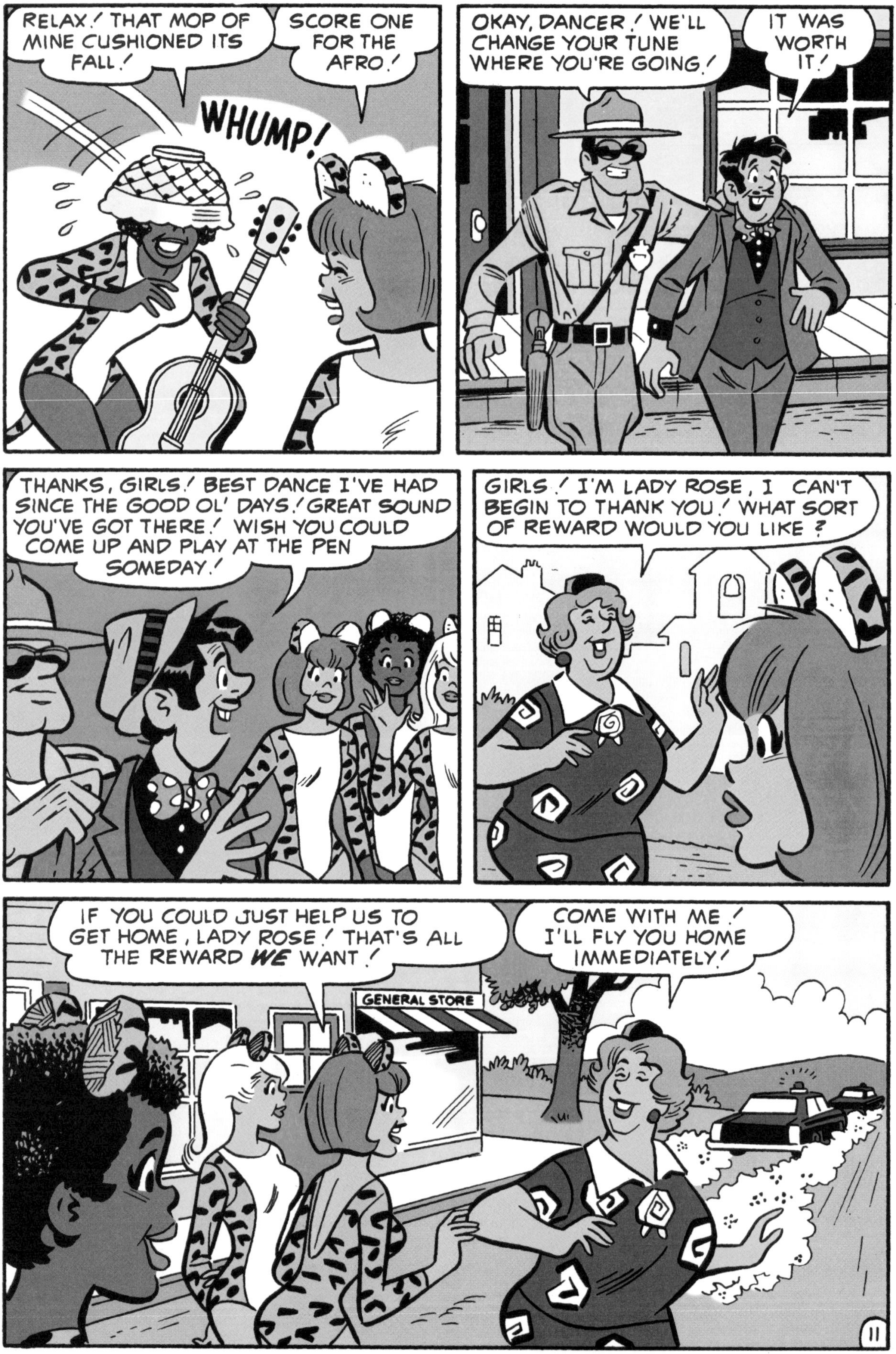
RELAX! THAT MOP OF MINE CUSHIONED ITS FALL!
SCORE ONE FOR THE AFRO!
WHUMP!
OKAY, DANCER! WE'LL CHANGE YOUR TUNE WHERE YOU'RE GOING!
IT WAS WORTH IT!
THANKS, GIRLS! BEST DANCE I'VE HAD SINCE THE GOOD OL' DAYS! GREAT SOUND YOU'VE GOT THERE! WISH YOU COULD COME UP AND PLAY AT THE PEN SOMEDAY!
GIRLS! I'M LADY ROSE, I CAN'T BEGIN TO THANK YOU! WHAT SORT OF REWARD WOULD YOU LIKE?
IF YOU COULD JUST HELP US TO GET HOME, LADY ROSE! THAT'S ALL THE REWARD WE WANT!
GENERAL STORE
COME WITH ME! I'LL FLY YOU HOME IMMEDIATELY!
11

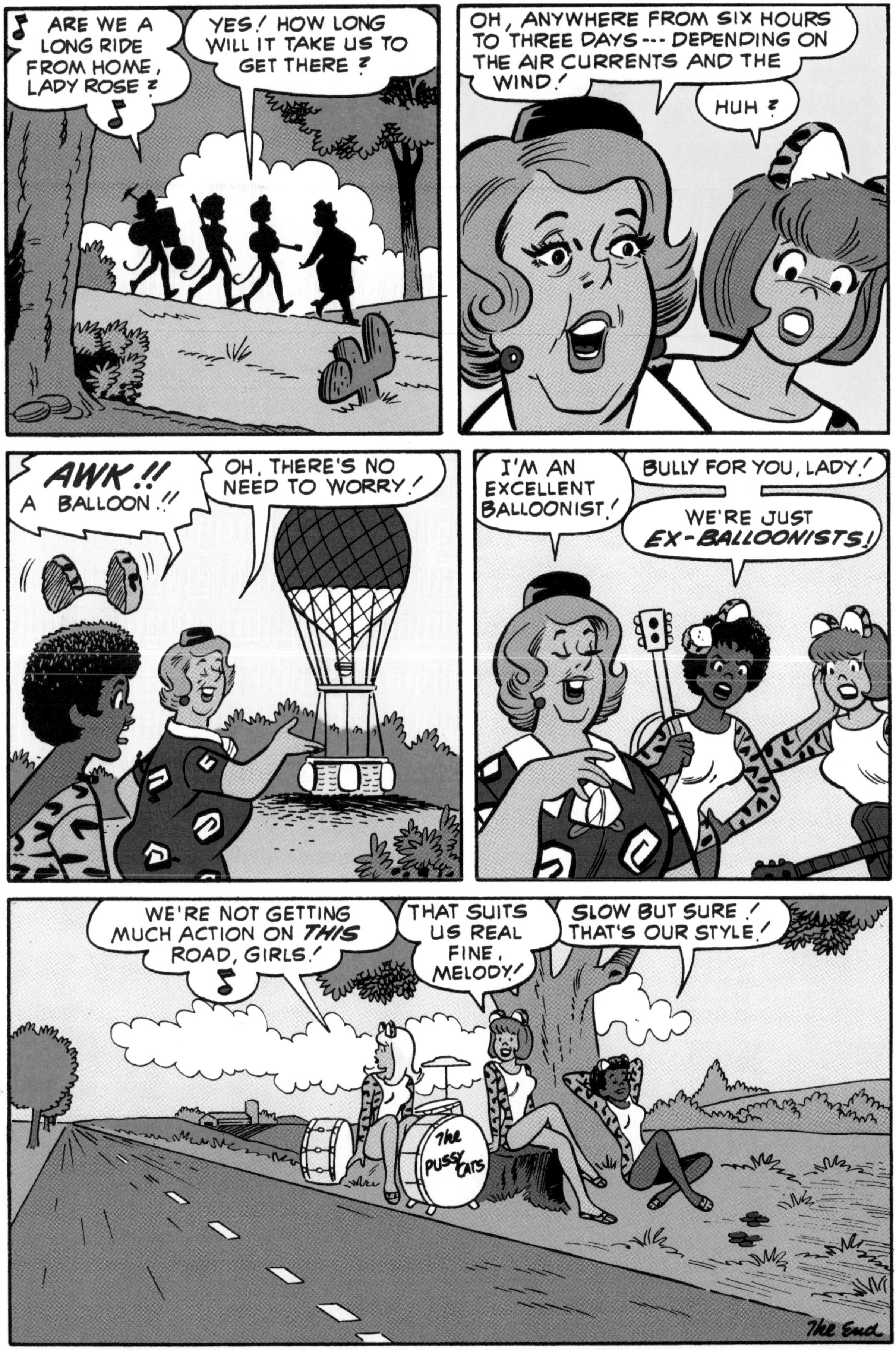
ARE WE A LONG RIDE FROM HOME, LADY ROSE?
YES! HOW LONG WILL IT TAKE US TO GET THERE?
OH, ANYWHERE FROM SIX HOURS TO THREE DAYS--- DEPENDING ON THE AIR CURRENTS AND THE WIND!
HUH?
AWK!! A BALLOON!!
OH, THERE'S NO NEED TO WORRY!
I'M AN EXCELLENT BALLOONIST!
BULLY FOR YOU, LADY!
WE'RE JUST EX-BALLOONISTS!
WE'RE NOT GETTING MUCH ACTION ON THIS ROAD, GIRLS!
THAT SUITS US REAL FINE, MELODY!
SLOW BUT SURE! THAT'S OUR STYLE!
The PUSSYCATS
The End

THE PUSSYCATS GET A NEW LOOK!

SPACE DOES NOT PERMIT US TO REPRINT THIS ENTIRE TALE, BUT WE'LL HUM A FEW BARS WITH SELECT PANELS FROM ARCHIE GIANT SERIES PRESENTS **JOSIE AND THE PUSSYCATS #540, AUGUST, 1984**

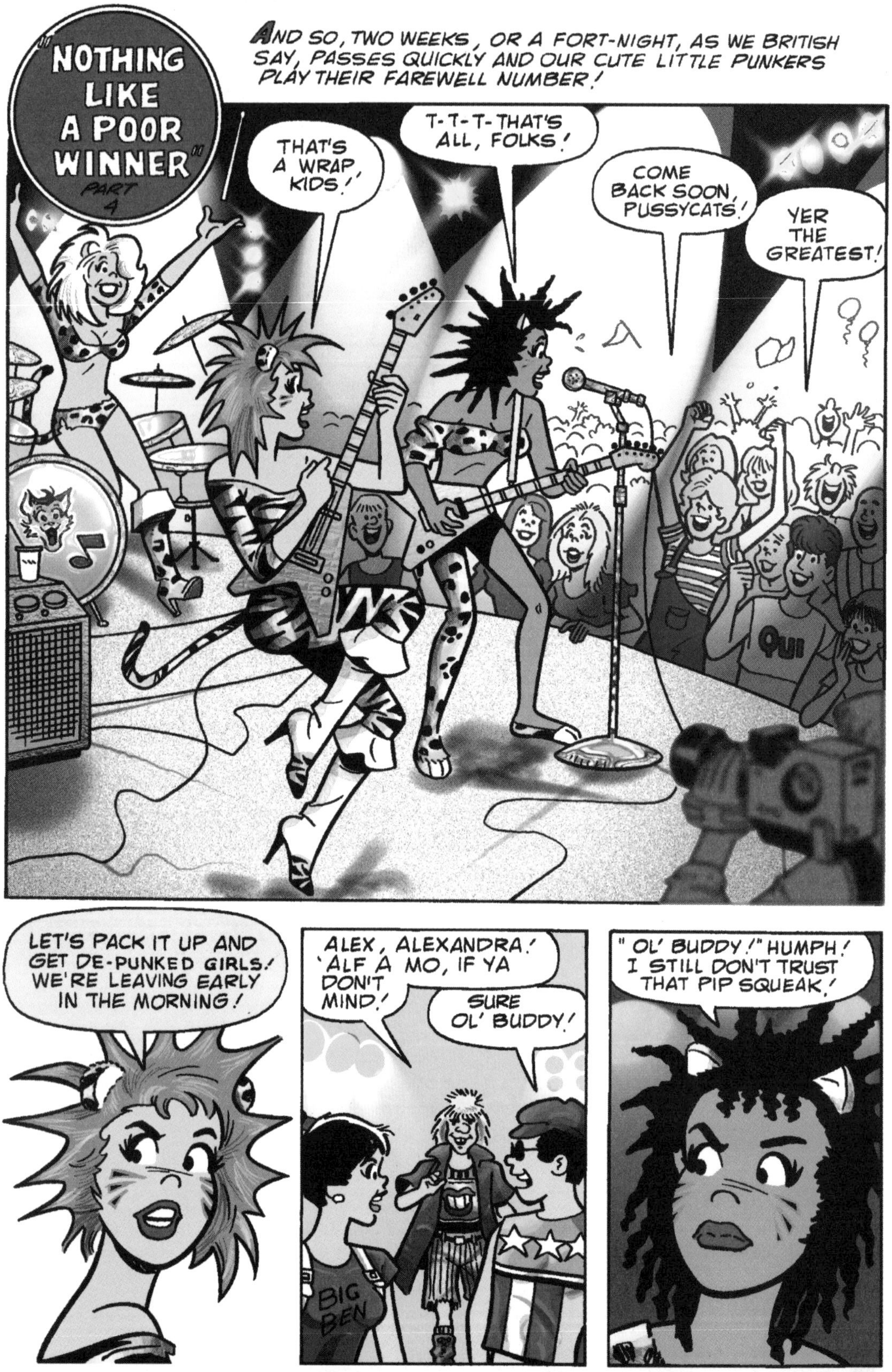
"NOTHING LIKE A POOR WINNER" PART 4
AND SO, TWO WEEKS, OR A FORT-NIGHT, AS WE BRITISH SAY, PASSES QUICKLY AND OUR CUTE LITTLE PUNKERS PLAY THEIR FAREWELL NUMBER!
THAT'S A WRAP, KIDS!
T-T-T-THAT'S ALL, FOLKS!
COME BACK SOON, PUSSYCATS!
YER THE GREATEST!
QUI
LET'S PACK IT UP AND GET DE-PUNKED GIRLS! WE'RE LEAVING EARLY IN THE MORNING!
ALEX, ALEXANDRA! 'ALF A MO, IF YA DON'T MIND!
SURE OL' BUDDY!
BIG BEN
"OL' BUDDY!" HUMPH! I STILL DON'T TRUST THAT PIP SQUEAK!

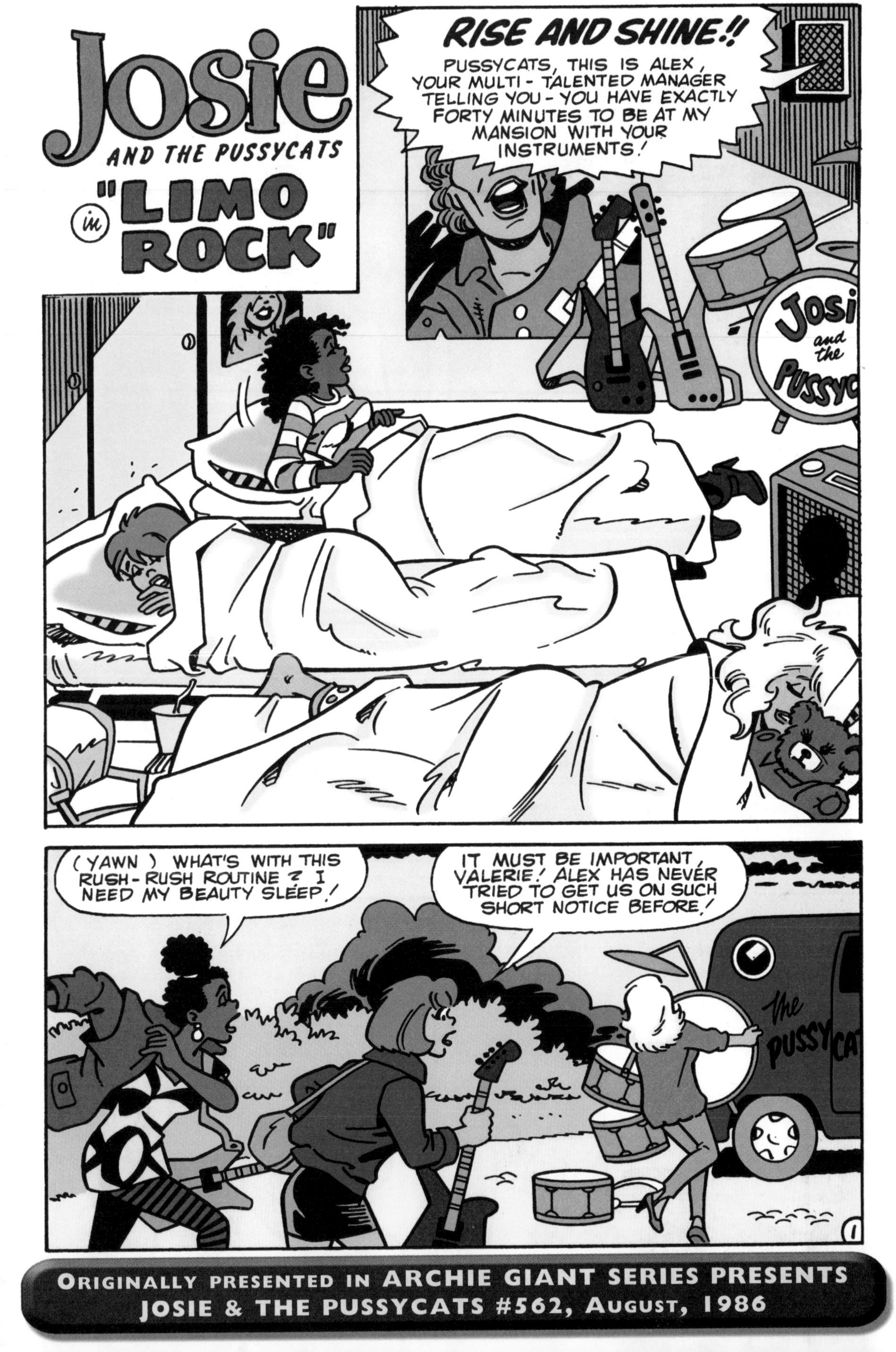
Josie
AND THE PUSSYCATS
in "LIMO ROCK"
RISE AND SHINE!!
PUSSYCATS, THIS IS ALEX, YOUR MULTI-TALENTED MANAGER TELLING YOU - YOU HAVE EXACTLY FORTY MINUTES TO BE AT MY MANSION WITH YOUR INSTRUMENTS!
(YAWN) WHAT'S WITH THIS RUSH-RUSH ROUTINE? I NEED MY BEAUTY SLEEP!
IT MUST BE IMPORTANT, VALERIE! ALEX HAS NEVER TRIED TO GET US ON SUCH SHORT NOTICE BEFORE!
1

ORIGINALLY PRESENTED IN ARCHIE GIANT SERIES PRESENTS JOSIE & THE PUSSYCATS #562, AUGUST, 1986

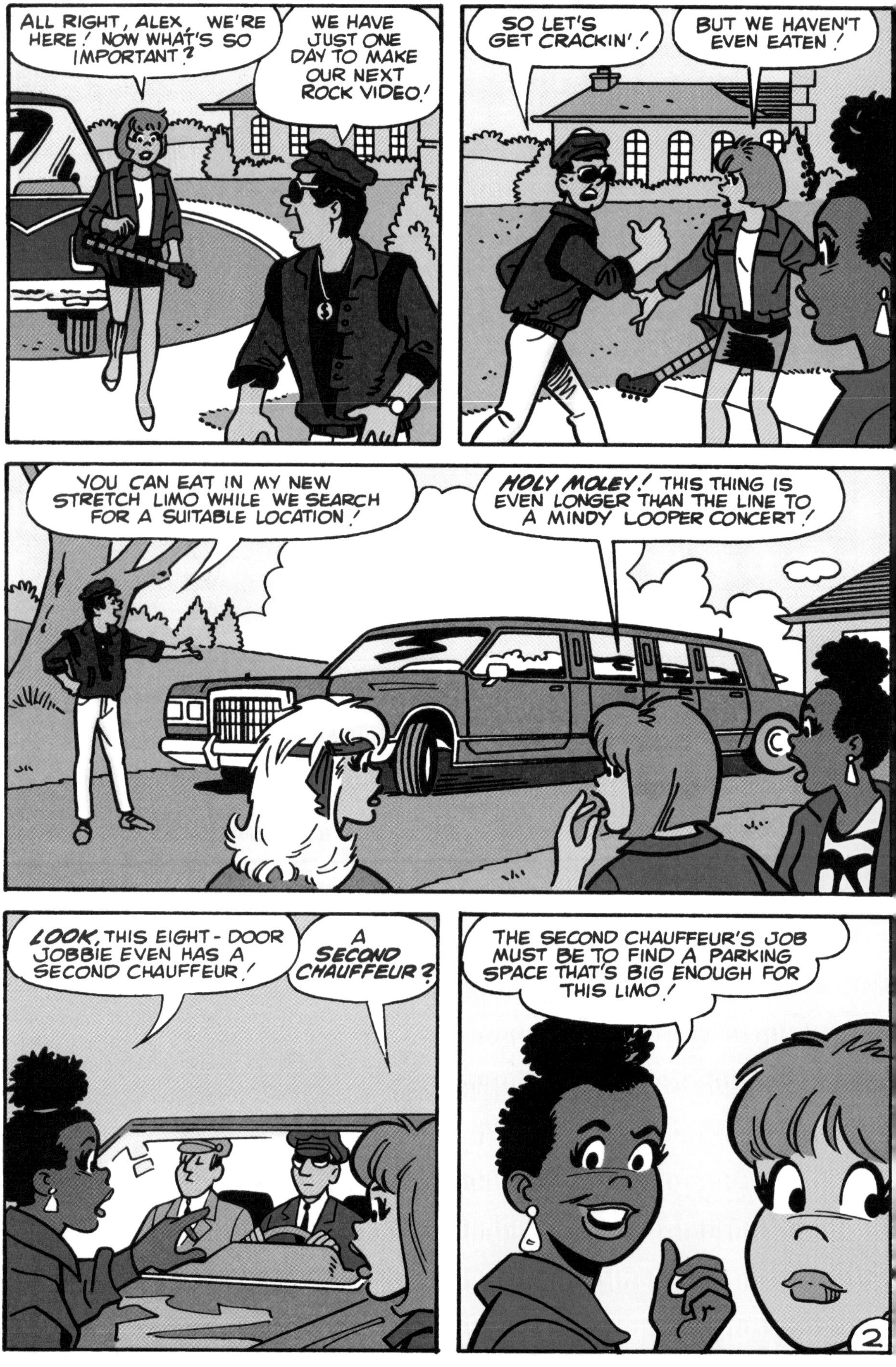
ALL RIGHT, ALEX, WE'RE HERE! NOW WHAT'S SO IMPORTANT?
WE HAVE JUST ONE DAY TO MAKE OUR NEXT ROCK VIDEO!
SO LET'S GET CRACKIN'!
BUT WE HAVEN'T EVEN EATEN!
YOU CAN EAT IN MY NEW STRETCH LIMO WHILE WE SEARCH FOR A SUITABLE LOCATION!
HOLY MOLEY! THIS THING IS EVEN LONGER THAN THE LINE TO A MINDY LOOPER CONCERT!
LOOK, THIS EIGHT-DOOR JOBBIE EVEN HAS A SECOND CHAUFFEUR!
A SECOND CHAUFFEUR?
THE SECOND CHAUFFEUR'S JOB MUST BE TO FIND A PARKING SPACE THAT'S BIG ENOUGH FOR THIS LIMO!
2

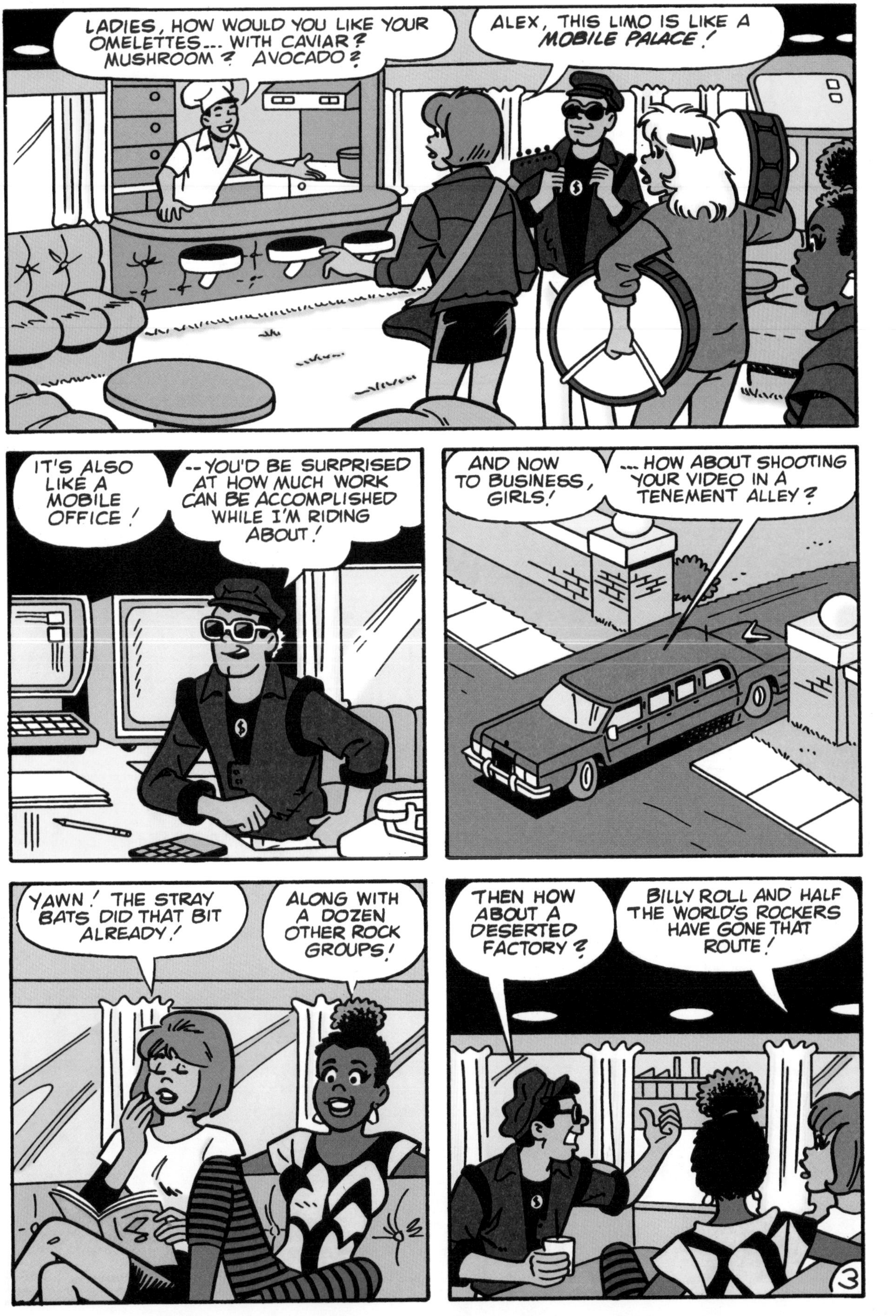
LADIES, HOW WOULD YOU LIKE YOUR OMELETTES... WITH CAVIAR? MUSHROOM? AVOCADO?
ALEX, THIS LIMO IS LIKE A *MOBILE PALACE*!
IT'S ALSO LIKE A MOBILE OFFICE!
--YOU'D BE SURPRISED AT HOW MUCH WORK CAN BE ACCOMPLISHED WHILE I'M RIDING ABOUT!
AND NOW TO BUSINESS, GIRLS!
...HOW ABOUT SHOOTING YOUR VIDEO IN A TENEMENT ALLEY?
YAWN! THE STRAY BATS DID THAT BIT ALREADY!
ALONG WITH A DOZEN OTHER ROCK GROUPS!
THEN HOW ABOUT A DESERTED FACTORY?
BILLY ROLL AND HALF THE WORLD'S ROCKERS HAVE GONE THAT ROUTE!
3

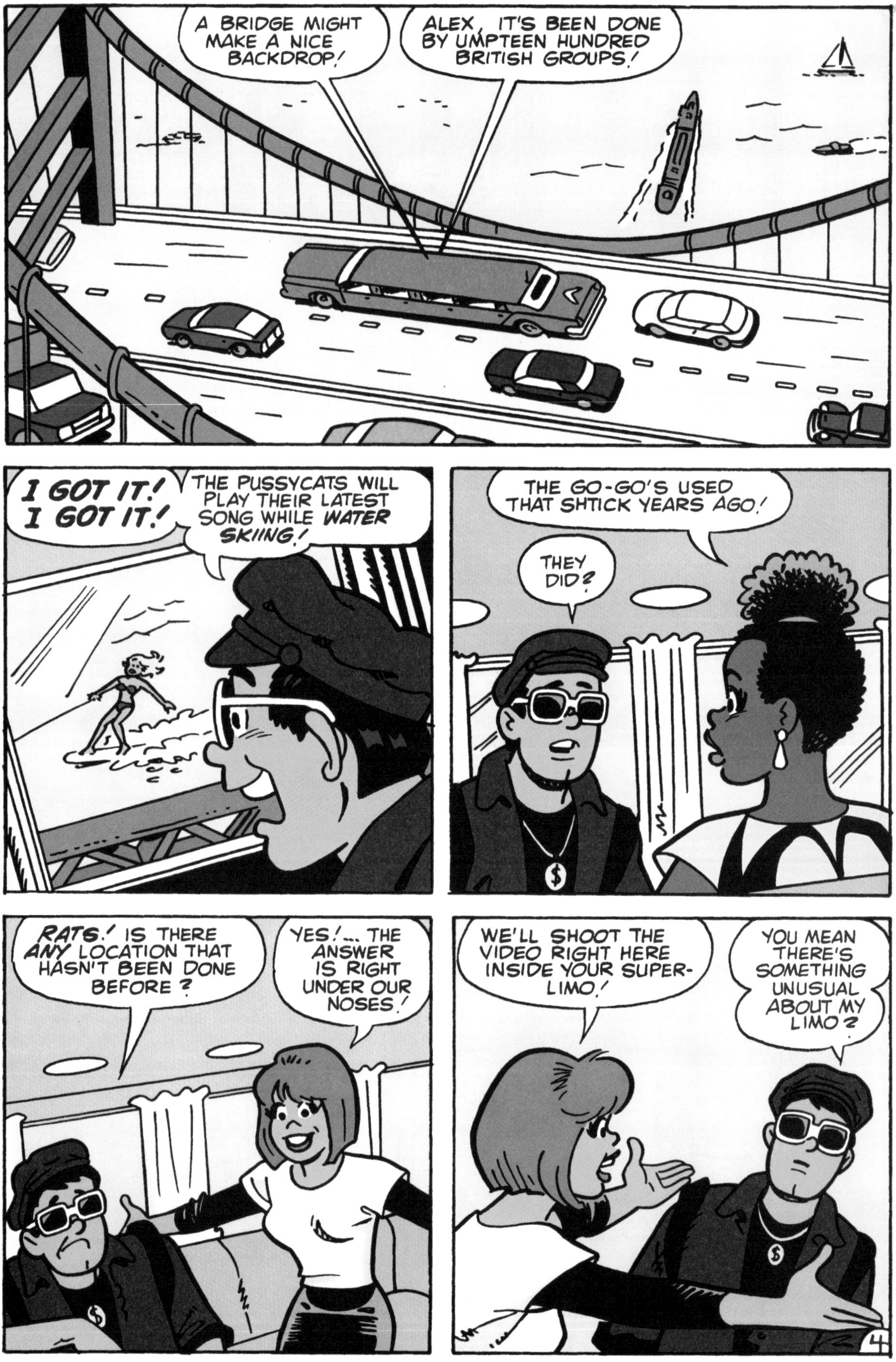
A BRIDGE MIGHT MAKE A NICE BACKDROP!
ALEX, IT'S BEEN DONE BY UMPTEEN HUNDRED BRITISH GROUPS!
I GOT IT! I GOT IT!
THE PUSSYCATS WILL PLAY THEIR LATEST SONG WHILE WATER SKIING!
THE GO-GO'S USED THAT SHTICK YEARS AGO!
THEY DID?
RATS! IS THERE ANY LOCATION THAT HASN'T BEEN DONE BEFORE?
YES!... THE ANSWER IS RIGHT UNDER OUR NOSES!
WE'LL SHOOT THE VIDEO RIGHT HERE INSIDE YOUR SUPER-LIMO!
YOU MEAN THERE'S SOMETHING UNUSUAL ABOUT MY LIMO?
4

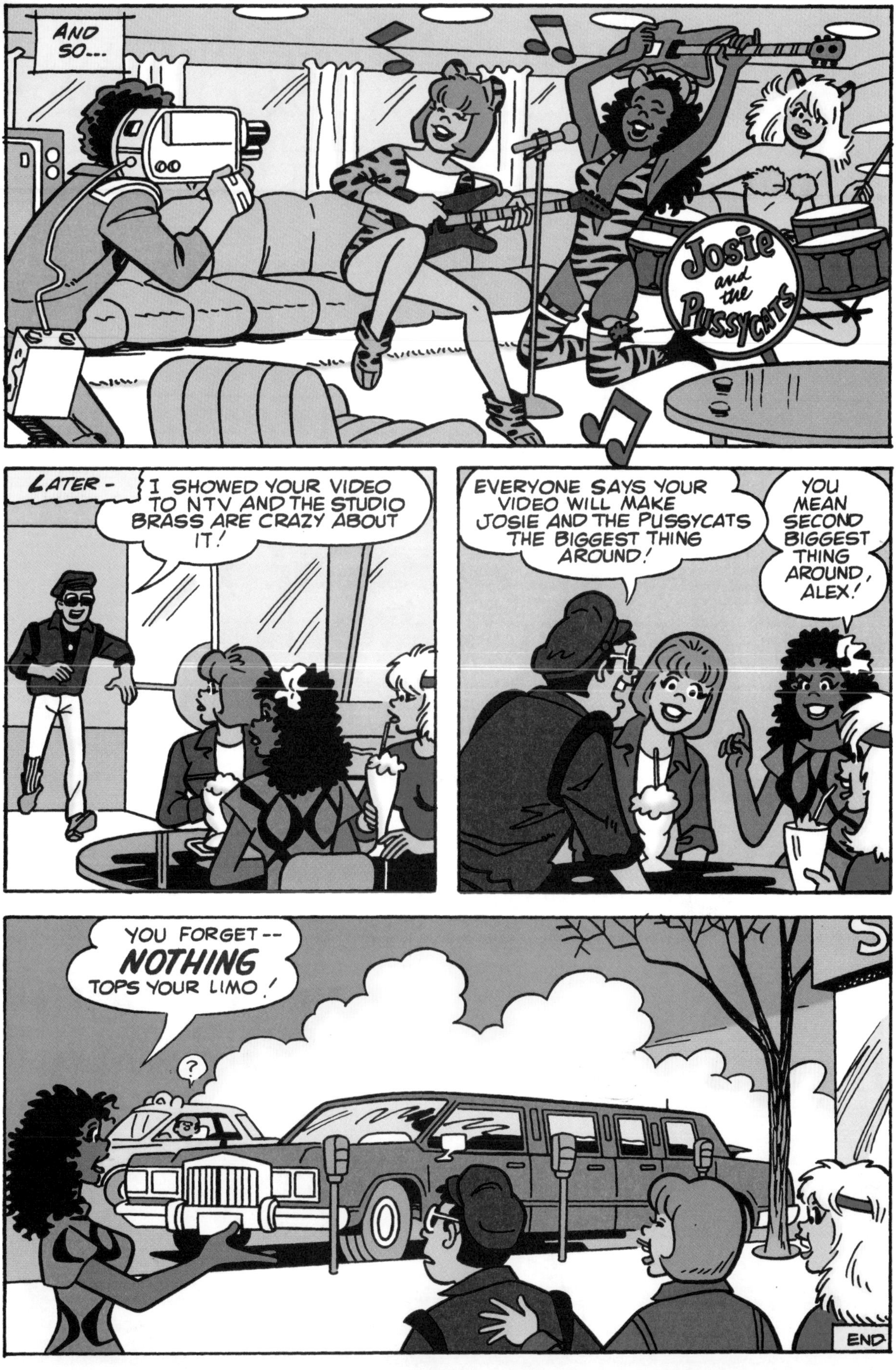
AND SO...
JOSIE and the PUSSYCATS
LATER -
I SHOWED YOUR VIDEO TO NTV AND THE STUDIO BRASS ARE CRAZY ABOUT IT!
EVERYONE SAYS YOUR VIDEO WILL MAKE JOSIE AND THE PUSSYCATS THE BIGGEST THING AROUND!
YOU MEAN SECOND BIGGEST THING AROUND, ALEX!
YOU FORGET -- NOTHING TOPS YOUR LIMO!
?
END

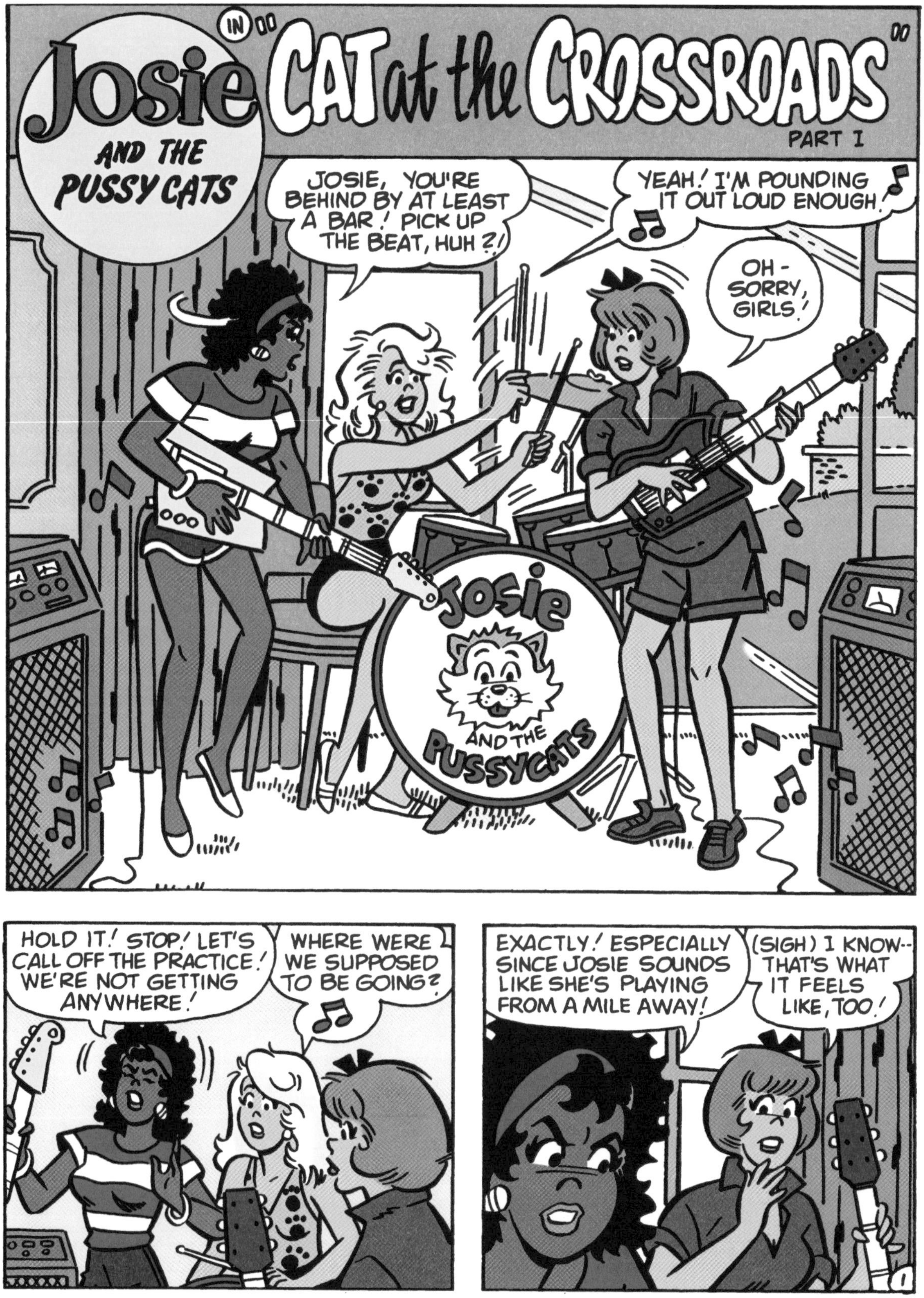
Josie AND THE PUSSY CATS
IN "CAT at the CROSSROADS"
PART I
JOSIE, YOU'RE BEHIND BY AT LEAST A BAR! PICK UP THE BEAT, HUH ?!
YEAH! I'M POUNDING IT OUT LOUD ENOUGH!
OH - SORRY, GIRLS!
JOSIE AND THE PUSSYCATS
HOLD IT! STOP! LET'S CALL OFF THE PRACTICE! WE'RE NOT GETTING ANYWHERE!
WHERE WERE WE SUPPOSED TO BE GOING?
EXACTLY! ESPECIALLY SINCE JOSIE SOUNDS LIKE SHE'S PLAYING FROM A MILE AWAY!
(SIGH) I KNOW-- THAT'S WHAT IT FEELS LIKE, TOO!
1

ORIGINALLY PRESENTED IN ARCHIE GIANT SERIES PRESENTS JOSIE & THE PUSSYCATS #584, SEPTEMBER, 1988

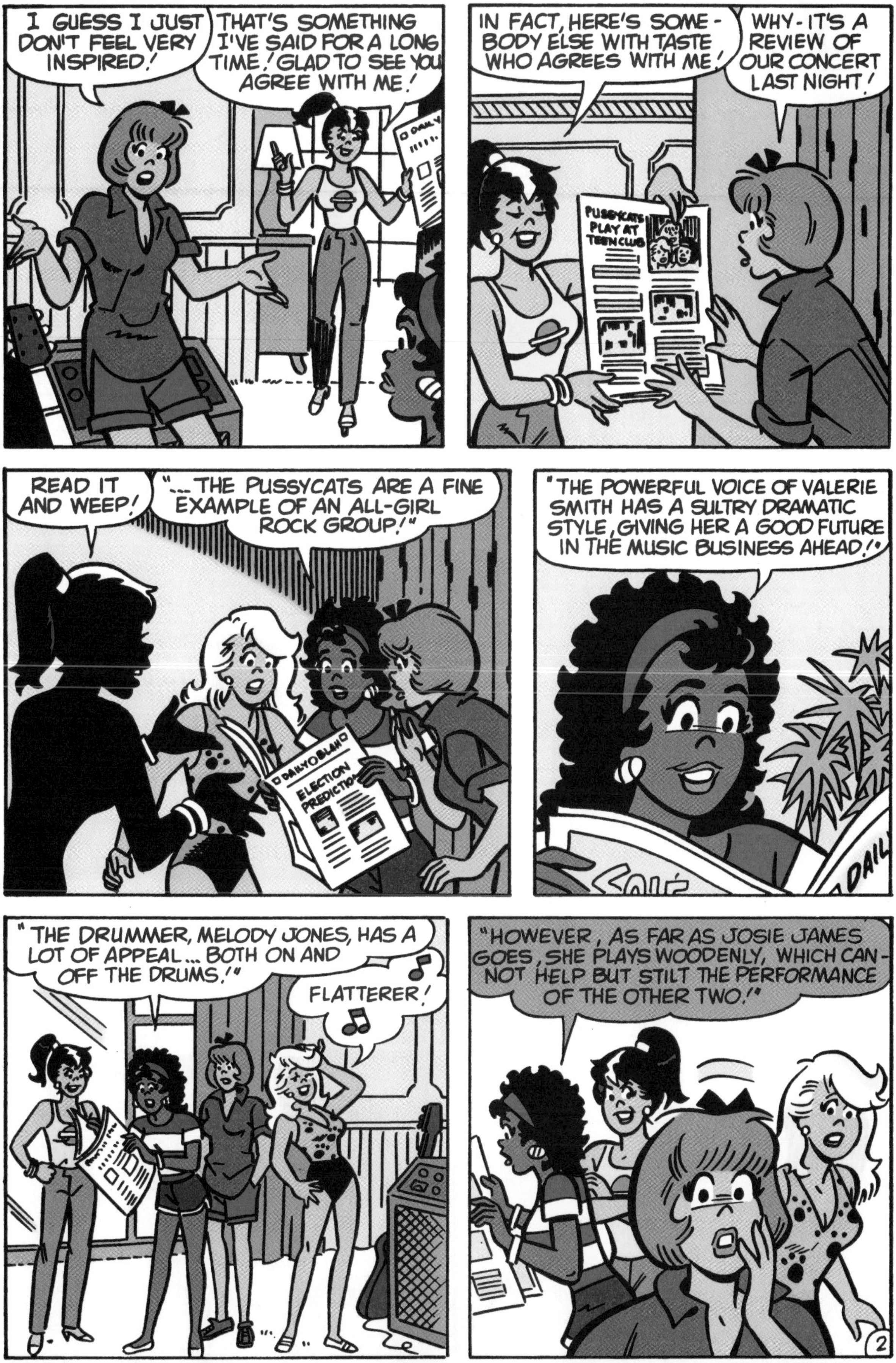
I GUESS I JUST DON'T FEEL VERY INSPIRED!
THAT'S SOMETHING I'VE SAID FOR A LONG TIME! GLAD TO SEE YOU AGREE WITH ME!
IN FACT, HERE'S SOMEBODY ELSE WITH TASTE WHO AGREES WITH ME!
WHY-IT'S A REVIEW OF OUR CONCERT LAST NIGHT!
PUSSYCATS PLAY AT TEEN CLUB
READ IT AND WEEP!
"...THE PUSSYCATS ARE A FINE EXAMPLE OF AN ALL-GIRL ROCK GROUP!"
ELECTION PREDICTIO
"THE POWERFUL VOICE OF VALERIE SMITH HAS A SULTRY DRAMATIC STYLE, GIVING HER A GOOD FUTURE IN THE MUSIC BUSINESS AHEAD!"
"THE DRUMMER, MELODY JONES, HAS A LOT OF APPEAL... BOTH ON AND OFF THE DRUMS!"
FLATTERER!
"HOWEVER, AS FAR AS JOSIE JAMES GOES, SHE PLAYS WOODENLY, WHICH CANNOT HELP BUT STILT THE PERFORMANCE OF THE OTHER TWO!"
2

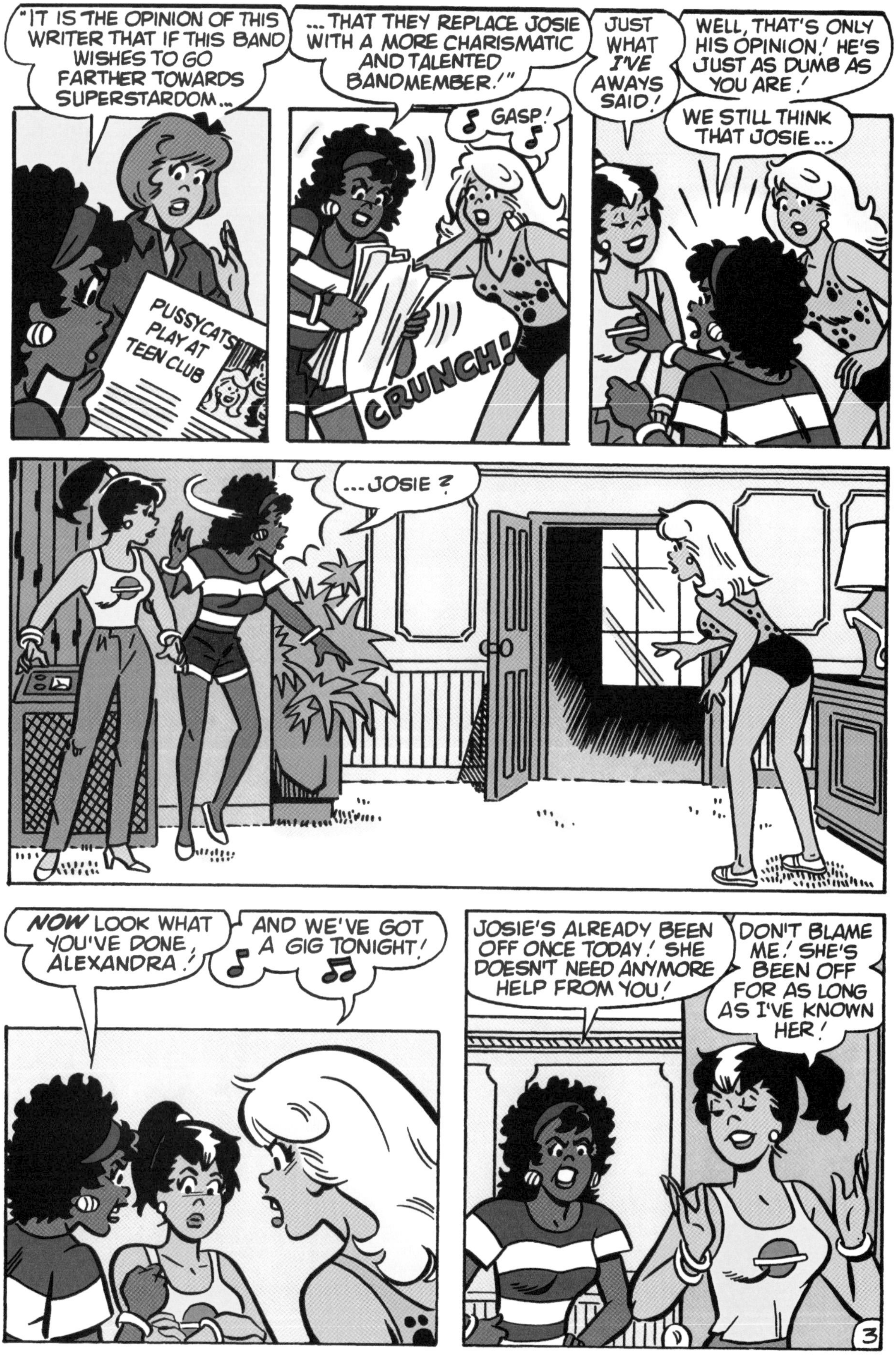
"IT IS THE OPINION OF THIS WRITER THAT IF THIS BAND WISHES TO GO FARTHER TOWARDS SUPERSTARDOM...
PUSSYCATS PLAY AT TEEN CLUB
...THAT THEY REPLACE JOSIE WITH A MORE CHARISMATIC AND TALENTED BANDMEMBER!"
GASP!
CRUNCH!
JUST WHAT I'VE AWAYS SAID!
WELL, THAT'S ONLY HIS OPINION! HE'S JUST AS DUMB AS YOU ARE!
WE STILL THINK THAT JOSIE...
...JOSIE?
NOW LOOK WHAT YOU'VE DONE, ALEXANDRA!
AND WE'VE GOT A GIG TONIGHT!
JOSIE'S ALREADY BEEN OFF ONCE TODAY! SHE DOESN'T NEED ANYMORE HELP FROM YOU!
DON'T BLAME ME! SHE'S BEEN OFF FOR AS LONG AS I'VE KNOWN HER!
3

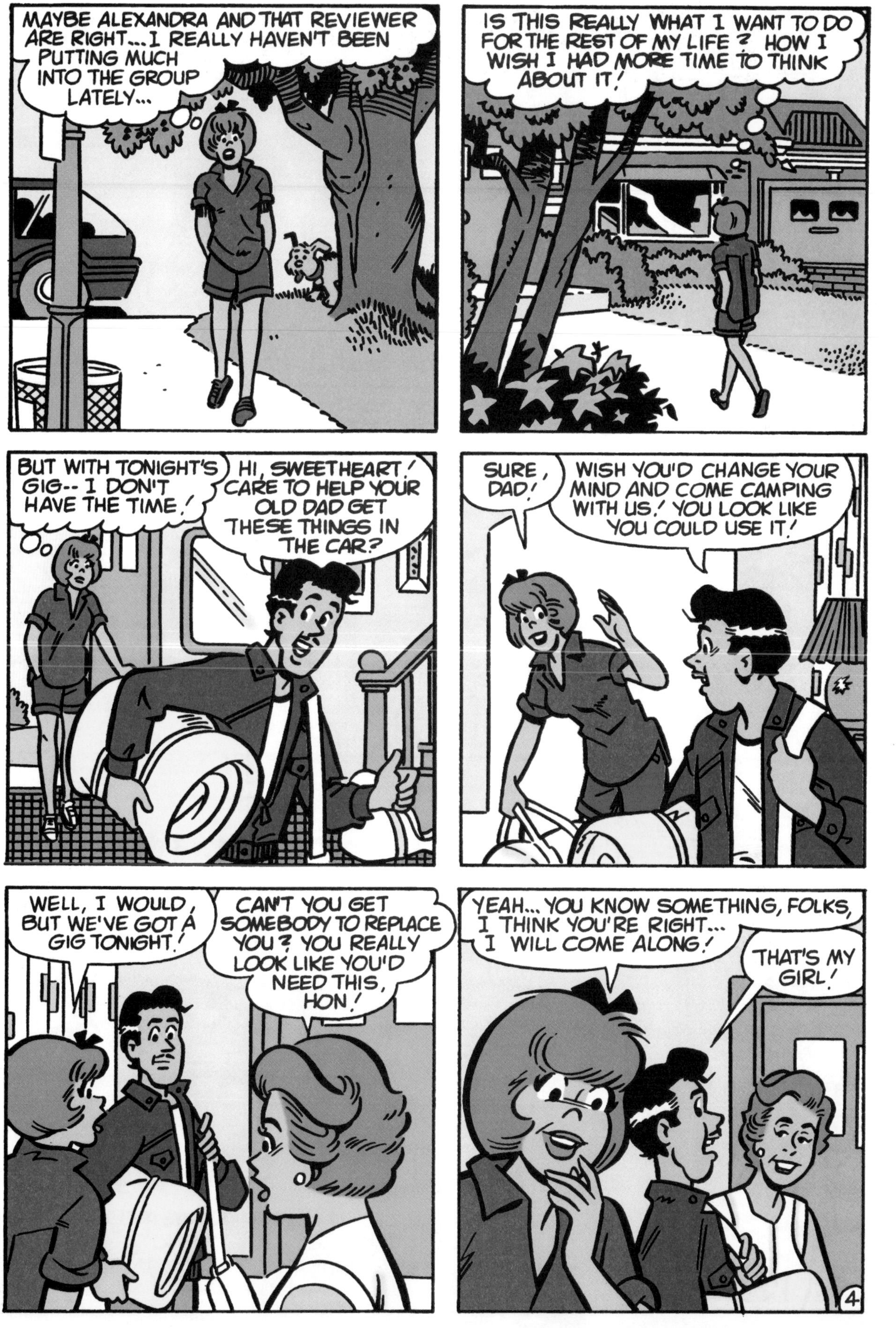
MAYBE ALEXANDRA AND THAT REVIEWER ARE RIGHT... I REALLY HAVEN'T BEEN PUTTING MUCH INTO THE GROUP LATELY...
IS THIS REALLY WHAT I WANT TO DO FOR THE REST OF MY LIFE? HOW I WISH I HAD MORE TIME TO THINK ABOUT IT!
BUT WITH TONIGHT'S GIG-- I DON'T HAVE THE TIME!
HI, SWEETHEART! CARE TO HELP YOUR OLD DAD GET THESE THINGS IN THE CAR?
SURE, DAD!
WISH YOU'D CHANGE YOUR MIND AND COME CAMPING WITH US! YOU LOOK LIKE YOU COULD USE IT!
WELL, I WOULD, BUT WE'VE GOT A GIG TONIGHT!
CAN'T YOU GET SOMEBODY TO REPLACE YOU? YOU REALLY LOOK LIKE YOU'D NEED THIS, HON!
YEAH... YOU KNOW SOMETHING, FOLKS, I THINK YOU'RE RIGHT... I WILL COME ALONG!
THAT'S MY GIRL!
4

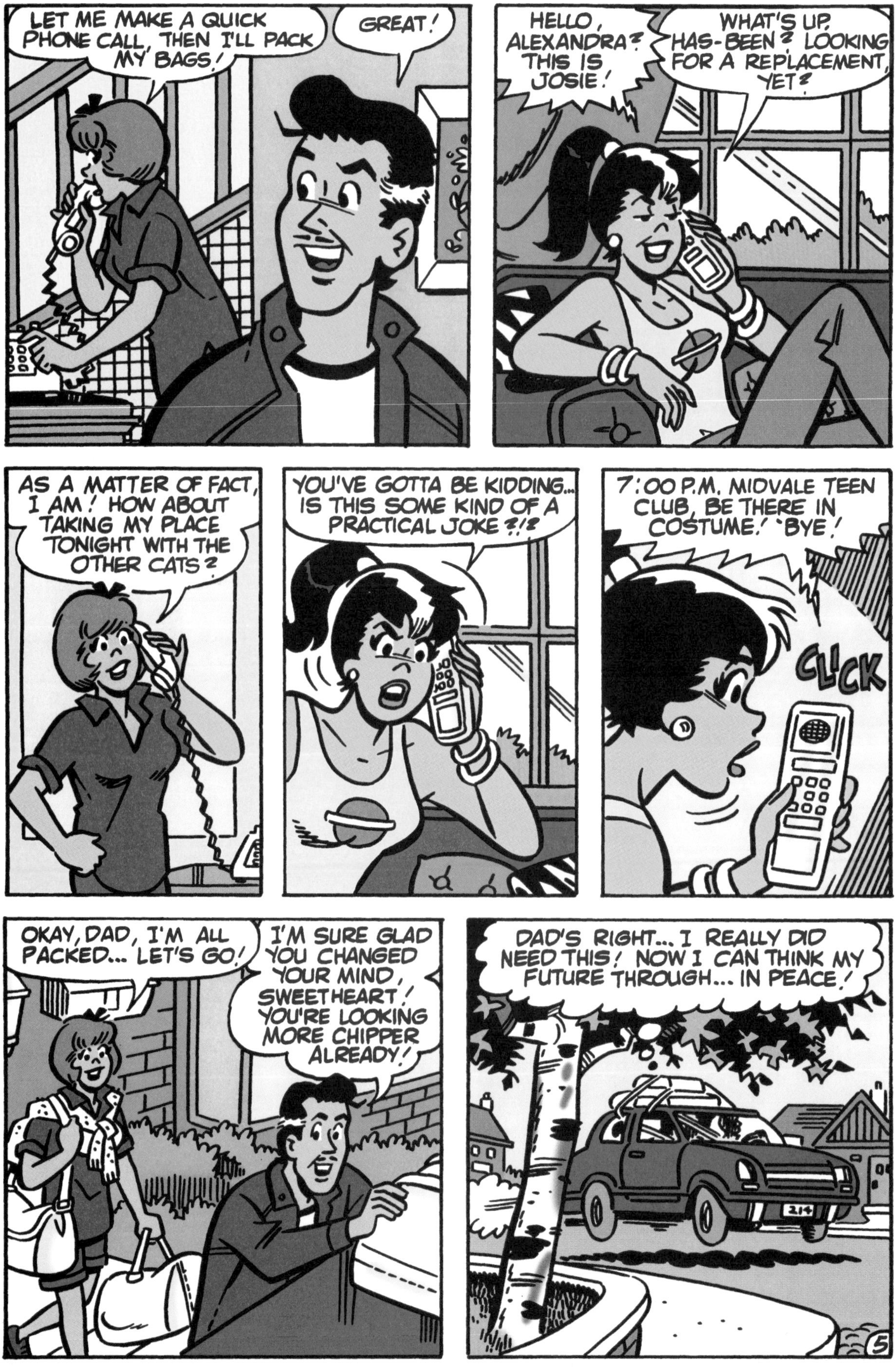
LET ME MAKE A QUICK PHONE CALL, THEN I'LL PACK MY BAGS!
GREAT!
HELLO, ALEXANDRA? THIS IS JOSIE!
WHAT'S UP, HAS-BEEN? LOOKING FOR A REPLACEMENT, YET?
AS A MATTER OF FACT, I AM! HOW ABOUT TAKING MY PLACE TONIGHT WITH THE OTHER CATS?
YOU'VE GOTTA BE KIDDING... IS THIS SOME KIND OF A PRACTICAL JOKE?!?
7:00 P.M. MIDVALE TEEN CLUB, BE THERE IN COSTUME! 'BYE!
CLICK
OKAY, DAD, I'M ALL PACKED... LET'S GO!
I'M SURE GLAD YOU CHANGED YOUR MIND, SWEETHEART! YOU'RE LOOKING MORE CHIPPER ALREADY!
DAD'S RIGHT... I REALLY DID NEED THIS! NOW I CAN THINK MY FUTURE THROUGH... IN PEACE!
5

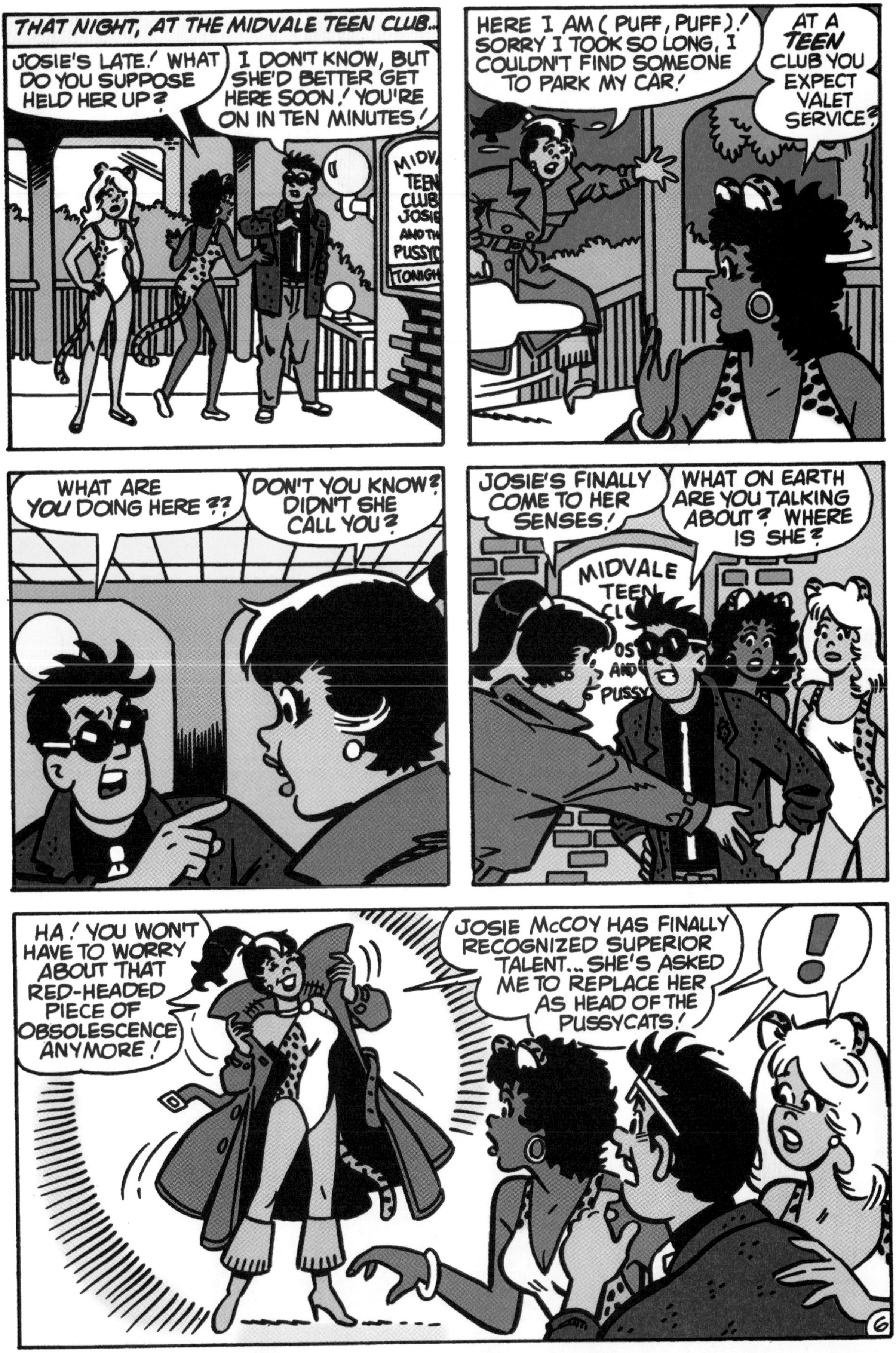
THAT NIGHT, AT THE MIDVALE TEEN CLUB...
JOSIE'S LATE! WHAT DO YOU SUPPOSE HELD HER UP?
I DON'T KNOW, BUT SHE'D BETTER GET HERE SOON! YOU'RE ON IN TEN MINUTES!
HERE I AM (PUFF, PUFF)! SORRY I TOOK SO LONG, I COULDN'T FIND SOMEONE TO PARK MY CAR!
AT A TEEN CLUB YOU EXPECT VALET SERVICE?
WHAT ARE YOU DOING HERE??
DON'T YOU KNOW? DIDN'T SHE CALL YOU?
JOSIE'S FINALLY COME TO HER SENSES!
WHAT ON EARTH ARE YOU TALKING ABOUT? WHERE IS SHE?
MIDVALE TEEN
HA! YOU WON'T HAVE TO WORRY ABOUT THAT RED-HEADED PIECE OF OBSOLESCENCE ANYMORE!
JOSIE McCOY HAS FINALLY RECOGNIZED SUPERIOR TALENT... SHE'S ASKED ME TO REPLACE HER AS HEAD OF THE PUSSYCATS!
!
6

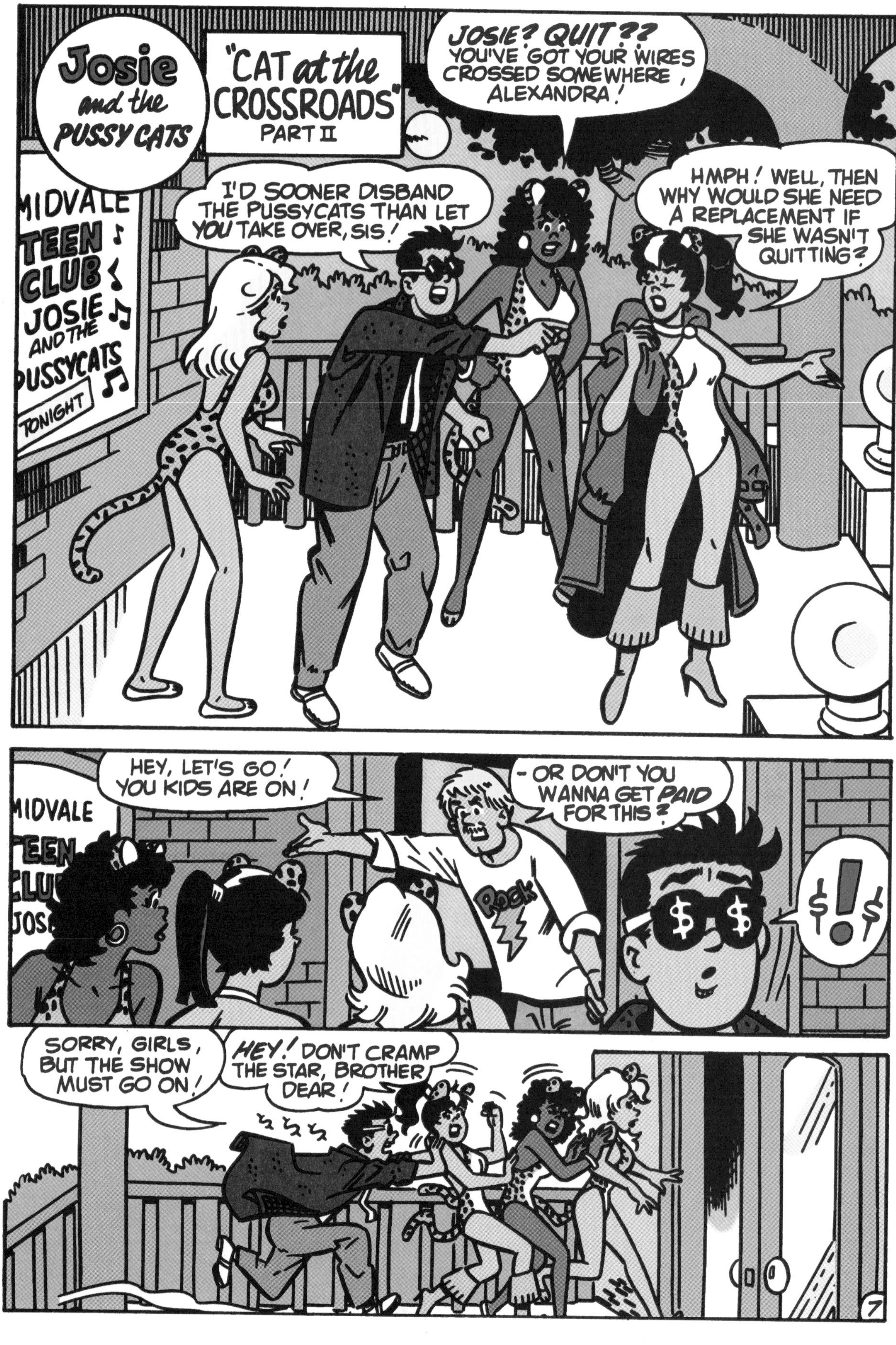
Josie and the PUSSY CATS
"CAT at the CROSSROADS" PART II
JOSIE? QUIT?? YOU'VE GOT YOUR WIRES CROSSED SOMEWHERE, ALEXANDRA!
MIDVALE TEEN CLUB JOSIE AND THE PUSSYCATS TONIGHT
I'D SOONER DISBAND THE PUSSYCATS THAN LET YOU TAKE OVER, SIS!
HMPH! WELL, THEN WHY WOULD SHE NEED A REPLACEMENT IF SHE WASN'T QUITTING?
HEY, LET'S GO! YOU KIDS ARE ON!
-OR DON'T YOU WANNA GET PAID FOR THIS?
ROCK
$!$
SORRY, GIRLS, BUT THE SHOW MUST GO ON!
HEY! DON'T CRAMP THE STAR, BROTHER DEAR!
7

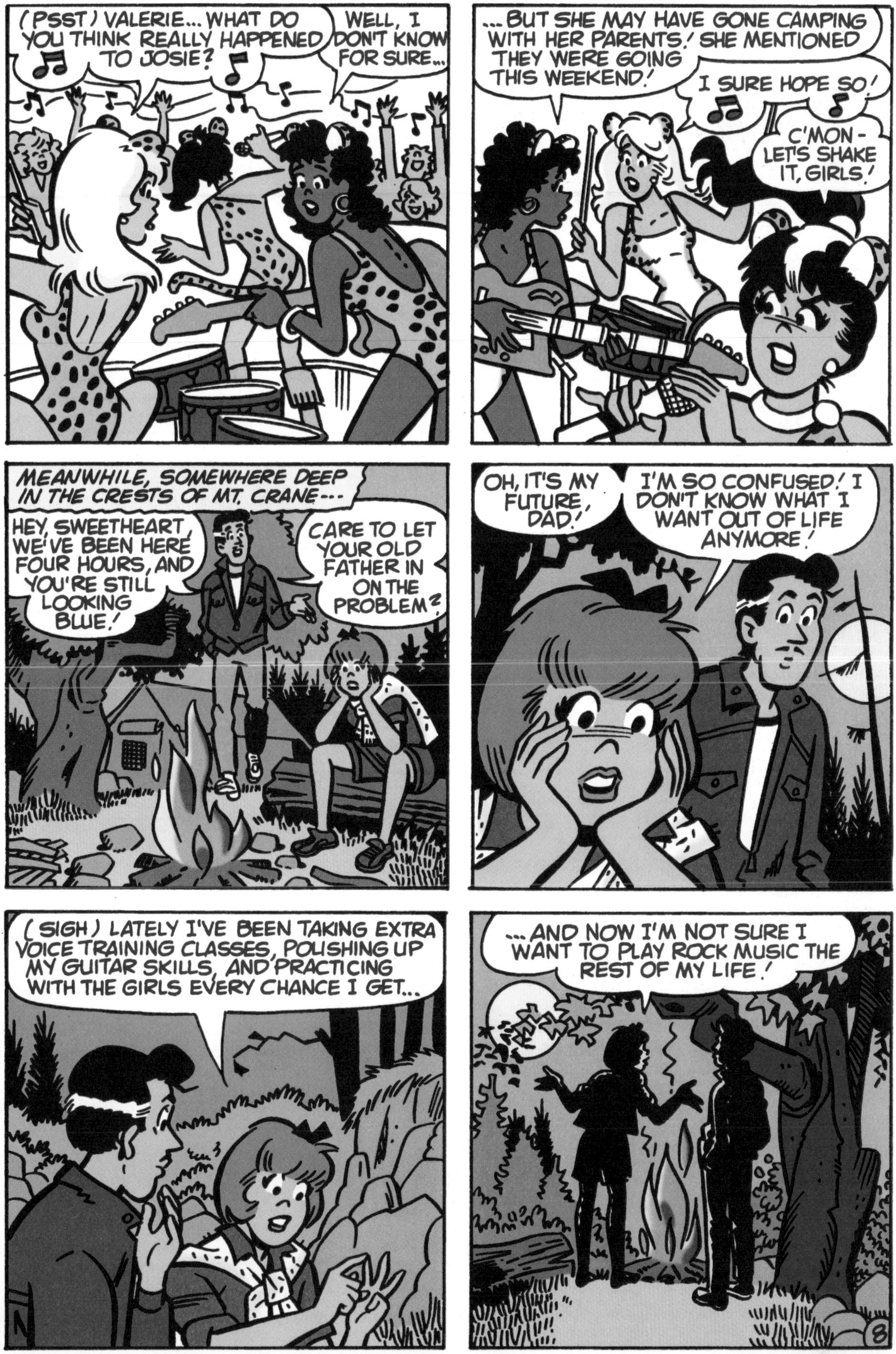
(PSST) VALERIE... WHAT DO YOU THINK REALLY HAPPENED TO JOSIE?
WELL, I DON'T KNOW FOR SURE...
...BUT SHE MAY HAVE GONE CAMPING WITH HER PARENTS! SHE MENTIONED THEY WERE GOING THIS WEEKEND!
I SURE HOPE SO!
C'MON - LET'S SHAKE IT, GIRLS!
MEANWHILE, SOMEWHERE DEEP IN THE CRESTS OF MT. CRANE---
HEY, SWEETHEART, WE'VE BEEN HERE FOUR HOURS, AND YOU'RE STILL LOOKING BLUE!
CARE TO LET YOUR OLD FATHER IN ON THE PROBLEM?
OH, IT'S MY FUTURE, DAD!
I'M SO CONFUSED! I DON'T KNOW WHAT I WANT OUT OF LIFE ANYMORE!
(SIGH) LATELY I'VE BEEN TAKING EXTRA VOICE TRAINING CLASSES, POLISHING UP MY GUITAR SKILLS, AND PRACTICING WITH THE GIRLS EVERY CHANCE I GET...
...AND NOW I'M NOT SURE I WANT TO PLAY ROCK MUSIC THE REST OF MY LIFE!
8

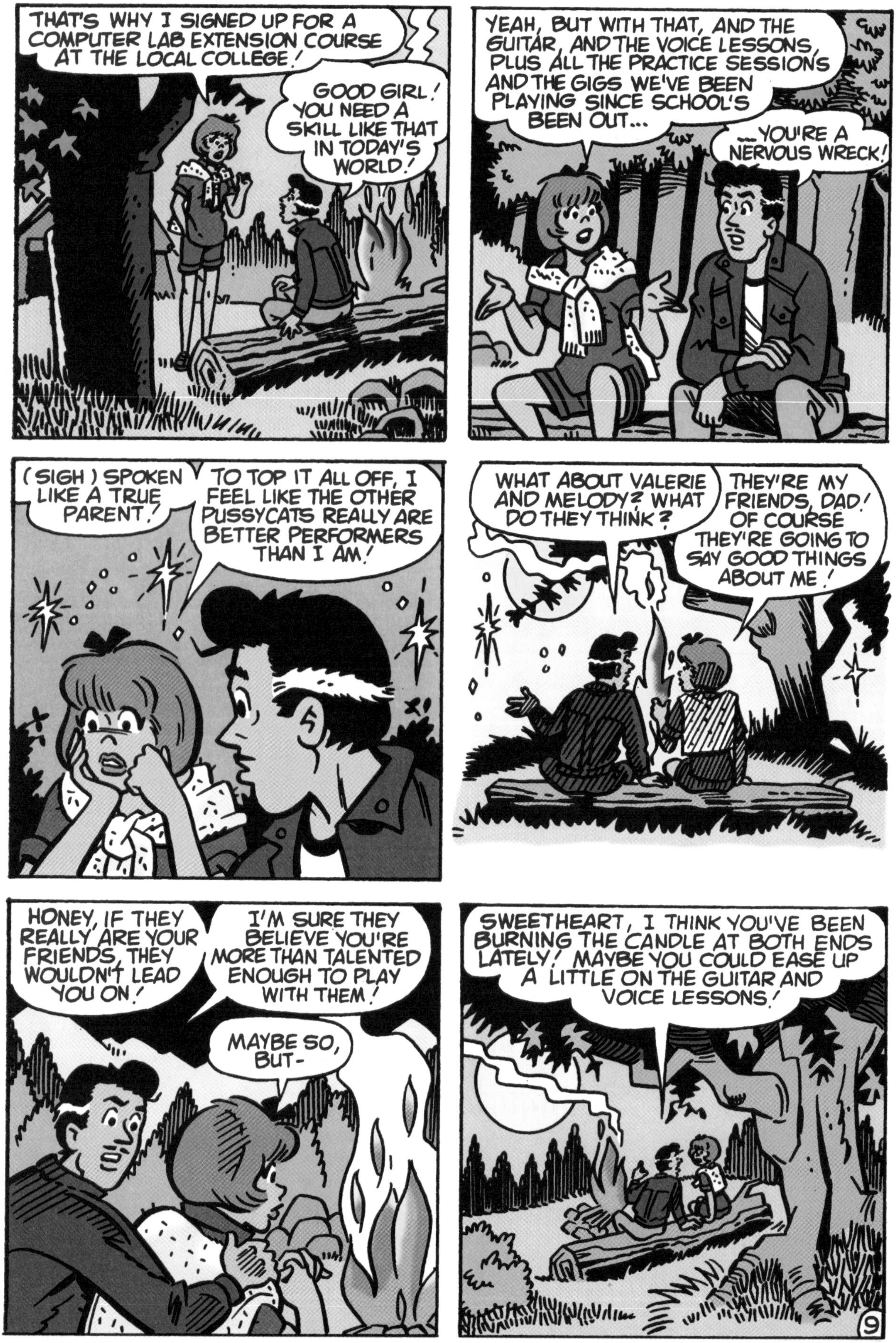
THAT'S WHY I SIGNED UP FOR A COMPUTER LAB EXTENSION COURSE AT THE LOCAL COLLEGE!
GOOD GIRL! YOU NEED A SKILL LIKE THAT IN TODAY'S WORLD!
YEAH, BUT WITH THAT, AND THE GUITAR, AND THE VOICE LESSONS, PLUS ALL THE PRACTICE SESSIONS AND THE GIGS WE'VE BEEN PLAYING SINCE SCHOOL'S BEEN OUT...
...YOU'RE A NERVOUS WRECK!
(SIGH) SPOKEN LIKE A TRUE PARENT!
TO TOP IT ALL OFF, I FEEL LIKE THE OTHER PUSSYCATS REALLY ARE BETTER PERFORMERS THAN I AM!
WHAT ABOUT VALERIE AND MELODY? WHAT DO THEY THINK?
THEY'RE MY FRIENDS, DAD! OF COURSE THEY'RE GOING TO SAY GOOD THINGS ABOUT ME!
HONEY, IF THEY REALLY ARE YOUR FRIENDS, THEY WOULDN'T LEAD YOU ON!
I'M SURE THEY BELIEVE YOU'RE MORE THAN TALENTED ENOUGH TO PLAY WITH THEM!
MAYBE SO, BUT-
SWEETHEART, I THINK YOU'VE BEEN BURNING THE CANDLE AT BOTH ENDS LATELY! MAYBE YOU COULD EASE UP A LITTLE ON THE GUITAR AND VOICE LESSONS!
9

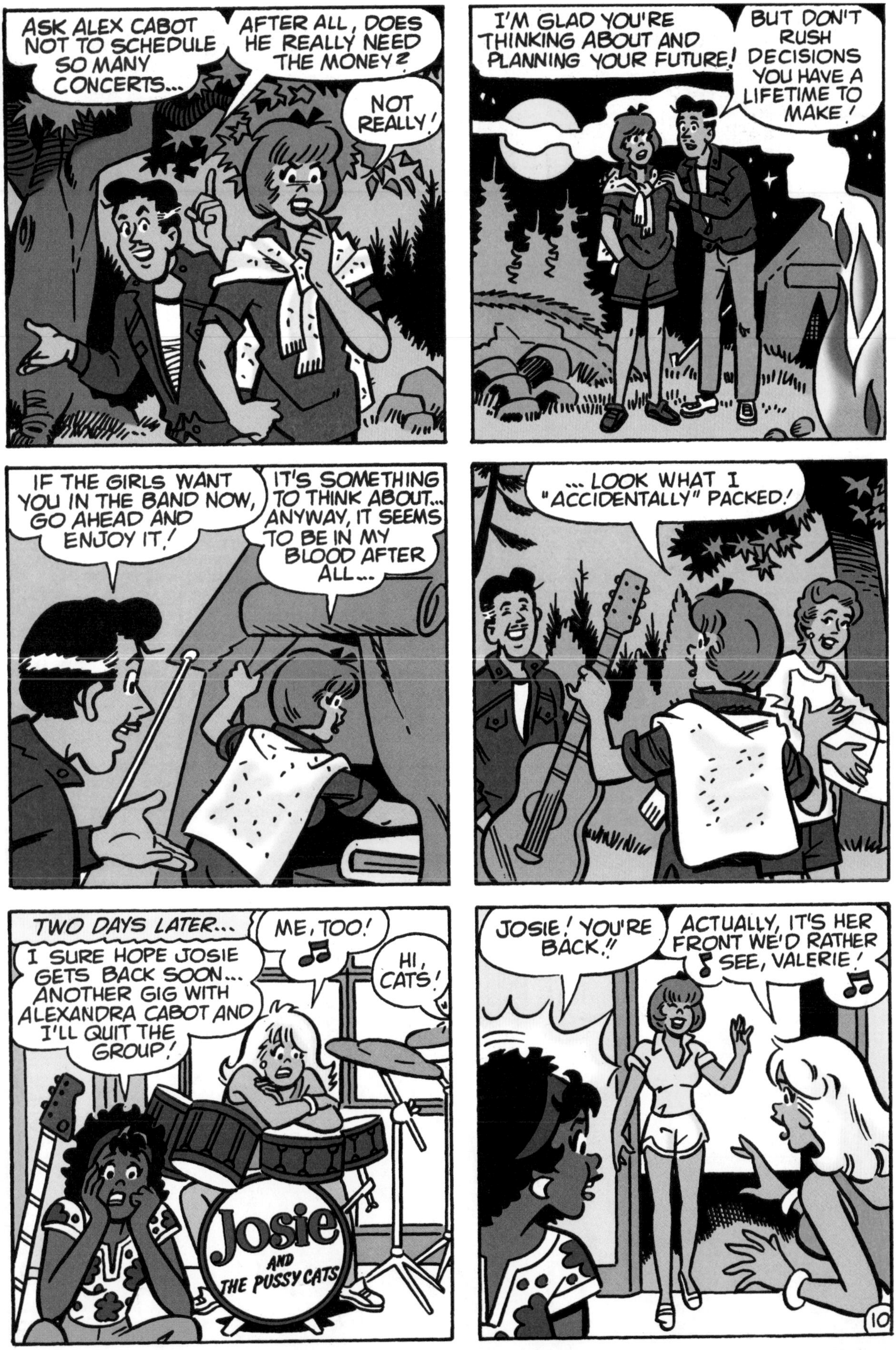
ASK ALEX CABOT NOT TO SCHEDULE SO MANY CONCERTS...
AFTER ALL, DOES HE REALLY NEED THE MONEY?
NOT REALLY!
I'M GLAD YOU'RE THINKING ABOUT AND PLANNING YOUR FUTURE!
BUT DON'T RUSH DECISIONS YOU HAVE A LIFETIME TO MAKE!
IF THE GIRLS WANT YOU IN THE BAND NOW, GO AHEAD AND ENJOY IT!
IT'S SOMETHING TO THINK ABOUT... ANYWAY, IT SEEMS TO BE IN MY BLOOD AFTER ALL...
... LOOK WHAT I "ACCIDENTALLY" PACKED!
TWO DAYS LATER...
I SURE HOPE JOSIE GETS BACK SOON... ANOTHER GIG WITH ALEXANDRA CABOT AND I'LL QUIT THE GROUP!
ME, TOO!
HI, CATS!
Josie AND THE PUSSY CATS
JOSIE! YOU'RE BACK!!
ACTUALLY, IT'S HER FRONT WE'D RATHER SEE, VALERIE!
10

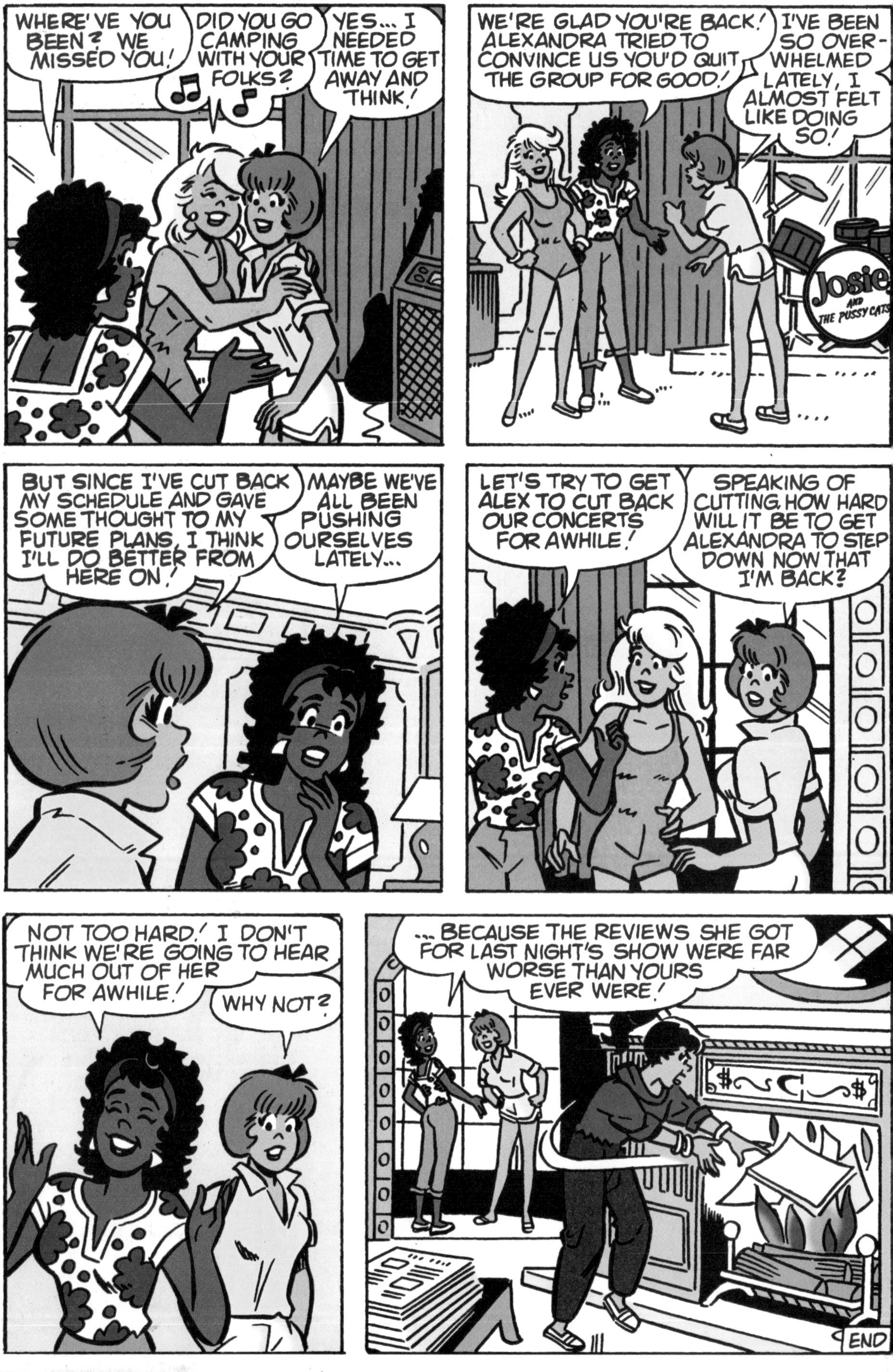
WHERE'VE YOU BEEN? WE MISSED YOU!
DID YOU GO CAMPING WITH YOUR FOLKS?
YES... I NEEDED TIME TO GET AWAY AND THINK!
WE'RE GLAD YOU'RE BACK! ALEXANDRA TRIED TO CONVINCE US YOU'D QUIT THE GROUP FOR GOOD!
I'VE BEEN SO OVER-WHELMED LATELY, I ALMOST FELT LIKE DOING SO!
Josie AND THE PUSSY CATS
BUT SINCE I'VE CUT BACK MY SCHEDULE AND GAVE SOME THOUGHT TO MY FUTURE PLANS, I THINK I'LL DO BETTER FROM HERE ON!
MAYBE WE'VE ALL BEEN PUSHING OURSELVES LATELY...
LET'S TRY TO GET ALEX TO CUT BACK OUR CONCERTS FOR AWHILE!
SPEAKING OF CUTTING, HOW HARD WILL IT BE TO GET ALEXANDRA TO STEP DOWN NOW THAT I'M BACK?
NOT TOO HARD! I DON'T THINK WE'RE GOING TO HEAR MUCH OUT OF HER FOR AWHILE!
WHY NOT?
...BECAUSE THE REVIEWS SHE GOT FOR LAST NIGHT'S SHOW WERE FAR WORSE THAN YOURS EVER WERE!
END